Check Up and Other Stories

Check Up and Other Stories

Wendi Lee

Five Star • Waterville, Maine

Copyright © 2001 by Wendi Lee

Additional copyright information may be found on page 6.

All rights reserved.

This collection is a work of fiction. Names, characters, places and incidents are either the product of the author's imagination, or, if real, used fictitiously.

Five Star First Edition Mystery Series.

Published in 2001 in conjunction with
Tekno Books and Ed Gorman.

Set in 11 pt. Plantin by Minnie B. Raven.

Printed in the United States on permanent paper.

Library of Congress Cataloging-in-Publication Data

Lee, W. W. (Wendi W.)
　　Check up and other stories / Wendi Lee.
　　　p.　　cm.
　　ISBN 0-7862-3552-7 (hc : alk. paper)
　　1. Detective and mystery stories, American.　I. Title.
PS3562.E3663 C48 2001
　813'.54—dc21　　　　　　　　　　　　　　　2001051237

Table of Contents

Salad Days 7

Miles Deep 23

Red Feather's Daughter 39

The Disappearance of Edna Guberman 57

Life of Riley 75

Dust and Ashes 91

The Other Woman 115

The Right Thing to Do 131

Winston's Wife 149

Feis 165

Indiscreet 187

Soft Day 207

Miami 223

Check Up 229

Additional Copyright Information:

"Salad Days." Copyright © 1994 by Wendi Lee. First appeared in *Noir Magazine*, Feb 1994.

"Miles Deep." Copyright © 1996 by Wendi Lee. First appeared in *Murderous Intent*, Spring 1996.

"Red Feather's Daughter." Copyright © 1996 by Wendi Lee. First appeared on *How the West was Read, vol. I*, Durkin-Hayes Audio.

"The Disappearance of Edna Guberman." Copyright © 1994 by Wendi Lee. First appeared in *Murder For Mother*, Signet.

"Life of Riley." Copyright © 1993 by Wendi Lee. First appeared in *Cat Crimes III*, D. I. Fine.

"Dust and Ashes." Copyright © 1997. First appeared on *How the West Was Read, vol. II*, Durkin-Hayes Audio.

"The Other Woman." Copyright © 1996 by Wendi Lee. First appeared in *Vengeance Is Hers*, Signet.

"The Right Thing to Do." Copyright © 1996 by Wendi Lee. First appeared in *Shades of Noir #2*.

"Winston's Wife." Copyright © 1996 by Wendi Lee. First appeared in *The Dark Frontier*, Carroll & Graf.

"Feis." Copyright © 2001 by Wendi Lee. Original to this collection.

"Indiscreet." Copyright © 1993 by Wendi Lee. First appeared in *Danger in D.C.*, D. I. Fine.

"Soft Day." Copyright © 1996 by Wendi Lee. First appeared in *Murder Most Irish*, Barnes & Noble Books.

"Miami." Copyright © 1995 by Wendi Lee. First appeared in *Murderous Intent*, Spring 1995.

"Check Up." Copyright © 1996 by Wendi Lee. First appeared in *Lethal Ladies*, Berkley.

This is the first Angela Matelli short story, originally published in the short-lived Noir *magazine.*

I wanted to put Angela into a situation in which she would be uncomfortable (something I do again and again—see the title story at the end). Despite the fact that Angela wore a uniform for eight years in the Marines, she has an aversion to silly-looking uniforms.

Salad Days

As I walked from the subway to the restaurant where I was working undercover, I kept feeling a draft up the back of my legs. I stared at my reflection in the glass front of the New Age vegetarian restaurant, Salad Days, and grimaced. My waitress uniform was bright green with a square neckline, puffed sleeves, a short, full skirt, and a bib apron with a vegetable motif. Oh, the things I did for relatives. On my little sister Rosa, the uniform looked cute. On me, an ex-Marine approaching thirty, it looked ridiculous.

When Rosa had been hired on a month ago at Salad Days, the hours had fit in perfectly with her school schedule. Then Joshua Cowan, manager of Salad Days, discovered that during the last month, someone had been systematically skimming fifty dollars a night from the dinner shift profits. Since Rosa was his newest employee, she was, in Cowan's eyes, the only suspect. He didn't want the publicity or the police, so he just let Rosa go.

"How could Mr. Cowan *do* this to me?" Rosa had sobbed.

After the initial shock wore off, Rosa got angry and decided to fight back. She suggested that I go to Cowan with a deal: I would find the real thief in exchange for Rosa being hired back. Since private investigation was my business, and since I had nothing in my appointment book for the next thirty years, I immediately agreed. Then the thought crossed my mind that Joshua Cowan might be stealing from Salad Days and covering for himself by firing Rosa. So I convinced Rosa to help me put an application together, under an assumed name, of course.

The next day, we concocted the perfect application, complete with high praise of my waitressing ability and glowing references to my reliability, all courtesy of an uncle in the restaurant business. I was hired on the spot and was told to report for work the next day.

Today was my first day. I stepped inside Salad Days and looked at the restaurant with new eyes. Paintings of eggplant, zucchini, tomatoes, and lettuce adorned the otherwise stark white walls. Square black tables each held a single red flower in a bud vase and place settings of white placemats and red cloth napkins. Ferns were hung from the ceiling in strategic places and rubber plants in large ceramic pots stood in corners and near posts. I took all this in before approaching a short, thin, woman in her thirties and introduced myself. "Hi, I'm Angie, the new waitress."

Her friendly smile told me that she was expecting me. "I'm Janice," she said. "I'll show you the ropes."

Mustering what little enthusiasm I had for waitressing, I replied, "Great. Let's get started."

Janice took me into the kitchen for introductions. Marcus, the cook, was a heavy man with a perpetual pout. "I do hope you can write clearly, my dear," he warned. "It would do well for you to remember that you are not a physician." I wondered if Marcus had any opportunity to steal from the till during or after work. I would be keeping my eye on the cash register all evening.

Next, Janice introduced me to Dennis, the dishwasher/busboy. He wore his dark blond hair slicked down and slightly long in back. The rest of him was pretty greasy as well, from his razor-thin, pockmarked face to his pointy-toed boots. When Dennis looked up at me, his eyes mirrored the boredom of his job, but he must have noticed my appraisal. "Nice to meet you," he said with a smirk. I noticed the gold Rolex on his wrist and wondered how he could afford something like that. Chances were that his restaurant job didn't pay well enough.

The next hour was filled with mind-numbing instructions such as how the tables were divided into stations, filling condiments, and how to make coffee and tea. While we were rolling the flatware into cloth napkins, Janice talked about herself.

"I just got divorced," she confessed, "and my kids are having a hard time adjusting."

"It sounds rough," I replied sympathetically. "Are you still friends with your ex?"

She gave a bitter laugh and replied, "When I hear anyone telling me that they had a friendly divorce, I don't believe it. I don't think any couple can remain friends after divorce. It's hardest on me when he comes over to take the kids for a day, which is getting to be less often."

I changed the subject. "Where's the manager today?" I wondered why I hadn't seen Cowan yet.

Janice had begun to fill peppershakers. She sneezed. "Oh, he rarely stays after three-thirty. He might drop in sometimes to see how we're doing, but he's usually here only through the lunch shift." Janice glanced at her watch and said, "We'd better move if you're going to get a chance to look at a menu before we open, Angie."

I attempted to memorize entrees and prices before Salad Days opened for business at five-thirty. By the time the first customers started trickling in, I had a pounding headache from trying to remember if the Eggplant Surprise was seven or eight dollars.

I kept my eye on the cash register as much as possible during my shift. Janice seemed to be the one who spent the most time at the till. As a new waitress, I had not been trained on the register yet. Dennis also worked in the front when business picked up. As the evening wore on, Dennis wore on my nerves. Whenever Janice called into the back for help, Dennis made sure to bump up against me on his way to the register. Despite this unpleasant distraction, I managed to notice that Marcus stayed in the kitchen all night. I don't think he even got a break. The hours went by swiftly and by the end of the evening, my feet felt as if I'd been on a fifty-mile march without a rest.

"So what do you think of this place? Is it anything like the restaurant you used to work at?" Janice asked as we wiped down the tables.

"I like it fine. The tips are better here than the last place I worked." I decided it was time to bring up Rosa. "I heard that the girl who worked here before me was fired for stealing. How long had she been here?"

Janice's face darkened and she shook her head. "Poor Rosa. She only worked here about a month. It's hard for me to believe she did it." Her expression brightened as she added, "But Rosa's young and she'll find another job."

I shook my head grimly. "Being accused of stealing is going to make it difficult for her to find work. I know that at the last place I worked, the owner didn't hire anyone with even a hint of scandal in their past employment. Was there an investigation?"

"No. Josh didn't want the publicity. He told us that he was sure it was her and that he just quietly let her go."

"That doesn't sound fair," I replied. My tone had an edge to it. I was getting angry, so I changed the subject. "What about you, how long have you been here?"

"About two years. I didn't think I'd be here this long, but the tips are great. We've even gotten a few celebrities in here." She proceeded to name a couple of actors and musicians who had frequented the place in the past. Finally, Janice surveyed the dining room and nodded her head, satisfied. "We're almost done here, except for the register. Why don't I show you how to count it out. Besides, I wouldn't mind someone watching me after the incident with Rosa."

I followed her over and we counted it out, separated the checks, cash, and credit card receipts into bundles, and stuffed everything into an official bank bag. While Janice brought the bag back to the office safe, I went over to the coat rack. As I pulled my black windbreaker down, a dark blue man's jacket fell to the floor. I stooped to pick it up. A small plastic bag fell out of a slash pocket. After a quick examination of the white powder residue in the bottom of the bag, I hurriedly stuffed it back into the jacket. The jacket had a recognizable label inside, the kind you would buy at a high-class store. I wondered if Cowan had left it behind this afternoon.

"That's mine," Dennis said. His voice startled me. He took the jacket from me and slipped it on.

"Nice jacket," I said, wondering how a dishwasher could afford a gold Rolex and brand-name clothes.

He smirked. "My brother owns an outlet." Dennis

looked me up and down as if he liked what he saw. Small wonder, he'd spent most of the night up close and personal with me. If he weren't a suspect, I'd have knocked his lights out hours ago.

Dennis moved in closer. "I could get you some real nice designer clothes like what I'm wearing. And you wouldn't have to pay much for them. You free now?" He slipped an arm around my waist.

"No, I have to go home and feed my goldfish," I replied, moving away quickly as if I hadn't noticed his moves. I put on my shabby windbreaker. "But thanks," I added with a tight smile, "I'll think about it."

When I got home, I went directly to Rosa's apartment. She tried not to laugh at the sight of me in my waitress uniform, but her sense of humor finally got the better of her. "You look like a crazed leprechaun," she managed to say, wiping a tear from her eye.

"Right. Get it out of your system," I said crossly. "I'll be upstairs, changing. Come up when you can keep a straight face." I stomped out of Rosa's apartment, accompanied by the sound of my sister howling with laughter.

Ten minutes later, I was in comfortable clothes and Rosa had stopped laughing. I asked her about the people I was working with.

"Marcus badly wants to have his own restaurant," she said. "It's all he ever talked about when I was there. Janice, well, she's a sad case. Her husband was abusive and she took it for ten years. When he started taking it out on the kids, she packed up and left him. He's paying child support and she has a restraining order. He can't go near her, except to pick up or drop off the children."

"What about Dennis?" I asked.

"He's an interesting case. I never got to know him very

well. During his breaks, he goes out in the alley for a smoke."

I nodded in understanding. Salad Days was a smoke-free restaurant. "What about that Rolex that he sports? How can he afford it on his salary?"

Rosa hesitated for a moment. "I've always suspected he sells drugs on the side."

More likely that he washes dishes on the side, I thought. As a drug dealer, he was a walking advertisement. A blinking neon sign around his neck couldn't have pointed it out more clearly. "What about Joshua Cowan?" I asked. "Do you think he might be in financial trouble?"

Although Cowan had accused Rosa of slipping the money out of the register while she was totaling checks, there was nothing to prove that Cowan couldn't have altered the bank slips before taking the night's total to the bank the next day.

"I don't know, Sarge," Rosa replied, shrugging. Ever since I left the Marines, Sarge was her affectionate nickname for me. "Digging up secrets is your department, right?"

I spent the next day getting information from Raina, an East Boston police dispatcher and my best friend.

"Wow, you sure don't ask for much, do you, Angie," Raina said as she sat down in my office and slapped the manila folders down on my desk. "Do you know how difficult it was for me to get this information on my day off?"

"I know, and thanks, Raina," I said, sincerely meaning it. "If it weren't for Rosa . . ." I trailed off.

She made a dismissive gesture with her hand. "I know, I know. I've known Rosa almost as long as I've known you and I think she got a raw deal. Which is why I moved so fast on this request of yours."

I flipped through the folders. Janice had some parking violations from a few years ago. Parking tickets were nothing new in a big city like Boston. Space was at a premium and after a while, the citizens begin to invent parking spaces. It was interesting to note that unlike most citizens, Janice had paid all her fines.

There was one more note of interest in Janice's file: the police had been called out to her home more than once for domestic violence. The reports always ended with "No charges filed" until the last one, about six months ago. Apparently Janice finally got tired of being beaten and filed for divorce. I caught a small notation in the report: "Evidence of battery on ten year-old girl, Melissa." So that backed up what Rosa had told me. As in most cases of domestic abuse, it had been all right if Dad beat up Mom, but when he turned violent with the kids, she suddenly found her backbone.

Dennis Holding's file was thick with arrest reports for selling and holding drugs. He never seemed to spend any time in jail, he just got arrested a lot. I would have loved to hang the restaurant's robbery on Dennis, but I hadn't seen him near the cash register more than a couple of times during my first night. Still, he was a suspect.

Marcus Freeley's file contained one arrest report. I scanned it, but found little to help me in my search for the truth. The cook had been arrested once back in the early seventies. He had been a college student in possession of a bag of marijuana and had only been given a slap on the wrist.

Cowan didn't have a file. He didn't have so much as a citation for spitting on the sidewalk. He was, by all accounts, a model citizen. It would take a little more digging on my part. I thanked Raina again and we made arrangements to get together when I was done working at Salad Days.

After she left the office, I started to make a few phone calls to check on my suspects' financial background. I started with Joshua Cowan—his Victorian house in Brookline, his family, his finances, everything. I discovered that he and his wife lived above their means, taking at least one expensive three-week vacation a year. Cowan also owned a cottage in Truro, an exclusive community on Cape Cod. And I couldn't figure out how he was paying for it all.

Although Cowan was still a suspect, I couldn't reconcile the amount of money skimmed from Salad Days with the lifestyle Cowan was living. The way Cowan handled firing Rosa did not look good, but I didn't see how skimming fifty dollars a night would add up to the amount of money Joshua Cowan would need to finance his extravagant lifestyle.

Marcus Freeley had been in serious financial trouble a few months ago, but suddenly his bank account turned flush. Although it was mysterious, his good fortune could not be explained by the small amount skimmed off the restaurant's profits.

Janice Gardner's finances were about what I had expected for a divorced waitress with two growing kids. She was barely making ends meet. She was still a suspect, but if she was having such a hard time, why wasn't she skimming more money to make life easier?

Dennis had no bank account. On paper, he had almost no financial history. I would have to dig a little deeper tomorrow.

I looked up from the paper on my desk and glared at the perky green uniform hanging on a coat hook on the wall. It was almost time to go to work. I had pored over the files and dug into the backgrounds of the suspects, and had come up with almost nothing. The cook was last on my suspect list, and as much as I would have liked to pin the crime on the man who fired my sister, I couldn't see any serious motive on Cowan's part. Dennis and Janice were the only ones left—a drug dealer and a former battered wife with dependents.

I was beginning to form a picture in my head, something that I wasn't sure I liked. But I followed my instincts and made a couple of phone calls. After confirming my suspicions, I picked up the phone one last time and called a friend on the police force.

"Lee? This is Angela Matelli."

"Good to hear from you, Angie," Detective Lee Randolph said heartily. "What have you been up to lately?"

"Moonlighting," I replied, "at a restaurant called Salad Days. How would you like to make a drug bust tonight?" I bent over, opened my bottom left desk drawer, and took out a camera.

The dinner shift was busy for a Thursday night. Sometime during the evening, Joshua Cowan stopped in. When he saw how busy we were, he stayed and ran the register while Janice and I ran back and forth from the kitchen to the dining room until I was certain I'd worn an inch off my pump heels. By the time the last customers were getting ready to leave and Janice was putting the CLOSED sign in the front window, I slipped into the kitchen. Marcus was wrapping up leftover chopped vegetables. Dennis was nowhere in sight. The back door was open.

"Where's Dennis?" I asked.

Marcus looked up, then jerked his head toward the open door. "He's taking his break."

I went over to the coat rack and pulled my handy pocket

camera from the pocket of my windbreaker. Then I walked over to the door and looked out. The alley was dimly lit and I hoped that what I was about to do would work. A few yards down, I spotted Dennis with a customer. It looked like a man, I thought, although the figure was too hunched over to get a clear picture. But that's exactly what I did. I fixed the camera on the two shadowy figures.

Just as money and drugs were being exchanged, I shouted, "Hey, Dennis!" He looked up at me, as did his customer, and I snapped the picture. The flash worked beautifully.

Dennis's customer turned and fled down the alley toward the busy avenue. Dennis's surprised expression turned into a snarl. He started toward me at a surprising speed. Before I knew what was happening, he knocked me to the ground. When I recovered my breath, I saw Dennis looming over me, a stiletto in his hand. He made slashing motions in the air before aiming the blade at my throat. I rolled out of the way, onto my side, and kicked him in the knee. Something snapped. He went down, howling and clutching his leg.

I picked myself up and brushed off my now torn and stained uniform. A big man, probably an undercover cop, helped Dennis to his feet. His leg wouldn't straighten out, but I figured he'd get treated at Mass General before being booked.

"What are you, a narc or something?" Dennis managed to growl at me.

I smiled and stood my ground. "No, but they are."

Detective Lee Randolph came up to us. I handed the photo to him before he started reciting the Miranda to Dennis. As I turned toward the restaurant door, I noticed that we'd drawn a crowd of three, Marcus, Janice, and Joshua Cowan.

"I think an explanation is in order," I said to all three. Once we were seated at a table in the dining room, I laid the whole story out for them. Cowan was irate when he found out that I had misrepresented myself, but he turned sheepish when I gently pointed out that he was the one who fired my sister without giving her a chance to prove her innocence.

"So Dennis was not only selling drugs out the back door during and after business hours, but was also skimming from our till," Cowan said when I was finished.

I nodded. "I can't prove it, but our boy has quite an arrest record. He served some time in jail, too."

Cowan's face went red. "He didn't mention it on his application."

I shrugged. "What's one more minor crime like lying on your application when you've got everything else stacked against you?"

Cowan rubbed the back of his neck. "I probably would have still hired him, but I wouldn't have let him near the till if I'd known about his record."

"That's why he didn't mention it, in the hopes that you wouldn't check into his background."

Marcus sighed and absently rubbed the table surface with a corner of his apron. "You must have suspected us all."

I nodded. "I did. But I checked into your backgrounds and you were all too nauseatingly normal to suspect for long."

Cowan got up. "Well, it's been a long day for everyone. Marcus, Janice, carry on and lock up. I'm going home." He motioned to me and I followed him to the front door. "Tell Rosa she can start back to work tomorrow."

I frowned. "That's all? You fire her, then hire her back so abruptly?"

Salad Days

He gave me a wry smile. "I do owe her an apology, so please convey that to her. When I see her in person tomorrow evening, I'll apologize again. Okay?"

I crossed my arms. "What about her lost work time?"

Cowan sighed. "You really drive a hard bargain. Okay, she gets two days' pay for her hardship."

"Including an average night of tips?"

"Don't push it, Matelli," he warned, then gruffly added, "Plus some money to compensate for lost tips. By the way, what did you find out about me? Just out of curiosity, of course."

"You live way above your means. Your credit cards are maxed out. You do not have an A-plus credit rating."

Cowan studied me for a moment, then nodded. "Who does?"

"That's why I said you were all nauseatingly normal. You didn't have a good enough reason to skim such a measly amount of money."

After he left, I was approached by a sheepish Marcus. "I was wondering what you found out about me," he said.

With a sigh, I patted him on the back. "I hope your restaurant is a success, Marcus. But how did you come up with the money?"

He flushed. "I have a silent partner. I can't tell you who it is. He comes in here sometimes. He's in the music business." I remembered that Janice had mentioned that some celebrities considered Salad Days too chi-chi for words.

I held up my hand. "Say no more. Just send me an invitation for the grand opening."

After Marcus left, Janice and I were the only ones left. She was putting her coat on when I approached her.

"Janice," I began.

She averted her eyes. "I suppose Rosa will be back to

19

work tomorrow. It sure was smart how you figured out Dennis did it all."

"But he didn't."

Her shoulders stiffened and her voice was timid. "He didn't?"

"Oh, he's guilty of selling drugs, but not of skimming. I was pretty sure that Joshua wasn't going to press charges once he found out who it was. After all, he fired my sister without an investigation." I paused, not knowing how to say it. "It was you who did it, right?"

She slumped over, suddenly looking very weary. "Yes," she said dully, "it was me. My ex is a deadbeat and I had no way of meeting all the monthly bills on just my salary. How did you find out?"

"I made a call to the county clerk's office to find out if you'd been getting your child support checks. Then I called your lawyer and he told me that you had contacted him when the checks stopped showing up a few months ago. And he'd told you that he didn't think he could help you."

"Because I didn't have the money to pay the lawyer," Janice replied bitterly. "And taking a second job would have meant less time with my kids. My ex, the vindictive son-of-a-bitch, would have fought for custody, saying that I wasn't a good mother for leaving my kids alone."

"But he couldn't have gotten custody, Janice," I pointed out gently. "He's on record as a child abuser."

"But his mother could have gotten custody," she replied in a hard voice. "I was going to pay it all back, every penny. I keep a running account. But I'm always behind on my bills. Something new comes along every month and, well . . ." A tear slid down her cheek and she turned her face away from me.

I put my arm around her. "I understand. And I think

your lawyer is a snake not to recommend some recourse. You can get your ex's wages attached. I know a good lawyer, a cousin of mine, who'll help you file charges against him. Pro bono. And I'll look into hidden assets, free of charge. But you have to promise me something."

"What?"

"Don't rob the till again. Dennis has taken the blame for this and I don't want my sister in trouble again."

"Agreed," Janice said with relief.

We locked up the place together and headed for the subway.

"Miles Deep" was my first attempt at noir. *I really enjoy writing this subgenre, probably because as I've gotten older, I've become more jaded, and writing* noir *stories alleviates some of the darkness within. "Miles Deep" was first published in the erstwhile* Murderous Intent, *my second story to be accepted by editor Margo Powers.*

Miles Deep

When I heard the sharp knock on the door, I felt my muscles tense. Cautiously, I sidled over to the curtained window and peeked out. A stranger stood huddled against the cold wind. He rapped again. While I willed the tall, broad-shouldered man to go away, I studied him. He wore lumberjack clothing covered by a green down jacket, the kind all men wore up here in backwoods country. And he was carrying an empty gasoline can.

I knew the can was empty from the way he jauntily swung it from his well-muscled arm. His sandy-colored hair was salon-styled, his beard too carefully trimmed, and his hiking boots so brand new that they probably came straight out of an L. L. Bean catalog. In my current frazzled state, it wasn't too hard for me to imagine that this stranger might have been sent here to kill me.

I'm a private investigator. That is, I used to be a private investigator until I testified in a murder trial a few months back. The man on trial was mob-connected and it was made clear to me that my testimony would make certain people very unhappy. Having a strong sense of right and wrong, I testified anyway. Ever since the trial ended, there had been a rumor floating around that there was a contract out on me.

When Miles arrived, he'd been jumpy, but I didn't learn why until just before he left to get my week's worth of groceries and propane.

"It's unconfirmed," he had said, a grim look clouding his face, "but it looks like it may be an inside job." I knew what that meant: a mole in the Bureau had taken mob money to kill me. "Jack down at headquarters heard it from a reliable source," Miles explained. "Keep those doors and windows locked while I'm gone. Don't let anyone in, even if they show you a badge."

"I'd rather go with you," I said firmly.

Miles brusquely vetoed that idea, explaining that I might be spotted riding around in his car. Even if I wore a disguise, I was a stranger to the nearby small town and I would be noticed. I'd known that, but I hated being left out here like a duck on a pond during hunting season.

After kissing my nose, Miles said lightly, "You've faced tough situations before, Bev. Don't go soft on me now. If you see anyone sneaking around the cabin, you have my permission to shoot 'em."

With that, he had gotten into the car and disappeared in the early afternoon.

The knock came a third time, so sharp this time that it startled me. I tried to brush off my discomfort as, in the fading daylight, I watched the man set down his gas can and, hands on slim hips, peer around the grounds.

Damn Miles, I thought. He would have to be away at this moment. He'd left at three-thirty this afternoon, and with the grocery shopping and stopping to talk to his partner, it should have taken him an hour and a half to get back. It was now close to five-thirty and getting dark. He was the Fed, he should have to deal with this bozo. On the other hand, he had given me permission to shoot anyone suspicious who came onto the property.

Miles Stewart is my only contact with the outside world right now. He's also my lover. My *married* lover. Lanky and raw-boned, Miles wears flannel shirts, jeans, and work boots when he comes up here to check on me. He probably wears dark blue suits with white shirts and gray ties in the city, but he'd be too conspicuous if he dressed that way up here in the backwoods of northern Minnesota.

We both know our affair will last only until I'm pulled completely underground. This is the first of several safe houses that I will stay in before my new identity is ready.

The stranger called out, "Is there anyone here? I ran out of gas and need to use your phone."

Sure. That was the oldest trick in the book. My hands were cold, whether from the temperature or from fear, I didn't know. I took another look at him and wondered if maybe I was being too paranoid. He could be a weekender, some stockbroker who likes to come out here, and do guy stuff like drinking beer and shooting a pellet gun at defenseless little squirrels in neighboring trees. He'd go back to his office on Monday and brag about what a great shot he was. The wildlife would breathe a little easier until the following weekend.

Then again, this guy could be a hired gun and that gas can could have a bomb in it. After considering my options, I decided I'd be better off answering the door. If he was some poor shmoe who needed gas, it was a long, cold hike to town, and if he was a killer, I would rather face him in the cabin. I had gotten very familiar with the cabin over that last two weeks. Either way, I was starved for company.

I took a deep breath and grasped the snub-nose .38 that

nestled in the deep outside pocket of my down vest. I opened the door just a crack.

The man was hunched over from the bitter wind that cut across the front property. He gave me an appraising look and said, "I was wondering when you'd get around to answering the door. I saw the curtains moving in the window."

I frowned.

Looking contrite, he continued, "I'm sorry to bother you like this, but I ran out of gas about half a mile down the road. Could I use your phone?" He set the gas can down and raised his cupped hands to his face and blew on them, stamping his feet slightly as if he wanted to make sure they were still attached to him.

I hesitated, then opened the door wider and let him in.

"My friend should be coming back any minute now," I said. "Maybe you can catch a ride into town."

"Thanks." Leaving his gas can on the porch, he stepped inside and added, "I think I'd better call a tow service. I wouldn't want your friend to have to stay out there any longer than he needs to."

"Sure. The phone's over there." I pointed to the contraption on the wall in the far corner of the living area.

The stranger scanned my cozy living quarters. It was a cheery little prison with pine paneling, a mounted deer head, and a roaring fireplace to take away the autumn chill. Knotty pine, dead deer, and fireplaces seem to be regulation requirements for all lakeside cabins. The braided rug was optional, but it lent a folksy touch to the room. All in all, it wasn't a bad set up, if I were a burly mountain man. But I was a city girl with a soft spot for fine restaurants, art museums, and the theater.

He strode over to the phone, picked up the receiver and

punched in some numbers. He talked low for a minute, then finally hung up and, at my urging, took a seat on the sofa by the fireplace. "Since we'll be keeping each other company for a while," he said, holding his hands out to warm them up by the fire, "my name's Pete."

"Katy," I replied. That was the name that had been temporarily assigned to me, if I encountered anyone who would ask. "Would you like some coffee? I have a pot brewing in the kitchen."

He nodded, rubbing his hands briskly and leaning toward the fire. "Thanks. That would be nice, Katy."

I went into the kitchen. Standing by a cutout window that looked into the living room, I filled two mugs with coffee and kept my eye on my buddy Pete at the same time. It's hard not to think in terms of conspiracies when you know there's a contract out on your life. My paranoia took hold again. I began to wonder why Pete hadn't removed his down jacket, in spite of the fact he was sitting so close to the fireplace. What was hidden underneath—a holstered gun with a silencer, perhaps? But paranoia can be a wonderful thing. After considering how he behaved and what he said within the first three minutes of entering the cabin, I was certain that Pete was not what he appeared to be. Now I just had to discover what he was and why he was here.

I looked at the wall clock, then glanced out the kitchen window. It was completely dark now. Miles had been gone over two hours. Pete might have waylaid him, and if that was the case, I would have to take matters into my own hands. "Cream or sugar?" I called out.

"I take mine black," Pete replied.

Clumsily balancing the handles of two steaming mugs with one hand, the other hand closed around the gun in my vest pocket, I walked back into the living room and set them down on the coffee table. Pete gratefully wrapped his hands around one of the mugs.

"So what brings someone like you out here?" he asked before sipping the brew.

I tried to shrug casually. "I like the quiet. And the lake is beautiful."

The first part was a lie. I was unnerved by the silence. No sirens, no city hustle, no constant jackhammer noise in the background. But right now, I'd give anything for Pete to go away and leave me alone in this wilderness cabin.

Here on Red Earth Lake, my nearest neighbor was a mile away. There were only three other cabins around the lake. Sometimes at night, I watched their faint lights glinting through the trees.

Red Earth Lake was small compared to most Minnesota lakes. It hadn't been turned into a tourist resort yet. There were still lots of pine trees edging the banks. If I followed a small path in back of the cabin, it would lead down to the lake.

There was a dock with a rowboat tied to it, although I'd never used it.

The locals who ran the grocery store once told Miles that there was a place in the middle of the lake so deep, they had given up trying to measure it. That confirmed my notion that I probably wouldn't be doing much boating or swimming. Besides, it was early November and I was pretty sure I wouldn't be here long enough for the warm weather.

"I like to get away, too," Pete said, putting his coffee cup down. "But I came up here for another reason, Miss Wisler. May I call you Bev?"

I put my mug down slowly, my muscles tensing up as I drew the gun out and pointed it at him. He stood up slowly, gesturing with his hands to show that he meant no harm.

"Take it easy, Miss Wisler."

"Okay," I said evenly, "you get a passing grade for knowing my name. And that's Ms. Wisler to you, bud."

"You're the private eye who testified at the Capelli murder trial," he said. "I'm here to help you. I'm a federal agent. I have identification."

"I already have a Fed helping me," I replied. "Miles Stewart. You should know that."

He started to slip his right hand inside of his jacket. Despite his reassurances, my sweaty grip tightened on the gun in my pocket. Thoughts raced through my mind. Was he on the level? He *couldn't* be! He was too casual, too controlled. Where was his back-up? All Bureau agents came in pairs; even Miles had a partner who hung around town and kept an eye out for suspicious characters. I'd only met her briefly a few times.

My stomach churned. I couldn't think straight. All I could think about was protecting myself.

"Keep away from me," I said, my voice coming out in a strangled whisper. I tried to take a deep breath, but it felt like there was a steel band constricting my chest. "Miles told me all about the hit. It's supposed to be an inside job. Maybe you're FBI, but that doesn't make you clean. Just put your hands where I can see them."

His face turned white. "Miles is the reason I'm here," Pete said slowly, bringing his hands out into view. "I'm not your killer. Search me. I brought proof . . ." He stepped toward me.

The last words didn't register for me until it was too late. I aimed the gun slightly to his left, just wanting to scare him a little. Everything happened in slow motion from that moment on. When I squeezed the trigger, Pete's eyes widened and I watched in horror as a slug caught him in the chest near the heart. I couldn't believe that I'd shot him.

It seemed to take an hour for him crumple to the ground. When he lay there on the braided rug with a surprised look on his face, I noticed the brown manila envelope that had slipped out from an inside pocket of his down jacket. I approached carefully, my gun still trained on the body. I picked up the envelope and opened it. A sheaf of photos slid out, photos of Miles, my protector, my lover. Photos showing a smiling Miles with one of the big bosses, Don Sabatini, shaking hands, patting each other on the back, looking around furtively for a hidden camera. Obviously, they had missed it.

Miles had been right. There was a traitor in the FBI. I sat back hard on my heels. Miles Stewart, the Fed I trusted, the guy who had been my only contact with the outside world these past few weeks, was the one who had been sent to kill me.

I turned back to the dead body and said, "Where the hell's the cavalry when you need 'em?"

Why hadn't they sent two men here to do this job? Would I have been any more reassured with two men standing outside my door? I tried to think like a G-man. Let's see . . . they probably sent just this one guy here because they were trying to salvage the situation. If two guys tried to come in, the witness—me—might get too nervous and do something stupid. Like maybe *shoot* someone.

It was typical Bureau logic. Here they had a corrupt agent to deal with, as well as the hapless witness—no sirens, no flashing red lights, no megaphones. Let's just do this as quietly as possible. Just get the witness alone and spirit her away. Then a swarm of FBI agents could come in and arrest Miles Stewart. The only problem is that they sent a guy who got himself killed by the witness.

The Witness Relocation Program: *We put you somewhere safe—like a nice deep grave in a cemetery.* Christ, I should have stayed on my own.

What should I do now, call the authorities? I could just hear the conversation: "Hi. I just killed one of your agents. Want to come pick him up?"

No, that was no good. The only thing I could do was get out of here before Miles made an appearance. If he were still alive, Pete would probably approve.

I reasoned that Pete must have come here in a car. I bent over the body to search for a set of car keys. I paused, sensing another presence in the room. The hair on the back of my neck prickled.

"Thanks for doing my work for me," said a quietly amused voice from behind me. I stiffened. Fear ran down my spine. I'd just run out of time. "I recognized this guy's car from down the road as a Bureau car." Miles came across the room, gun in hand, and took the photos out of my numb hands. After a cursory look at them, he tossed them into the fireplace and grinned at me. I watched the edges of the photos curl up and turn black as the fire ate away at its prey.

"Stand up slowly and put your gun on the table. Keep your hands where I can see them," he ordered. "We're going for a little boat ride."

Moving slowly over to the fireplace, Miles glanced over at Pete's body and laughed. "This is great. You kill the guy who came here to help you. I always thought women were too stupid to be private investigators."

I glared at him as I lowered my gun onto the coffee table. No sense in antagonizing Miles. He might decide to kill me on the spot. I sure as hell wasn't ready to die. I'd just have to wait for my opportunity to escape.

Funny, but it was the first time that I had noticed that his eyes were flat and cold. What I had once thought of as Miles' dark, brooding, good looks were suddenly stripped away to reveal the reptile behind them. How could I have once thought Miles was attractive? I shuddered as I recalled the nights by the fireplace and the mornings we woke up in each other's arms.

Maybe he was thinking similar things about me. I had to try. I tried to keep my voice steady and seductive. "Look, baby, we can go away, the two of us. I'll lay low for a while and—"

He shrugged, gave me a sardonic grin, the bastard, and said, "Sorry, Bev baby, but you're expendable. It was fun while it lasted, though." I became all the more anxious to wipe that smarmy look off his face. Out of the corner of my eye, I noticed the poker to my right.

"Yeah, expendable," I said, backing toward it. "Just like that poor dope on the floor."

Miles glanced again at the dead body. I took advantage of the moment, grabbed the poker, and swung it. He was prepared and leaned away easily. But his superior sneer turned to surprise when he stepped backwards and stumbled on the apron to the front of the fireplace. I lunged at him, brandishing my weapon. He reached out and tried to catch the free end of the poker.

If he wants the poker so much, I thought, he can have it. With that thought in mind, I swiped the poker at his free hand. Miles yelped in pain. Startled by my vicious attack, he dropped his gun and used both hands to grab the other end of the poker. I yanked it away from his grasp and went for his gun. Just when it was within my reach, Miles kicked the gun away and it went skittering across the wood floor.

"Shit," I muttered as I dove for my .38 on the coffee

table. Miles kicked my legs out from under me and I fell hard to the floor. My knees thrummed with pain, but I staggered up on my feet, ready to charge him. I looked up in time to see that Miles had recovered his gun.

I froze, wondering if this was the end. Instead, he smiled and said lightly, "Oh, no. You're not getting off that easily. You'll live long enough to drag the body down to the boat." He had his wounded hand tucked into his armpit.

I got up slowly, the anger still building in me until I thought I would explode.

"You son-of-a-bitch!" I said in a low voice.

Miles seemed to think about it for a moment, then said, "I'm a very rich son-of-a-bitch now, and soon I'll be free to leave. As soon as I get rid of you both." He turned all business, coldly ordering, "Get going."

I reluctantly took hold of Pete's feet and dragged the body out of the cabin toward the lake. Miles walked behind me. I could feel his gun trained on the spot between my shoulder blades. It wasn't easy to walk down to the dock in the dark, and even harder to drag a corpse along. I stumbled a couple of times, and each time, I could feel Miles' finger tighten on the trigger.

I managed to reach the dock alive. With one foot, Miles helped me push Pete's body into the boat's bow. Water slapped against the rocking hull. He gestured for me to get in. I clambered into the back of the boat.

"No," he said shortly. "You row."

Grudgingly, I moved forward and took hold of the two oars. I studied them as Miles pushed the boat away from the dock. The oars might make good weapons.

As if he could sense what I was thinking, Miles growled, "And don't try anything with those oars or you're dead."

"A gunshot will be heard by the people in those other

cabins," I reminded him.

"Maybe," Miles replied, "but they'll probably think it's a car backfiring, or someone shooting at hungry raccoons."

He had a point. Besides, if anyone looked out at the lake, it was too dark to tell what was out here. It was a moonless night. Massive clouds covered the sky and the air felt heavy with the promise of rain or, more likely, snow.

My eyes adjusted to the darkness, and I could make out the bulk of the body stuffed in the bow. My arms were beginning to ache from rowing. Every time the boat started to drift toward shore, Miles barked orders, steering us toward the middle of the lake.

"More to the left, Bev."

"Row stronger on your right side."

"Point the boat more toward the middle."

I was getting annoyed with Miles' orders. Besides, I was still curious about a few things and I felt that Miles owed me a few answers.

"When did you become a flunky for the mob, Miles?" I asked. "Before or after you took on this assignment?"

He ignored my jibe. "After. I was approached by one of the don's soldiers and was made an offer I couldn't refuse." He chuckled at his own clichéd joke.

"Do you mean that you were offered a lot of money, or that your loved ones were threatened if you didn't kill me?" It was a thin hope, but if it were the latter, maybe I could appeal to his sense of decency.

Unfortunately, he replied, "The money was too good to refuse. In fact, the only reason you're still alive is that I've managed to keep squeezing Sabatini for more money while I waited for the right time to dump you."

He chuckled again. His gallows humor was getting on my nerves.

"What about your partner?"

"Yeah, Mary's on vacation. She'll come back to an empty cabin and no partner." He grinned. "When I've finished with you and your friend here, I can disappear, leave the wife and kids. Start over." What a prince, I thought. "This money came at a good time for me."

Yeah, and a bad time for me. And Pete. So here I was in a boat in the middle of Red Earth Lake with a turncoat FBI agent, and a dead body that used to be an FBI agent. When I first went into the Witness Relocation Program, I'd expressed reservations. But the bureaucrats assured me that their agents were trained professionals. They were trained and professional, all right. But the one still alive was twisted.

"Stop right here," Miles said. I put the oars up slowly. This was it. In another minute, I was gonna be fish food.

I almost forgot Miles was still nursing his smashed hand.

"Bev, you're going to reach slowly under your seat. There's a length of chain there."

I did as I was told. It was a long chain, just right for weighing down dead bodies, but the links were small enough for me to handle.

Miles spoke again. "Now move to the front of the boat and wrap it around your friend's ankles."

I carefully slid up to the bow and with cold, stiff fingers, began to wrap chain around the dead man's feet.

I'd soon be joined to him at the bottom of the lake. If there was a bottom.

"That's enough," Miles' voice came from right behind me. "Now it's your turn."

I swung around, the free end of the chain whipping around in my hand. Miles leaned back in time and the chain left only a bloody welt on his cheek. He touched the wound and his fingers came away with blood. How appropriate.

I shifted my weight and swung the chain again, aiming for his gun hand. The piece went into the drink. Miles looked stunned. Then he narrowed his eyes and lunged at me, grabbing my throat with his good hand.

"You little bitch!" he snarled. He tried to lift me up, but I kneed him in the groin. It was like watching an inflatable pool deflate—all the air went out of Miles as he doubled over. His hold on my throat loosened, but not enough for me to break free. With as much strength as I could muster, I wrapped the cold iron links around his neck. He took one of his hands off my throat to grab at the chain, but I kept a firm grip on it and pulled it taut in opposite directions.

His grip became slack and I redoubled my efforts. Miles struggled to get free, his hands clawed at the chain noose. His betrayal, and the fact that I had killed an agent because of his lies, ran through my mind and I gave the chain another vicious yank. Miles' eyes widened, his tongue swelled up, then he slumped over. Whether he was unconscious or dead didn't matter much to me. I was still alive.

I thought about going back to shore and calling in the appropriate people. Yeah, Don Sabatini would send in another assassin and the FBI would spirit me away to another "safe house." Right.

Besides, what good was it going to do poor old Pete now? He was dead by my hand. I could spin a story—Miles shot my protector with my gun—but it would only cause more paperwork for everyone. I was better off taking care of myself. I decided to finish what Miles had started. It would be best for everyone, including his wife and kids. They would think he died a hero. I doubted the Bureau would tell them any different now.

I fished the car keys out of Miles' pocket and took money from his wallet as well. I'd need every cent I could get my hands on if I was going underground. After I dumped the bodies, I would row back to shore and use Miles' car to get as far away from the FBI and the mob as I could possibly get without a passport.

I sat back for a moment to catch my breath. The trembling in my hands was still there. The lake was so peaceful and quiet. Maybe I'd find another place similar to this one. A place where they would never find me. Of course, I could never work as a private investigator again, but I'd find work. It would have to be work I'd never done before. Falling back on familiar haunts and work you're qualified for makes it easy for the mob to find you.

When I felt strong enough, I wrapped a length of chain around Miles' arms and legs and secured it in a way that, if he regained consciousness, it would be impossible for him to get free.

Then I pushed both bodies overboard, sending them to the bottom of the lake. If there was a bottom.

I went back and forth about whether to include my Jefferson Birch short stories, but Birch was my first series character, and he is a private detective, albeit in the 1800s West. The novels featuring Birch were considered traditional westerns, the anthologies in which the short stories appeared were western anthologies. However, two of the three Birch stories included have only been offered in audio form. Here, for your consideration, is "Red Feather's Daughter", one of two stories included in the Hayes-Durkin audio anthologies, How the West Was Read. *I believe the actor George Kennedy read the first volume, which was a thrill for me.*

Red Feather's Daughter

Jefferson Birch had to admit it: This was the strangest meeting place his employer, Arthur Tisdale, had ever arranged. Birch shifted in his saddle and his horse Cactus shook his head nervously as they left Nez Perce territory. The animals seemed less nervous now that they were headed for the town of Coeur d'Alene. A few hours earlier, Birch had entered the Nez Perce camp with a guide and encountered his employer, Arthur Tisdale, who ran a detective agency out of San Francisco called Tisdale Investigations. An ex-army man, Tisdale was short and always neatly dressed in a suit, even on the hottest summer day. He had shaved off his mustache recently, and his upper lip shone like a beacon in contrast to the rest of his tanned face. They shook hands and Tisdale led the way to the main lodge, obviously the village head's home.

"His name is Red Feather and his daughter is missing," Tisdale had explained.

"I don't mean to sound ungrateful, Tisdale, but we are in Indian Territory. I didn't know you hired out to Indians."

Tisdale turned around, forcing Birch to stop short to avoid bumping into him.

"Do you have a problem with this assignment?"

Birch blinked. He never really thought about it. His only encounters with Indians up to now had been when he was a Ranger back in Texas. Town Apaches and Navahos had populated El Paso and he had the occasional run-in with groups of drunken Apaches that had destroyed some homesteader's ranch. He had met some men who hated Indians. Birch never thought of himself that way. Indians were just like white men in some ways. You could like some of them and dislike some of them. It all depended on his mood and the Indian's mood.

Birch found himself inside the village head's lodge, being introduced to Red Feather, the man whose daughter was missing, and Bear Who Touched the Sky, who turned out to be the daughter's betrothed. Red Feather was a squat, sad looking elderly Indian who didn't speak English. Bear Who Touched the Sky was a tall, handsome Nez Perce whose attitude toward Birch and Tisdale was just a small sign of the bitterness that was beginning to seep into the relations between whites and Indians. Birch understood, having read the accounts of what was happening to the Nez Perce.

Greedy miners had come into their territory, the land that had been set aside for the Nez Perce, and found gold. The miners had been putting pressure on the government to make the Nez Perce abandon the land, so that they could

Red Feather's Daughter

stake claims. Until now, the Nez Perce had always welcomed the white men, always willing to share the land. But bitterness was setting in as talk between government officials and Indian representatives continued. And the officials were trying to pressure the Nez Perce Chief Joseph into moving his people onto a much smaller reservation to be shared with other tribes. So far Chief Joseph was resisting the efforts, and Birch had a feeling that this time his government would push the agreeable Nez Perce too far.

Through Tisdale, who served as interpreter, Birch found out that Red Feather's daughter, Morning Star, had been missing over a week. And that she had last been seen walking by a stream that ran half a mile beyond the Nez Perce village. Birch also learned that Morning Star had been educated by a local missionary, and had been sent back East to finish up her education, courtesy of a rich family, the Proux, who lived in Lewiston.

She had been christened Anna Christine by the missionary, a Reverend Thomas Kirk. Birch turned to Bear. "Were you looking forward to Morning Star becoming your wife?"

Bear, after Tisdale translated Birch's question, showed no emotion. Birch didn't need Tisdale to translate Bear's answer. He said, "Yes" in Nez Perce.

Birch wondered how it must feel for a proud, fierce warrior like Bear Who Touched the Sky, to be marrying a woman from the same tribe who had been brought up partially in the white man's world. For that matter, Birch wondered how Morning Star felt about the impending union.

He asked Red Feather. "How did your daughter feel about marrying Bear Who Touched the Sky?"

"She was looking forward to her duties as a good wife to Bear Who Touched the Sky," was Red Feather's answer.

But Birch caught a troubled look on his face. There was more to it, but Birch had a feeling that Red Feather wouldn't tell him the entire truth. He thought of another line of questioning.

He addressed Red Feather. "Have you talked to this reverend, the one who helped send your daughter back East to complete her education?"

Red Feather and Bear Who Touched the Sky glanced at each other before answering. "Yes, we have talked to him. He is the first person we thought to talk to when Morning Star disappeared."

"And what was his reaction to her disappearance?" Birch asked.

"He did not seem very concerned," Bear said in a fierce tone. Birch noticed that his fists were clenched tightly at his sides.

Tisdale took out his Waltham pocket watch. "Well, Mr. Birch, there seems to be nothing more to be learned here. I must be in Lewiston within the week." He gave no explanation beyond that and Birch had no reason to stay beyond the time he had already spent.

Through Tisdale, Red Feather gave Birch several names of people Morning Star had known in Coeur d'Alene, where she had been educated.

"I expect," came Tisdale's short reply, "I'll be in touch soon."

With that, Tisdale headed southwest, Birch due south. It took several hours for Birch to ride to the town of Coeur d'Alene.

He found Reverend Thomas Kirk's house easily. It was a modest dwelling, but it looked comfortable. Birch knocked on the door, and a few minutes later a plump, red-cheeked man with a perpetual smile on his face and a shock of thick, white hair came to the door.

"Reverend Thomas Kirk?" Birch had taken off his hat in deference to the man of the cloth.

"That's me," the man said with a chuckle. "What can I do for you, young fellow?"

He hadn't called Birch stranger, the common greeting for anyone who wasn't known to the general populous of a small town. He had used the term "young fellow." Very friendly. Birch wondered how friendly he would be when he was questioned about Morning Star. He explained why he was there.

The reverend surprised him by opening the door wider and stepping back. "Come in, come in."

They sat in the front room and were waited upon by Reverend Kirk's wife, a woman as spare as the reverend was round. "Come here, wife. This is Jefferson Birch. He has come for some information about Morning Star, known to us now as Anna Christine," Reverend Kirk said, gesturing to his wife.

She sidled over to him and he took her hand. "Mr. Birch, this is my wife, Marie."

"Please to meet you Mr. Birch," Marie Kirk replied, bobbing her head. Her eyes darted towards the back of the house. "Let me put some water on for tea." She slipped out of her husband's hold and left the room.

The reverend lowered his voice. "Marie will be back in a few minutes with a tray of bread and jam as well as tea. I hope you haven't eaten yet."

As a matter of fact, Birch hadn't eaten since early morning and the promise of something to eat was most welcome. "Reverend, I'll come straight to the point. I have just come from the Nez Perce village and Red Feather is very concerned about the fate of his daughter. He thinks you have some knowledge of her whereabouts and would be grateful if you would cooperate."

The Reverend frowned and took a pair of bifocals from a side table by the chair he sat in. He rubbed them absently with a large handkerchief. "Sorry if I left him with that impression. But I do not know where Anna Christine is." He didn't look all that concerned.

Birch was getting the same feeling that Red Feather and Bear Who Touched the Sky had gotten. He decided to get the information from another angle. "Did she have any friends here in Coeur d'Alene?"

"Oh yes," the Reverend said obviously pleased to get off the subject of Morning Star's disappearance, but just as pleased to talk about her. "She didn't look very Indian, which was one of the reasons why I had chosen her to tutor. She fit very well into Coeur d'Alene society and she has several friends who live here in town."

"Can you give me their names?"

Reverend Kirk hesitated for a fraction of a second and then smiled. "Of course, if you think it would help." He got up and went over to his desk. He took a sheet of paper and dipped his pen in the ink well. Then he wrote down a couple of names with a flourish, blotted the paper and handed it to Birch just as Mrs. Kirk brought in a tea tray.

The Reverend rubbed his hands together as his wife poured tea. "Now, Mr. Birch, shall we partake of this repast?"

Birch wasn't sure how the Reverend's wife had come up with such an elaborate tray in such a short time. There were thick slices of fresh baked bread, homemade gooseberry jam and sweet churned butter, molasses cookies, some kind of sweet cake with brown sugar topping and tea with cream and sugar.

While they ate, Mrs. Kirk withdrew again to the kitchen. The reverend didn't seem to notice this time. His hand reached greedily for another cookie, his tea sloshing over his cup.

Birch decided that while the reverend's guard was down, this was a good time to talk to him. "Why did you offer to send Anna Christine back east?" Birch asked.

Reverend Kirk swallowed a bite of cookie and slurped some of his milky tea. "Anna was a quick learner, and I could see that she enjoyed our world. As I said earlier, she fit nicely into Coeur d'Alene's society. Sometimes I think her mother might have been a white woman."

"What about her father, Red Feather, and the man she is betrothed to, Bear Who Touched the Sky?"

The reverend stopped sipping tea and looked at Birch curiously. "What about them?"

"Well, you don't seem very concerned about Anna's well being, so I'm assuming you know where she is. Don't you think her father has the right to know that she is well?"

The Reverend frowned. "Mr. Birch, I don't think you understand Red Feather's concern very well." His cup clattered onto its saucer and he started.

"Enlighten me."

"Red Feather wanted, well, the whole Nez Perce nation wanted, Anna Christine to become a symbol of their new nation. They wanted her to be," here, Reverend Kirk seemed to be searching for a word or description, "they wanted her to be another Sarah Winnemucca."

Birch was aware of who Sarah Winnemucca was, a Paiute woman who had been taught by Christian missionaries. She had become a negotiator and a spokeswoman for the Indian nation. Still she was a controversial figure. Her own people did not always trust her. She had been married twice to date and from what Birch had read about her, he did not imagine that she felt comfortable in either the white man's world or in her own tribe. Without telling him anything specific, the reverend was filling in the picture of Morning Star, Anna Christine, for Birch. The only thing Birch needed to do now was to figure out where Anna Christine was staying and go to speak to her.

"Reverend," he began. "I think I understand part of the reason why Anna Christine left her tribe. But it will do no good to keep her in hiding." Birch finished off his tea and stood up, taking his hat up ready to leave. "Please tell me where she is and let me go speak to her. Her father needs to know where she is, needs to know that she wasn't taken away against her will. And if she is unhappy with the plans her father and Chief Joseph have for her, she should confront her father."

The reverend looked up at Birch with sad eyes and shook his head. He put his teacup down and stood up to shake Birch's hand. "I'm sorry Mr. Birch, but you know how women are treated. I don't think the girl would have much of a choice. Besides," he smiled regretfully here, "I gave Anna Christine my word and I can't go back on it. Please convey my sympathies to her Indian family." He turned and called to his wife, who appeared quickly enough.

"Please show Mr. Birch the door, dear. I have a sermon to write."

Mrs. Kirk walked Birch to the door and went outside with him.

"If I don't bring news back to her father," Birch told Mrs. Kirk, "there could be trouble for the reverend and yourself. Possibly, the entire town."

He wasn't sure that would happen, but Bear Who

Touched the Sky seemed to be the sort of man who would take things into his own hands if he didn't see results soon. Birch looked the Reverend's wife straight in the eye. "You could avert a tragedy, Mrs. Kirk."

She hesitated, turning away for a moment and catching her breath. When she turned back there was determination in her eye. "My husband gave his word, but no one asked me to give mine. I love Anna Christine as I would love my own daughter, but I've been against her decision to leave her father and tribe since the beginning. But I cannot in good faith tell you where Anna Christine is living. However, I can tell you a name of someone who might help you."

She told him and Birch thanked her and left.

It was ninety miles to Lewiston through the Coeur d'Alene Mountains and it took Birch three days to get there. The Proux name was well known in Lewiston, hanging above a general store, a hotel and a saloon. Even a street was named after them. In one of the saloons in Lewiston, he learned more about the family. Gene Proux had been a merchant who had made his money by moving West and opening up a trading post near Fort Hall during the early days of the immigrant trail. When he had amassed his fortune, he moved his family to Lewiston and they had been there for ten years. Birch learned that Jason, the youngest, had recently returned from back east where he had attended Harvard College.

It was early in the evening when Birch left the saloon to pay a visit to Gene Proux. He had just entered the stable and was getting ready to saddle up Cactus when he heard two men approaching. Birch thought little of it since this was a boarding stable. The first man caught Birch off-guard with a blow to the head. The second man pinned his arms back and let the first man throw a few more punches to Birch's gut. Through all of this, Birch could hear Cactus prancing around nervously eyeing the attackers. When the men stopped beating him up, Birch fell to his knees on the hay-strewn floor, his arms clutching his middle as he tried to catch his breath.

"We hear you've been asking questions about the Prouxs," one of the men said.

Birch couldn't have identified either of them. He had been too busy taking blows to take notice of what they looked like.

"Stay away from the Prouxs. In fact it would be better for your health if you leave town tonight."

When Birch finally recovered enough to look up, they were gone. Nothing made Birch more determined to find out the truth than someone who told him he couldn't investigate.

He rode out to Gene Proux's house, his hand near his gun, all the time wary of possible ambushes. When he got to the house, a large, handsome mansion befitting a man of Proux's status, Birch dismounted and climbed the steps to the imposing front door. A stiff butler with a British accent answered and, looking down his nose at Birch, left him outside while he went in search of his employer. Ten minutes later a barrel of a man, thick graying mustache, monocle in his left eye, cigar clenched between his teeth, came to the door.

"I'm Gene Proux. Who are you?" He eyed Birch warily. "Are you a messenger?"

Birch didn't feel much like playing games. He came straight to the point. "Yes, I've been hired to give you a message from Red Feather and Bear Who Touched the Sky. Red Feather wants to see his daughter."

Proux went stoned faced. "I don't know what you are talking about, Mister. But I'm calling my guards to throw you out."

"The way you called the other men who sucker-punched me back at the stables back in Lewiston?"

A strange expression crossed Proux's face. "What are you talking about? I sent no men to come after you. I don't even know you."

Birch was getting tired of facing hostility and secrecy. "Well, someone in the Proux family knows me, knew that I was coming here. Reverend Kirk had three days to send a wire to someone. And I can go down to the telegraph office to find out who it was. And then I can bring the marshal."

Birch had checked earlier on the Lewiston marshal, and discovered that he was an honest lawman, not bought and paid for by powerful men like some lawmen. Gene Proux went pale, then took a few moments to think about it. He seemed to make up his mind quickly as to who had sent the men and why.

"We better settle this right now." He ordered a horse saddled up and led Birch to his son's house about a mile away. "My son is recently returned from Harvard in Boston. He was just married the other day," was all that Gene Proux would say on the ride over.

No expense had been spared on this house either. Birch wondered if it had been a wedding gift to the young couple. Ornate wrought-iron work and gingerbread cutouts decorated the house. Proux knocked on the massive carved mahogany door, hat already in his hand.

A maid opened the door and looked curiously at him. "Mr. Proux, your son is indisposed at the moment. Would you like to come in and wait while I tell him you are here?" She opened the door wider to usher him in and then seemed to catch sight of Birch.

"He's with me, Martha," Proux said. "Is the lady of the house at home as well?"

"Yes sir. I'll tell her you are here." She threw another interested look at Birch before withdrawing from the parlor.

A few moments later, a young woman came into the room. She was beautiful in an exotic way, her black hair held back with diamond and ruby combs, her ebony eyes sparkling brighter than the jewels that graced her hair. She had that special glow that only newlywed women can wear and Birch hated to bring up her past. She glanced at Birch, then went over to Gene Proux. He took her hands as she lightly kissed him on the cheek.

"You must be Morning Star," Birch said. She withdrew her hands from her father-in-law and took a few steps back. Her complexion turned pale and she put a hand to her mouth. "I'm sorry, sir, there's no one by that name here," came a voice behind her. A handsome young man outfitted in the latest fashion from back east, put his hands on her shoulders and tried to draw her away from the door. He noticed Birch's companion. "Father, what are you doing here?"

Gene Proux gazed steadily at his son. "And I might ask you what you meant by hiring two men to beat up this man for asking questions?"

Jason Proux paled. "I . . . I don't what you mean."

His father's brow darkened. "Don't lie to me, my son. You've never been very good at it."

Morning Star stepped between the men. "Please, Father, don't be angry with him. He did it for me, for us."

All of the anger drained out of Gene Proux. He looked kindly at her and put a hand to her cheek. "I know dear, I know." He looked tired. "But it's time to tell the truth. No more deception."

She nodded and turned to Birch. "I am sorry about what happened to you, Mr. Birch." She glanced at her new husband who stared at Birch in a hateful, protective manner.

"I have been hired by your father to find you."

"Well you can tell him that there is no Morning Star here." Jason had shouldered his way past his father and threw a weak punch at Birch, who easily avoided it. "Come on, step outside and show me you are a man."

Birch studied him and then said, "Son, one thing your father obviously hasn't taught you, never pick a fight with an armed man." He pulled back the edge of his duster and showed Jason his gun. Jason deflated and stepped back.

"Jason, it's time." Morning Star, now Anna Christine, turned back to Birch. "I'll be happy to talk to you, Mr. Birch." Anna Christine sat on the seat and indicated that everyone else should sit. Birch liked the fact that she had taken charge of the situation. Her husband sat next to her. "Mr. Birch, is it?" He nodded and waited. Anna Christine continued. "Mr. Birch, please convey my apologies to my father for any worries that I may have caused him." She glanced at her husband. "As you can see, I am well taken care of."

Jason Proux put a hand over her hand and smiled. It was clear to Birch that he loved her and would do anything to protect her. "Mrs. Proux, may I ask one thing?"

She turned her bright smile to him and said, "Of course. Ask anything."

"Why?"

Her smile dimmed a bit as if a stiff wind had blown through her heart, and she looked down. "Mr. Birch, I met Jason when I was being tutored by the Reverend and his wife." She paused here and laughed a bit. "You went to see the Reverend, didn't you. That's how you found out I was here." Birch felt the Reverend and his wife needed defending, but he didn't have to say a word. The question was rhetorical. Anna Christine shook her head. "The Reverend probably didn't give up my whereabouts, it was Mrs. Kirk wasn't it?"

Birch shrugged, wanting to remain noncommittal.

She continued. "I bear her no ill-will. Mrs. Kirk has always counseled me to face my father and she knew it was just a matter of time." The maid came in with a tea tray. It would be the first time today that Birch had eaten. As the maid poured tea, Anna Christine said, "You must have given Mrs. Kirk a pressing reason why she should violate my confidence. Even though she didn't approve of the way I left, she would not have told you unless there was some threat." She looked up as if an unpleasant thought had just occurred to her. "You didn't scare her badly, did you?"

Birch smiled and shook his head. "I just told her what might happen if your father and his tribe didn't find you. The Kirks are not good liars and both your father and your betrothed knew that the Reverend was lying to them."

Her husband had remained quiet until now, but it was clear that he was getting restless. "Anna, you don't have to talk to him."

She eyed Birch speculatively. "Is that right, Mr. Birch, I don't have to talk to you?"

Birch shook his head. "No, I can't make you talk to me."

"But my father will hear only what I have told you so far." She looked at her husband who met her gaze, and then reluctantly nodded his understanding that things had progressed too far for her to stop now. She stood up abruptly, her arms crossed and paced languidly as if she'd been born to this life. "As I said before, I had grown up partly in the Reverend and Mrs. Kirk's house. And I knew Jason and his family. We didn't fall in love until we were both in Boston. We saw each other more frequently there, going for Sunday buggy rides in the countryside, walks in the Boston Common, and to the opera and the theatre, all with a chaperone, of course." Birch nodded and sipped his tea. He was getting tired of tea and wished for something stronger. As if reading his mind, Gene Proux stood up and went over to a table on which a cut glass brandy decanter and four snifters stood. He poured three healthy shots and offered one to Birch and one to his son. Anna Christine turned to look fondly at her husband. "We fell in love, and decided that nothing would keep us apart."

"Not even Bear Who Touched the Sky?" Birch could feel Jason Proux's tension.

"Not even my father's plans for me for the future of our tribe," Anna Christine replied pointedly.

"So you were running away from expectations?" Birch suggested.

Anna Christine gave him a warm smile. "No, I was running to my future." She looked out the window and then turned back to Birch. "Come for a walk with me in my garden."

It was not a suggestion. It was a command. Birch complied. It was a hot spring day and rows of daffodils, irises and crocuses were springing up. Even a peony bush had buds on it, ready to burst into flower at the end of May.

"You have heard something of my father's expectations for me, haven't you?" Anna Christine asked.

"Yes, it seemed to me that he was trying to do some good for your people by getting you an education in the white man's world."

She smiled bitterly. "He got the idea after meeting Sarah Winnemucca many years ago, when she was first becoming known to Indians and white men alike. When Reverend and Mrs. Kirk offered to take me in, he saw it as an opportunity to do some good for the people. He saw me as destined to become just like her."

"Well, that had to be hard to live up to," Birch said.

She nodded. "I had the opportunity to meet Miss Winnemucca at a lecture at Harvard. Jason escorted me, and afterwards we were introduced. I found myself telling her about my dilemma. She seemed to understand my vacillation between doing what was expected of me and what I really wanted. She saw the love between Jason and me." Anna Christine stopped and faced me. "And do you know what she told me?"

"I have a pretty good idea," he said.

She started to walk again, slower this time. "She told me that some people were born to a destiny, and others were pressed into it against their will. I felt as if she could see right through me. Then she encouraged me to do what was right for me."

"She sounds like a wise woman," Birch replied.

Anna Christine nodded decisively. "She is. But it's been hard not knowing how to tell my father, and eventually Chief Joseph. Not wanting to dash their hopes and dreams of a better day for our people, but I don't think I'm their answer." She paused and then said in a sad voice, "I don't think there is an answer."

"It must be hard to live with someone else's expectation and not be able to live your own life."

She nodded. "You understand," she sighed. "But I suppose that I have to face my father. It has been a little over two weeks since I left, and it's time to make things right." She held out her hand. "Thank you, Mr. Birch."

He stood up to shake her hand. She had a firm, dry

handshake. She would have made a fine translator, but she would have been unhappy. In the background, Jason was coming toward them. Gene Proux stayed in the background.

"I'll have to consult with my husband."

"I think he will support you, Mrs. Proux," Birch said. The Prouxs escorted him to the front of their house where he swung up in the saddle. "I'll be riding back to your father's village. When should I tell him to expect you?"

She looked at her husband, talked softly a few moments and then replied, "We will be packing today and should be there a day behind you, Mr. Birch."

He tipped his hat to them, wheeled Cactus around and headed back north.

Although it was not the ending Red Feather or Bear Who Touched the Sky would have wanted, at least he could assure them that Morning Star was safe and happy. But Birch had to wonder if she had bought her own happiness at the expense of her nation's future.

I unabashedly love this story. It was included in a crime fiction anthology entitled Murder for Mother, *and it had to take place around Mother's Day. My Angela Matelli stories vary from dark to light, and this one definitely tips the scales toward light humor.*

The Disappearance of Edna Guberman

I leaned back in my chair and tried to put my feet up on the desk, the way I'd seen so many private eyes do it in the movies. When the chair tipped so far back that I thought I'd slide out of it and through the open window onto the unforgiving pavement below, I tried to get my feet off the desk. But the heel of my running shoe was snagged on a tack that, in a moment of boredom and stupidity a few days ago, I'd stuck halfway into the desk surface. So I tried to make myself as comfortable as possible and, phone clamped to my ear, listened to the voice on the other end of the receiver. It was my mother, and she was talking about my upcoming visit to her.

"Aunt Sarah will want to see you girls when you and Rosa get here," she was saying as I tried to figure out how the hell I was going to get myself out of this pretzel position.

"No one likes Aunt Sarah, Ma," I replied. "And I don't think she's too crazy about our family. Besides, how come Sophia or our brothers never have to come along?"

"They all have their own families, darling," Ma explained to me patiently. Once again, in that subtle motherly way, she was reminding me that I hadn't gotten married and produced any grandchildren for her. But I outsmarted her—I ignored the dig. My little sister Rosa would have completely lost it and confronted Ma on her outmoded notions.

Aunt Sarah was this creepy old lady who is distantly related to us by marriage. Although she never seems to appreciate it, Ma insists that we go visit her several times a year, always bringing casseroles and desserts. The inside of Aunt Sarah's house was lined with old newspapers that were stacked to the rafters, creating a surrealistic maze for visitors that rivaled some of the best British garden mazes. It was a fire hazard, and whenever I tactfully brought this up to Ma, she would just say, "She's thrifty."

The place was also thick with cats. During our visit, Aunt Sarah would spend half the time carrying on silly one-way conversations with the sullen felines who were draped over the furniture, the mantelpiece, and every other square inch of space in the living room. The cloying, musty smell of old cat litter hung heavily in the air, and cat hair was everywhere.

"Anyway, you and Rosa will be here tonight, right?"

I managed to extricate one foot from the lip of the desktop. My chair did a crazy tilt to the left, and I reached out to steady myself, dropping the phone receiver in the process. My office door opened at that precise moment, and a worried woman walked in. I must have looked pretty silly with one foot on the desk and the receiver dangling from its cord over the desk, Ma's squawking coming from it. "Angie? Angie? Are you okay? Are you there?"

Trying to maintain as much dignity as possible, which wasn't much, I pulled my other foot off the desk and righted my chair. Somehow I managed a businesslike gesture to the only empty chair in the room as I picked up

The Disappearance of Edna Guberman

the receiver at the same time.

"Ma? I have to call you back. Someone just walked in."

"Angie! Don't you dare take a case this time. You missed Mother's Day last year." Ma sounded like she was going to cry.

I winced, remembering how I had come up with some lame excuse for not visiting her on Mother's Day a year ago. Something about car trouble and paperwork. I enjoy visiting Ma, but not on holidays when my older sister Sophia is there. We don't get along, and I don't think it adds to the festive atmosphere when the two of us—the three of us, actually, because lately my youngest sister Rosa has been joining in the fracas—start arguing at the top of our lungs.

Frankly, I think Mother's Day is Ma's way of getting back at us kids for all the trouble we gave her during our formative years. There's never any question that her single children will be spending Mother's Day with her. Since my brothers are all married, they can get out of it. They get to skip the feast once in a while and all the fighting and back-biting and guilt trips that go with it—to visit their mothers-in-law. It almost makes marriage sound appealing.

"I promise I'll be there, Ma, but I have to eat, too." I threw an ingratiating smile at my potential client, who looked through me as if she was thinking of something else. When I had hung up, I turned my attention to her. "Now, what can I do to help you?"

She was about forty, although her elfin features, framed by a shiny dark cap of hair and large gray eyes, made her look younger at first glance. She was thin to the point of anorexia, but was well dressed in designer business attire. I guessed that she either worked as a stockbroker or ran her own company. She started to say something to me, but before she could get a word out, her chin trembled and she tried to gulp back great big sobs. I pushed a box of tissues across the desk, and she grabbed a fistful, pushing it to her face to get control of herself. It's a weird experience to see a career woman in tears.

"I-I don't kn-know where to begin," she began with a huge shuddering breath. After blowing her nose, which had turned a shiny red from the crying, she introduced herself. "My name is Carol Zakowski, and my mother's missing."

Bingo, I thought. This is how I can get out of driving out to Malden to visit Ma tomorrow. "When did you discover she was gone?" I asked, grabbing a pencil and paper.

"I came home from work early, about two hours ago." That would be about two o'clock, in my brilliant estimation. "I live, we live, a few blocks from here," she continued, dabbing at the flow of tears in the corners of her eyes. "My mother's name is Edna Guberman, and she's lived with me for almost three years. Ever since my divorce became final, it just seemed convenient to share an apartment. Neither of us are interested in getting married again."

It turned out that Edna Guberman was sixty-two years old and widowed, according to Carol. I was given a picture of the two of them sitting on the sofa next to last year's Christmas tree. Edna was a sweet-faced woman with a halo of fluffy, curly white hair. She looked like the perfect mother.

"I was planning on surprising her tonight with a trip to Hawaii. She's always talked of how much she wanted to go back—my parents honeymooned there in the 1940s—and I thought how nice it would be to take her." Boy, did *that* make me feel guilty for wanting to postpone the inevitable family event at Ma's tonight.

"How do you know she's not coming back?" I asked.

The Disappearance of Edna Guberman

Carol dug into her purse and produced a hastily scribbled note on the back of a grocery receipt that said: *Carol, I know what you're planning and I can't let it happen. Don't worry about me. Love, Mom.*

"I had packed her bag and left it in my bedroom this morning, but it was gone, too," Carol explained. "We were supposed to leave tonight on an eight-thirty flight from Logan Airport. I know she's not fond of flying, or traveling of any kind really. When we flew to Chicago for my grandma's funeral last year, Mom had to down two glasses of white wine before I could get her on the plane."

"Do you have any siblings she might drop in on?" I asked.

"Jane, my sister in Tulsa. But I checked all the flights out, and she's not on any of them. I also called Jane to find out if she knew anything, but she hasn't heard from Mom either."

I let out the breath I had been holding. "What about anyone local?"

Carol gave me the names of several people her mother knew: her beautician, the local grocer, the neighbor, Edna's best friend, her bridge partners, and her brother, Carol's uncle. But no, Edna couldn't go to Uncle Harry—he lived at the YMCA. Besides, Carol had called him, and he'd told her he hadn't heard from Edna. They weren't all that close anyway.

"Okay," I said. "What about this best friend, Marilyn Strickland? Have you called her?"

"I couldn't reach her," Carol said. "Maybe she's out or something. I can keep trying." She got up. "I only have a few hours before the flight. It's worth hiring you for these few hours if you can find her quickly."

"You haven't had a disagreement with your mother

lately? It seems strange that she would leave so suddenly."

Shaking her head, Carol said in a puzzled voice, "She must have found out about the trip, but I can't believe she would be this upset about going to Hawaii."

I didn't say anything because there was no use in alarming my client over nothing, but I was wondering if Edna Guberman had left of her own accord.

I called my mother to tell her I would be late. At first she yelled at me, but after I explained that this was about a vanishing mother, she said, "Disappearing daughters happen all the time, but a disappearing mother? Something's fishy. Take all the time you need." I thought she was being sweet until she added, in the tone a drill sergeant uses with his men, "Just be here tomorrow at noon for dinner."

Maxine's Cut 'n' Curl was right down the street from my office. I walked into the perm-and-shampoo-scented salon and asked to speak to Maxine. While I waited, I checked the place out. The walls were painted yellow, and the chairs were pink.

Maxine came over to me. She was a large woman in a pink smock and bright yellow hair was pinned up in an elaborate do. She went with the decor. I introduced myself.

"So you're a private eye," she said with frank curiosity. "Just like in the movies, right? Wow! Never met one before, but to think I've met a female P.I." She eyed my hair. "What can I do for you?"

I got straight to the point. "I'm looking for Edna Guberman. She's moved out of her daughter's apartment, and Carol only has a few hours to find her." I explained the circumstances. Normally private eyes don't discuss their cases with the people who are being questioned. But with the limited amount of time we had to find Edna Guberman, I figured that the gossip circle could spread the information in about half the time it would take me to question everyone.

"I saw her early this afternoon, about one o'clock, for a touch-up perm. She'd just come off of her hospital volunteer work at Brigham's." Maxine reached out and felt my hair. "You really need a hot oil treatment. It shouldn't be this dry. And you could use a trim, too."

I smiled. "Thanks. Maybe I'll make an appointment with you after we find Edna."

Maxine smiled and nodded. "I think one of Edna's bridge partners is here. Lori," she called over her shoulder. A shapely nineteen-year-old girl with lots of hair and thick black eyeliner completely outlining her eyes came up. She was chewing and cracking a wad of gum. "Lori, is Louise Harris still here?"

"Yeah," Lori replied before popping her gum. "She's under a dryer."

Maxine led me back and introduced me, raising her voice above the sound of the dryer. "It's an emergency, Louise."

Louise Harris was a dumpy, middle-aged woman with bright red lipstick. Her hair was all done up in small pink rollers with a big strip of cotton keeping the perm solution from running into her eyes. We had interrupted her reading. "Eh?" she replied.

Maxine repeated herself, and Louise shook her head. "Haven't seen Edna since last Tuesday," she said loudly, then looked at me and shrugged. "Sorry," she shouted before going back to reading her copy of *People* magazine.

I thanked Maxine and left.

Since Marilyn and Edna and Louise were three of the four who played bridge every Tuesday night, I headed for the home of Phyllis McKay. We had agreed that Carol would stay at home and keep trying to get in touch with

Marilyn while I tracked down and questioned the others.

Phyllis McKay, the fourth bridge partner, lived a few blocks north of my office in a high-rise. She let me in only after I explained my mission over the intercom in the lobby. Once inside her apartment, it was obvious that Phyllis lived well. I'm not good with antiques, but I recognized a few things, French chairs and Italian commodes and a nice tapestry hanging on the wall in the foyer. I wondered what she was doing hanging out with dumpy Louise and widowed Edna. I hadn't met Marilyn yet, so I had no way of knowing just how out of place Phyllis was in the group.

"I'm afraid I haven't heard from either Edna or Marilyn since—"

I finished her sentence for her. "Last Tuesday. Tell me, has she seemed depressed lately?"

Phyllis wrinkled her perfect forehead, which I suspected of having been worked on, and brightened. "I remember a few months ago, she was a little upset when she came to bridge night. Carol had discussed putting her in an old-age home. At least, that's what she told me." She shook her head. "But that wouldn't help you, would it. Edna was her usual self the next week, and it was never mentioned again." Phyllis turned her attention to flowers in a large vase and started to arrange them. "Would you like some coffee?"

I told her coffee would be very nice. Before she went out to the kitchen, I asked permission to use the phone, then called Carol at her home.

"I haven't heard anything," she said in a sad voice. "And Marilyn still isn't home." There was a moment of silence, then she said in a whisper, "You don't think anything . . . *bad* has happened to them, do you?"

I assured her that she was probably blowing it out of pro-

The Disappearance of Edna Guberman

portion. "I'll go over to Marilyn's place as soon as I finish questioning Phyllis." We hung up.

Phyllis and I talked a few more minutes, but when I finished my coffee—a dark, aromatic Italian blend—and looked at my watch, it was already six o'clock. I had only two and a half hours to go. I thanked her and left. The only place left to go was that of Edna's best friend, Marilyn Strickland.

Marilyn's apartment was only a few blocks away, but the neighborhood wasn't as nice as Phyllis McKay's. The apartment building was still fairly well maintained with the smell of lemon-scented ammonia in the hallways and all the hall lights working. I knocked on her door, but there was no answer. A woman balancing a bag of groceries in her arms came down the hall and stopped at the door of the apartment across the way. I thought she hadn't taken notice of me, but as she pulled her keys out, she said, "Looking for Marilyn Strickland? I don't think she's back yet."

"Do you know when she'll be back?" I asked.

The woman opened her door and put her groceries on a table just inside the apartment, then turned back to me. "I don't know that, but I do know she went out earlier today about four-thirty. There was a woman with her who was carrying a suitcase. Looked like she was going somewhere."

I nodded and pulled out the photo of Edna Guberman. "Is this the other woman?"

Marilyn's neighbor nodded. "That's her. She looked real upset as they were leaving. It looked as if she had been crying."

I couldn't believe my luck. "I don't suppose Marilyn told you where they were going."

The woman thought for a moment, then said, "I think I

heard Tulsa in their conversation, but I couldn't swear to it."

Well, if Edna wasn't taking a plane, there were only two choices—the train station and the bus terminal. I called Carol and told her what I had just learned.

"Oh, she probably wouldn't take the train," she replied. "She doesn't like trains. All forms of travel involve either Dramamine or a good, stiff drink. Buses stop more frequently so she can get off and walk around, have a drink."

Edna Guberman was beginning to sound less like the perfect mother and more like a lush, but I kept my thoughts to myself. I hung up the phone and took the subway to Arlington Street. The bus terminal is the very definition of a pit. Gum wrappers and spilled soft drinks littered the sidewalk outside, and inside was a haven for the homeless, the hopeless, and the insane. I scanned the apathetic faces of those who would soon be boarding the departing buses, but Edna was not among them. I checked the restroom downstairs, but there was no one at all down there. Somehow, an hour had already gone by and I only had a little over an hour to find her and pop her in a cab headed for Logan.

I pulled out the photo of Edna and went over to the counter. When my turn came, I went up to the first open window. "Has this woman bought a ticket in the last few hours?" I asked.

The clerk gave me an exasperated look. "Lady," he said, "you gotta be kidding. You expect me to remember? Geez, I've only seen a couple hundred people since my shift began at four."

I was relentless—and desperate. "She bought a ticket to Tulsa. Probably within the last two hours. And she was with another lady about her age."

The Disappearance of Edna Guberman

He looked at me for a minute, a disgusted look on his face. But when he saw that I was not going to leave without some information, he sighed heavily and checked his computer monitor. A few minutes later, he said, "Three people have bought tickets to Tulsa since five o'clock. That's all I can tell you. We don't require names or anything like that."

"Can you tell me if a bus has left for Tulsa since then?"

"No," he replied, "we only have two heading out that way each day—one at twelve-forty-five, and one at eight-oh-five tonight."

I felt a surge of hope. "Thank you," I said before turning and scanning the faces of the crowd one more time. There was still a possibility that she was here in Boston, here in this very terminal, or she was very close by. I looked at my watch. It was seven-fifteen. If she had bought a bus ticket, she and Marilyn had gone out, maybe for a cup of coffee. The coffee shop! There was one attached to the terminal that was just as greasy and depressing as the bus station itself. I entered it and looked around, but there was no Edna Guberman sitting at a booth, sipping java with her good friend Marilyn.

I supposed I could wait until eight, but I was restless. I started to walk out of the coffee shop when I had a thought—Edna wasn't going to be drinking coffee right before she boarded a bus for a long ride to Tulsa. She'd find a bar, something close by.

Outside, I looked around. There wasn't much choice in the way of bars. You'd think in an area like this, there'd be a dozen seedy joints surrounding the bus terminal. But the weird thing about the area was that across the street from the terminal was one of the more elegant hotels, Park Plaza. Of course, these days, it was a bit worn around the gilt edges, and there were an awful lot of businesses occupying the first floor, but it still had Trader Vic's and a few upper-class shops for the discriminating traveler. Then I spotted a likely place: The Wishing Well Lounge.

It was dark inside, but then, it was dark outside, too. A steady beat throbbed in the main lounge area, and colored lights fleshed on and off. What kind of place was this? I asked myself:

"Five dollars," someone said. I looked around until I found a woman sitting at a small table just inside the door. As my eyes adjusted to the darkness, I talked to her. "I'm not here for a drink, I'm trying to find someone." I started to pull Edna's photo out of my pocket, but she waved it away.

"That's what they all say," she said in a flat voice. She stuck out her palm again, and I paid up, making a mental note to bill it to my client.

"Woo, woo!" some woman screamed. Another squealed. Then I saw why they were shrieking—a man was doing a bump and grind on the stage, wearing only a sequined G-string. Women crowded each other along the foot of the stage. It was a truly frightening spectacle to watch. Anonymous hands waved dollar bills at the stripper, and his G-string kept getting pulled and tugged in various ways. My eyes traveled up to his face, which wore an expression of phony rapture, presumably at the touch of these women's dishpan hands.

As the music wound down, he bent down and kissed a few of his admirers. Then he slowly turned around so we could see his muscled ass, and picked up his costume and left the stage. The lights came up, and the women drifted back to their seats. I picked my way through the milling crowd in search of Edna and her friend. I found them at a table near the stage.

The Disappearance of Edna Guberman

"Edna Guberman?" I said. She had a pleasant smile on her face and when she didn't respond right away, I realized that her pleasant smile was the result of being totally sozzled.

The woman standing next to her, Marilyn, I presumed, was a little taller than me with pale blond hair braided and wrapped around her head. Some of the pins that were holding it in place had come loose, and her normally sharp face was out of focus. She answered me readily. "Yeah, that's Edna." Her eyes were too bright from drinking, but at least she wasn't incoherent. She leaned across the table and shook Edna's arm. "Hey, Edna! Someone's here to see you."

Edna shook her head a little and took a sip of some concoction with pieces of fruit and little umbrellas decorating the edge of the fake coconut. Edna perked up a little and looked my way as if she were seeing me for the first time—which she probably was. "So who're you? Do I know you?" She sucked the dregs of her drink and managed to signal a passing cocktail waitress.

"You drinking?" she asked me. I shook my head.

"Actually, your daughter sent me."

"Who, Jane? I haven't even tol' Jane I was comin' to Tulsa."

"No, your *other* daughter, Carol."

"I ain't got no other daughter," a surly Edna snarled at me.

Marilyn leaned toward me and patted my arm. "She don't like to talk about the other one."

I must have looked mystified because Marilyn explained it to me. "She came home this afternoon and found her bag packed in Carol's room. Doesn't want to be shipped off."

Didn't want to go to Hawaii? That was the first time I'd

ever witnessed anyone go to such extremes to avoid the sunny islands. Besides, how did Edna find out about Carol's surprise trip? Maybe an unsuspecting travel agent called to confirm the plans, and Edna took the call. I was about to ask the by-now-almost-comatose Edna about this, when the lights went down again.

"And now, ladies," a disembodied Barry White-type voice announced, "here's the man you've all been waiting for, the one, the only, White Lightnin'!" The women rose as one big mass. I put my hand on Edna's arm, still trying to get her attention, but she shook it off. "Gotta see Lightnin'," she said before staggering off toward the stage with a fistful of dollars in, her hand.

I turned to Marilyn, who seemed about the only one in the room who wasn't insane with misplaced lust. "Is she really going to Tulsa?" I asked.

Marilyn shrugged. "Who knows? She bought the ticket, but if she keeps drinking at this rate, we'll be lucky to get her across the street to a room in the Plaza." She shook her head and lit a cigarette. "I'll tell you, I always thought Carol was a nice daughter. But she turned out to be a real piece of work."

"What do you mean?" I was still mystified.

Marilyn looked at me sharply and put out her match, taking a deep drag of her cigarette. "You mean you don't know? She's planning to put Edna in a nursing home. They talked about it a couple of months ago. Carol was worried that her mother didn't have enough to do, not enough friends and all. So Edna took up hospital volunteering at Brigham and the bridge club. I'd been wanting her to join us for ages. I guess that wasn't enough for Carol."

"You think Carol packed that bag to put her mother in a nursing home?" I was screaming now, not because I was

The Disappearance of Edna Guberman

mad, but because I was competing with some disco dance number to which White Lightnin' was gyrating and peeling off his costume. "Carol planned a surprise trip to Hawaii for Edna. The plane leaves in a little under an hour."

Marilyn's mouth dropped open, and she stood up, her cigarette falling onto the table. She had the presence of mind to grind it out, then turned to me, businesslike. "We'd better get Edna on that flight before she passes out." Together, we battled the crowd of women, most of whom thought we were trying to elbow our way to the front to tuck a tip in White Lightnin's white sequined G-string. We found Edna waving five-dollar bills at the stripper; her hair a wild mass around her head. Marilyn grabbed one elbow, and I got the other side. Together, we carried Edna out of the place.

"Wha's goin' on?" Edna asked, her forehead puckering up in concentration. As Marilyn explained, Edna started to come out of her self-induced stupor. By the time she had the full story, Edna's face was crinkled up in disappointment. "I'll never make it. I've ruined Carol's surprise."

"We can salvage this," I replied. I ordered Marilyn and Edna to get the suitcase, which was in a locker at the bus terminal, and meet me out front. Then I ducked back inside the bar, found a pay phone and, over the body-vibrating beat of the music, I shouted instructions to Carol.

Outside the bus terminal, I hailed a cab and stuffed the three of us inside, ordering the cabbie to get us to Logan as fast as possible. Boston cabs are vehicles of wonder and terror combined. No one can get you anywhere in Boston faster than a cabbie. They know all the streets and all the back roads. Our cabbie was especially fearless, passing a slowpoke driver to the right of a merge when exiting for the tunnel that took us to East Boston. We were at Logan Airport in under fifteen minutes.

Edna was fading fast. We hustled her inside the terminal and looked up the gate number on the departure monitor. I'd had the foresight to ask Carol what airline and flight number. While I moved Edna along, Marilyn checked the bag with a skycap.

Once at the gate, we waited for Carol to arrive fifteen minutes later and out of breath, just in time for the boarding announcement. Edna was peacefully snoring in the seat between Marilyn and me.

"What the—?" Carol exclaimed, looking at her mother, then at Marilyn and me.

I shook my head. "Don't ask. No time." I bent over Edna and shook her. She snorted and mumbled something, her eyes still half-closed. "We're getting on the plane now, Edna."

"Is she all right?" Carol asked, looking worried.

Marilyn patted her arm. "Don't you worry about your mother, dear. We've never done this sort of thing before."

"What sort of thing before?" Carol asked, a befuddled look on her face.

"Let's just say that I think the bridge club has a new hobby, and leave it at that," I said dryly.

Carol and I hoisted Edna between us and waited in line. By the time we got to the airline employee who took the boarding passes, Edna was walking under her own steam, with a little help from Carol.

Carol sniffed the air. "She smells like—"

I shot her a sympathetic look. "She's had enough to last her till you get to Honolulu."

"Thanks," she said, with a grateful look.

"Oh, don't worry," I replied cheerfully. "You'll get my

bill." I wondered how I would explain the five-dollar cover charge from The Wishing Well.

Marilyn and I shared a cab out of Logan, and I was dropped off at my apartment in East Boston. She went back to wherever—maybe the Wishing Well Lounge. Who knows?

Rosa was waiting for me. "So I thought you'd never get here. Ma called and told me you had a last-minute case. She didn't sound too put out over it, which was surprising."

"I'll tell you all about it on the way to Malden. You all set?"

Rosa grimaced. "As set as I'll ever be." She hoisted her overnight bag over her shoulder, I picked up my bag, and we headed out the door, ready to do the Mother's Day battle.

I have fond memories of "Life of Riley," which found its way into the third volume of Cat Crimes. *I was going for light Hitchcock, and I'm very proud of the results.*

Life of Riley

As Freddy Wilson drove back to the mansion, the litany kept running through his head like a slow, steady drumbeat: "The stupid cat, the stupid, rich cat." It was not until Freddy turned into the driveway that he added, "The stupid, rich, lost cat." Parking the Mercedes haphazardly in the driveway, Freddy's only thought was to find Riley. How could he tell the lawyer that he had tossed Riley out on his furry rear end without so much as a nugget of kibble to his name?

The will reading had not gone as Freddy had expected. Two days after Calvin Harding's funeral, Freddy showed up at the lawyer's office at the appointed time and surveyed the room. The maid, the cook, and the gardener, along with representatives from several of old man Harding's favorite charities, were already gathered there.

Freddy Wilson had been Old Man Harding's companion for close to seventeen years. Since the rich old man had no immediate relatives, Freddy had been led to believe that Harding had come to think of him as the son he'd never had. Often, when they would sit before the fireplace with their brandies, Riley firmly planted in the old man's lap, Harding would turn to Freddy and, with a grand sweep of his arm around the room, would say, "Someday, Freddy, this will all be yours."

Oh, he had been given everything he wanted, Freddy thought, ruefully remembering the will reading. After Fichter's little speech about the sad circumstances under which they must all meet and what a fine man Calvin Harding had been, Freddy barely paid attention to the first part of the reading—the servants and charities had been given very generous sums. Harding had bequeathed the cottage on the edge of the grounds to his faithful gardener, Bert Hill. Freddy only came out of his self-induced trance when Mr. Fichter came to the bulk of the estate.

"And now we come to the last part," Mr. Fichter said, beaming in Freddy's direction. He cleared his throat and read, "The bulk of my estate, which includes the house and the remainder of my fortune will heretofore be left to my faithful companion." Here was where Freddy stuck out his chest with pride. He was Harding's faithful companion, after all. Seventeen years of his life and he was getting his reward "—my companion, Riley."

Freddy felt his chest deflate like one of those kiddie swimming pools. He listened to the rest in stunned silence. "In the event of my beloved Riley's death by natural causes, and if there are no living relatives to inherit, the money shall revert to my companion and valet of nearly two decades, Frederick Wilson."

The lawyer put the will down, the smile still on his face, and faced Freddy. Although Freddy was tempted to punch him out, he refrained. He was curious as to why Harding had left everything to his cat.

"Well, what do you think of that, Mr. Wilson?" Fichter asked smugly. "Mr. Harding has left specific instructions that you should remain in the house. I think that was very generous of him. Of course, your duties will be to see that Riley's needs are taken care of. Your salary shall remain the same, with the usual raise every year, your expenses in regard to Riley shall be taken care of out of the estate, and, since Riley cannot drive," Fichter paused to chuckle at his sorry sense of humor, "use of the Mercedes is part of the deal."

"But why *Riley?*" Freddy heard himself whine.

"Just before he made this will, Mr. Harding began to worry about how his death would affect Riley," Fichter explained. "He felt this was the best way to ensure a long and happy life for Riley."

"Uh, yes," Freddy managed to say, too dumbfounded to think of a better response.

Fichter interrupted Freddy's thoughts. "Well, we'll work all the details out in the next few days. I will stop by the mansion tomorrow afternoon to further discuss the arrangements with you."

"F-fine," Freddy managed to say as he shook hands with the lawyer before he left.

As Freddy got out of the Mercedes, his thoughts remained on the cat, the stupid rich cat. All his life, Freddy had been someone's servant. First he was a shoe salesman, and when he tired of catering to bunions and smelly feet, he became a chauffeur for a wealthy businessman. Then he met Calvin Harding, who took a liking to Freddy and asked him to become his valet and companion. And so Freddy had spent the past seventeen years catering to an old man's every whim, including putting up with Riley.

Riley had been just a year old, but firmly established in the household, when Freddy came into service. Freddy, who was a dog lover, had never cared for cats in general, and had never taken to Riley in particular. Of course Riley had never taken to Freddy either; over the years they had reached a tacit agreement to stay out of each other's way as much as possible.

Freddy had never understood why Calvin Harding, a wealthy industrialist, had taken in an orange alley cat with one white paw. Here was a man who could have the best of everything, cigars, brandy, cars. Yet when it came to a pet, he chose a marmalade tomcat and gave it the same treatment that would be expected if Riley were an exotic breed or had a pedigree, even to the point of letting the cat out of the house only if he were on a harness and leash.

"He's a constant reminder of where I came from," Harding had once explained while absentmindedly puffing on his cigar.

"Even his name, Riley, reminds me of a fighter, someone who won't take anything for granted. If all this was gone tomorrow, Riley would be able to take care of himself."

Now Freddy regretted last night's rash decision to throw the beast out of the house. He had been so sure that he was getting Harding's millions that he had grabbed the unsuspecting Riley by the scruff of the neck and tossed him out the kitchen door. All night long, Freddy had been kept awake as Riley incessantly yeowled his anger below his bedroom window. By morning, the cat was no longer there.

Now Freddy circled the grounds, searching for a tough and wily marmalade tomcat with one white paw. He wondered if the gardener might have taken Riley in. Bert Hill had, in Freddy's opinion, one cat too many. It was a little orange-and-white tabby. Bert had once told Freddy that he kept her around not only because she was a good mouser, but she was a good companion as well.

As Freddy moved in ever-widening arcs, he called, "Riley, oh, Riley, here kitty, kitty, kitty." But Riley did not answer. Freddy spent the entire day searching the property. He passed Bert's cottage several times, but the gardener was nowhere to be seen.

In the late afternoon, just beyond the hedge that bordered the cottage, Freddy caught sight of a flash of orange. His heart leapt to his throat. "Riley," he whispered in a voice hoarse from shouting. A small orange-and-white cat emerged from the hedge and looked up at Freddy with luminous green eyes, a quizzical expression in her face. Freddy's heart sank. It was the gardener's cat, Sarabelle. Sighing, turning away, Freddy had an uncanny feeling that Riley had been there with Sarabelle, hovering just on the edge of his guardian's peripheral vision.

The day wore on and there was still no sign of Riley. Freddy began to panic. He would be entertaining the lawyer tomorrow, and if Riley hadn't returned by then, he would have some explaining to do. Freddy tried to think of ways to get around it. Telling the lawyer the partial truth—that Riley had gotten outside—was a possibility. But Fichter might suspect Freddy of foul play. He then thought about searching for a look-alike cat at the pet stores and the humane society, but it occurred to him that there was a chance that someone might put two and two together. After all, when he had inherited Harding's estate, Riley had been featured on the front page of the local paper. Besides, Riley's veterinarian might discover the imposter during a checkup.

By dusk, Freddy had covered every inch of the grounds, and he was now covered with mud and leaves. Just as he was about to give up, Freddy spotted lights on at the gardener's cottage. He hesitated about going to Bert with his story. If he told the gardener that Riley had got out, would Bert believe him? Freddy sighed, remembering the times Bert had been in the house to collect his pay. Riley would invariably pad into the library and coil himself around Bert's legs, purring loudly.

And every time the gardener, chuckling, would stoop down to scratch behind the marmalade cat's ears. "You must smell Sarabelle on me, old boy," Bert would say softly. "She's a good mouser, she is." How could the gardener miss the lack of affection Riley had for Freddy, and vice versa? Freddy took one last look at the gardener's cozy cottage, then trudged back to the cold and dark mansion at the other end of the property.

He had a hard time getting to sleep. Whenever he started to drift off, he would hear the loud, mournful meows of cats outside under his window. Then he would sit bolt upright, leap out of bed, and run to the window, hoping to catch a glimpse of Riley. But each time, the cats were gone by the time Freddy got into view. Then he would try to get back to sleep, but the problem of the missing cat would gnaw at him until he had paced the length of the floor a few times. He would finally crawl into bed, start to drift off, and the meows would start in again.

The dawn finally came, gray and damp, just the way Freddy was feeling. As he made breakfast, he had a sudden inspiration. Pouring a little cream in a bowl, he set it just outside, leaving the kitchen door open. Half an hour before the lawyer was to arrive, Freddy was sitting before a crackling fire, puffing on one of Harding's cigars, the kind Freddy used to cut and light for the old man. This might be the last cigar I have, the last time I can enjoy this fire, Freddy thought. I'll be out on my ear in a short while.

Riley entered the study, interrupting Freddy's black contemplation. Freddy narrowed his eyes and watched the large orange tomcat jump up on Harding's favorite chair, sniff the cushion, turn counterclockwise three times, then curl up and go to sleep.

"So you decided to join me after all," Freddy said with a

false heartiness. The cat solemnly lifted his head and gazed at his guardian as if he were the lowest form of life on the planet. Freddy found himself shrinking into his chair. After all, he had tossed Riley out on his ear, but now here he was with cream on his whiskers. The cat began to studiously clean his left paw.

"No hard feelings, eh, chum?" Freddy said in as cheery a voice as he could muster. Riley ignored him.

Fichter arrived to witness this peaceful scene, completely unaware of what had gone on the day before. Freddy silently thanked his stars that cats were unable to communicate.

"Well, everything seems to be in order here," Fichter said, looking around. "Of course, you know there is an inventory of the contents of the house. You cannot sell or give away anything in this house, or redecorate in any way, without my express permission—with the exception of your own quarters." The lawyer stroked Riley's fur. "And this fellow must go in for a check-up and grooming once a month. He's getting on in years and needs to be looked after." Riley was on his side now, yawning and stretching his four legs out, tensing them for a moment before relaxing them completely. "In any case, I don't think we need to meet more than three times a year."

After Fichter had left, satisfied that all was well with Riley, Freddy continued to chew thoughtfully on the end of his cigar, which had by now gone out. He gazed at the sleeping cat. Fichter had unwittingly pointed out something that Freddy had almost forgotten. Riley was over seventeen years old. Cats didn't live forever.

It had been a month since Harding's funeral and it was time for Riley's physical. Freddy was waiting in the outer office when Dr. Anason, a large man with curly graying hair, came out with Riley in his pet carrier. Freddy silently hoped that Riley wasn't as healthy as he looked. He had been fantasizing about the vet telling him that Riley only had a few weeks to live.

Freddy stood up to take the carrier. "How's he doing, Doc?" he asked, mentally crossing two fingers.

"He's a fine, healthy cat, Mr. Wilson. You should have him around for a long time," the veterinarian said with a smile.

"But he's over seventeen years old," Freddy stammered.

Dr. Anason dismissed Freddy's worry with a wave of his hand. "Oh, I wouldn't worry about losing him, Mr. Wilson. Cats are known to live for twenty-five or thirty years. I personally know a cat who lived to be thirty-five. Don't worry. You might have Riley around for company for at least another ten years."

It was on the drive home that Freddy decided to kill Riley. It wasn't that he hated the cat, but he hated the fact that Riley was the heir to a fortune. No animal should inherit money. Besides, he was a dog man himself. He had wanted to get a couple of big dogs, German shepherds or Weimaraners, for company. A dog was an affectionate creature, giving unconditional love for no more than a pat on the head.

Over the last seventeen years, Riley had shown no more affection to Freddy than he would to a statue. The cat acted like he deserved to be waited upon like a king. But what galled Freddy the most was having to clean the litter box. There was nothing more humiliating than cleaning a rich cat's litter box while the cat regally looked on. No, the cat definitely had to go and if he wasn't willing to do it gracefully by dying of some cat disease or of old age, Freddy would help him along with an undetectable poison.

When they got back to the mansion, Freddy went straight to the kitchen to fix dinner for Riley. He settled on a can of sardines. The moment he opened it, the orange tom arrived and sat by his bowl, impatiently waiting for his dinner. As Freddy bent down to empty the sardines into the dish, he had to restrain himself from kicking the animal.

"After all," he cooed as he straightened up, grateful that he didn't have to cook pheasant under glass for the cat, "you are the master of this house, right?"

As if in response, the tom grunted just before diving into his dinner, dismissing Freddy's presence as if he were only the hired help.

Freddy sighed. "That's all I am, aren't I? Just the help these days. And what thanks do I get?" he asked aloud, addressing the orange cat who so disdainfully ignored him. "Mr. Harding doesn't leave me a small gift of money like the others, no. Instead he names me as your guardian, you ungrateful, miserable creature."

Riley finished his meal and sat back smugly to wash his paws. Freddy studied the orange cat for a moment, musing that Riley's left front paw looked as if he had stepped in white paint.

After completing his duties, Freddy went straight to the public library. He found the book he was looking for: *The Complete Guide to Poisonous Plants and Fungi*. He knew he couldn't take the book out; he would be the first suspect in a suspicious death when an autopsy was done on a dead Riley. Freddy didn't want to lose the inheritance through a careless oversight. He made photocopies of several entries on poisonous plants and mushrooms, one on fool's parsley and another on a mushroom called Caesar's fiber head; both of these could be ingested by Riley without arousing suspicion. Both were common to the area and Freddy was confident that finding them wouldn't be a problem.

The next day, it was still drizzling outside. Impatient to get his rightful inheritance, Freddy dressed in jeans and a windbreaker, then took the cat harness and lead from the hall closet shelf. Shaking it gently in front of Riley, Freddy softly asked, "Wouldn't you like to go out?"

The big orange tomcat stared at him, then pointedly looked out the window at the rain. Freddy got the distinct impression that Riley was reading his mind. The cat got up and turned around, his tail as high in the air as a social climber's nose, and started to stalk away. Freddy lunged for the cat and after a short but tiring struggle, managed to get the harness on. "There," he told Riley through labored breathing, "now we're going for walkies."

As he dragged the reluctant cat out the door, it occurred to him that walkies was a term used for dogs, not cats.

"Doesn't look like he wants to go with you," remarked a man who emerged from behind a hedge in the backyard. Even on such a crummy, gray day, Bert Hill's face was as tanned as a cowhide.

"It's the first time I've taken him outside the house since Mr. Harding died," Freddy explained as he yanked at the lead. Riley was trying to get to the gardener while Freddy just wanted to get on with his plan. "It looks like the rain has let up."

"You should be fine for about half an hour, but it'll start up again soon. I wouldn't stay out longer than that," Bert warned.

What does he know? Freddy thought. Just because he's the gardener, suddenly he's an expert on the weather. Bert had crouched down and held his hand out for the cat to sniff. This was one struggle of wills that Riley won. The

Life of Riley

gardener was on his knees now, accommodating Riley by scratching behind his left ear. "That's a nice fella," he cooed. "Yeah, you like a little attention, don't you? Sarabelle sure would like to see you."

Freddy said with forced heartiness, "Since one of the provisions of the will was that Riley should never be allowed to roam on his own, I thought he might appreciate a brisk walk in the woods."

"It can't be easy for you," Bert replied mildly, "knowing that all that money and a perfectly good house has gone to a tomcat."

Although a lump of rage had formed in his throat, Freddy managed to sound casual. "It was Mr. Harding's money, not mine. I was only his companion. At least I get paid for my trouble. Besides, Riley isn't such a bad old guy." Freddy bent down to prove that they got along famously, but Riley pointedly turned away from him and stalked off toward the woods.

Bert straightened up and gave Freddy a quizzical look. "Guess he's anxious for that walk after all."

Freddy's laugh sounded hollow even to his own ears. "Yeah, see you later." He followed the insistent tug of the leash until they got into the woods.

While Riley rooted out scents under dead leaves, pounced on insects, and was taunted by squirrels, Freddy kept an eye out for his poisonous plants. Eventually, he found the mushrooms under a group of white pines. Freddy picked several of the small, brown, fibrous fungi and, after glancing around, stuffed them in the deep pocket of his windbreaker.

But now Riley wasn't ready to go back to the house. Freddy picked him up and started back. Riley protested by squirming so much that Freddy ended up half carrying the cat back to the house. When they were in sight of Bert's cottage, the rain had started again. Although the gardener's wheelbarrow was still resting on the front lawn, Bert was nowhere in sight. There were no witnesses to the cat's plaintive yeowling and efforts to break free of his guardian's hold.

By the time Freddy got Riley back in the house, the rain had drenched them both and Freddy had deep scratches and claw marks on his shoulders and halfway down his arms. The right sleeve of his windbreaker was ripped down to the elbow.

As he dabbed antiseptic on the wounds, he glowered at the cat, who sat calmly by, cleaning the blood from his paws after the battle. "First you didn't want to go out, then I couldn't get you back in here without suffering through this," Freddy said with exasperation, wincing as the peroxide bubbled in the scratches.

When he was finished tending to his injuries, Freddy headed for the kitchen, muttering, "Well, at least I won't have to put up with this much longer."

Freddy wasn't sure if cats ate mushrooms. Other than the tuna and sardines that he had always fed Riley, Freddy had never taken the trouble to find out what else Riley liked. He wanted something soft that could easily hide the taste and texture of poisonous mushrooms. After a short search, he discovered a can of crab-flavored cat food, the expensive kind, up in a cupboard. Freddy whistled as he mixed the minced mushrooms into the cat food; even Riley's pointed meow didn't irritate him.

"Here you go, fella," he said, setting down the bowl. "Happy eating."

Freddy left Riley to eat in peace. A short time later, he came back in to check Riley's bowl and was satisfied that it

Life of Riley

had been licked clean. In the library, a sated Riley was curled up on Harding's chair by the fireplace, lazily washing his face with his white paw.

Guilt overcame Freddy's sense of greed. He hesitated when faced with leaving Riley to die alone. He had never thought of himself as a hardened criminal, killing in cold blood. Rather, Freddy saw himself as just dispatching a minor problem that stood between him and ten million dollars. It wasn't the cat's fault that Old Man Harding had left his fortune to the damn thing. Besides, Freddy thought as he settled into the other chair, he wanted to make sure his handiwork had left nothing to chance.

Fifteen minutes later, Riley began to look a little drowsy. Freddy leaned forward eagerly—could this be it? Someone cleared his throat, making Freddy jump out of his chair and turn around. Bert stood in the doorway.

"Just wanted to let you know that next week I'll be uncovering the tulip bulbs and planting rose bushes."

"Fine, fine," Freddy replied anxiously.

The gardener looked at him strangely. "Are you okay?"

He said quickly, "I was just watching the cat."

Bert walked over to Riley. "He looks so peaceful."

Freddy's heart leapt. That was what so many people had said at about Harding at the funeral: "He looks so peaceful."

The gardener bent down to scratch Riley's head, then stopped and frowned. "Say, I don't think he's breathing." He checked more closely, then announced, "He's still breathing, but barely."

"Isn't that normal for cats when they go to sleep? He is an old cat, seventeen years old." Freddy realized he was babbling.

The gardener shook his head. "My son-in-law's a vet

and he says cats can live to be thirty. In fact, I had an eighteen-year-old cat and he was as healthy as a week-old kitten till the end. Maybe you should call a vet."

There was nothing Freddy could do but call Dr. Anason. He was already regretting his rash decision to kill Riley with poison. With a guardian who stood to inherit the estate, an autopsy would definitely be done on Riley and poisoned mushrooms would definitely look suspicious. Surely Bert would mention Freddy's strange behavior, and then the money would be lost.

Ten minutes later, the vet was inducing Riley to vomit. Then he pushed a pill down the woozy cat's throat and listened to his heart.

"He should be all right now," Dr. Anason said as he stood up. "Tomcats are troopers."

Freddy crossed his arms. "Do you know what made him sick?"

The vet scratched his head. "You took the cat for a walk in the woods today, right?"

"That's right," Freddy said, not being able to resist elaborating. "He'd been cooped up in this house for three days. I thought a walk would do him good."

"Cats love the exercise," Anason enthused. "But sometimes they find plants in the woods and eat them. You'll have to be more aware of what he eats outside. I could get this analyzed," he gestured to the mess Riley had made, "and tell you—"

"No, no, that's okay," Freddy said quickly. "I'll just keep a closer eye on him when I take him out for exercise."

The vet bent over to gently rub the cat's head. "He's a beautiful animal and very healthy for his age. I'd just be careful what you feed him," the vet said, looking up at Freddy.

Life of Riley

★ ★ ★ ★ ★

Two months went by since the poisoning incident and Freddy had come to terms with his subservient position. He was just getting used to the idea that Riley was going to live for five to ten more years when it happened one bright, sunny morning in June. Freddy found Riley curled up in old man Harding's chair, looking very much as if he were asleep. But he wasn't breathing.

Freddy realized he was holding his breath as well, and he let it out in one great big sigh of relief. Riley appeared to have passed away peacefully in the night. At least, he hoped the cat had done so. The first order of business was to phone Fichter, then the vet to verify Riley's death.

Within half an hour, Dr. Anason declared Riley dead.

"Well, he certainly lived a good life, such as it was," Freddy replied, upon hearing the news. He hoped he didn't sound as exultant as he felt. In his mind, he was already collecting the money, the house, and the Mercedes. All he'd had to do was wait. Riley hadn't been half bad, Freddy reasoned, for a cat.

The lawyer entered the study. "I understand our heir has died," Fichter said solemnly.

"Yes," Freddy replied, "I knew something was wrong when he didn't come to breakfast."

Fichter clucked his tongue and shook his head. "He was in such good health, too."

Dr. Anason looked up. "That he was. But all cats are different and I think the old fellow's heart just stopped pumping last night sometime."

"Of course, there will be an autopsy," Fichter said. Freddy realized that the lawyer was watching him carefully for a reaction. But Freddy had a clear conscience.

Bert appeared in the doorway with a box. Freddy looked

at him with annoyance. "What do you want, Bert?" he asked impatiently.

"Well, I thought I ought to show you something," the gardener said, glancing over at Riley's still form. He suddenly looked sad. "Aw, did the little guy die?"

"Yes, and it looks like his inheritance will go to Mr. Wilson here," Fichter said. He was looking curiously at the box now. Freddy heard mewling noises coming from it.

"Aye, I guess so." Bert nodded to Freddy and said, "I'm sorry Riley's gone. He never got to see his kittens." The lawyer and Freddy moved closer. Inside, Sarabelle was curled up in the center while four roly-poly orange kittens climbed over her and each other. Each kitten sported a white left front paw.

Freddy chuckled. "Those have to be Riley's, all right. The same white paw. That must have happened the night he got out." He felt free to admit it now. "I spent the whole day looking for him. I was frantic with worry."

Fichter was frowning. "I'm sorry, Mr. Wilson, but this means that you won't be receiving the inheritance after all. Of course, you may stay on as guardian."

Freddy felt his heart drop down to his ankles. "Wha-what do you mean?" he asked in a stricken tone. "Riley is gone, and Mr. Harding doesn't have any living relatives. I'm next in line."

"You've got it backwards, Mr. Wilson. The way Calvin Harding wrote his will, it states that the bulk of his estate went to Riley first, then any living relative. Any living relative of Riley's, that is." Fichter's face softened and he stuck a finger into the writhing orange mass. "My, aren't they cute? You'll have years of employment ahead of you, Mr. Wilson. *Years* of enjoyment as Riley's kittens grow older. They do live for quite a long time, I understand."

This is the second Birch story published by Durkin-Hayes for the How the West Was Read *audio western anthology, never published in print before. When you read this you'll understand why I had to include it.*

Dust and Ashes

While most of Jefferson Birch's cases had something to do with capturing bank or train robbers and murderers, he had never gotten the message from Arthur Tisdale with the word *urgent* in it. Birch was curious about what type of case made Tisdale use such a word.

It was a fortunate coincidence that Birch happened to be in Abilene when he received the wire. Dodge City wasn't far away, no more than a day's ride on his horse Cactus, less if he took the Santa Fe Line, which he did. As he rode the rails, Birch tried to remember what he knew of Dodge City. Like so many cattle towns, Dodge City was a rough-and-tumble place known for its gambling, saloon dance halls and whorehouses. Birch recalled reading a description of Dodge as "hell-popping" in one newspaper article.

As Birch rode down Dodge's Front Street, he noted the posters that stuck in every window of every shop. There was an election in the fall and two names kept coming up, Bat Masterson and Larry Deager, both running for county sheriff. Outside the Dodge City jail, an older man sat in a creaky chair, packing a wad of tobacco in his cheek. Birch stopped in front of him. The man looked up from under the brim of his ten-gallon hat.

"Is the marshal around?" Birch asked.

"That's me," the man replied.

He had to weigh close to three hundred pounds, and it surprised Birch that someone so out of shape could hold the position of marshal in a cattle town where cowboys came into town to drink and fight on Saturday nights. Birch introduced himself.

The marshal looked carefully unimpressed. "So what's your business here in town?" When he shifted his bulk, Birch thought that the chair might fall apart.

Before he had a chance to show Tisdale's wire to the as yet nameless marshal, a man came out of The Long Branch Saloon and crossed Front Street. He was in his mid-twenties and was clean-shaven with the exception of an impeccably groomed dark mustache. He wore a black suit and a bowler hat with an upturned brim. But what distinguished him from the average dandy was the pair of silver plated pearl handled guns that peaked out from beneath his suit coat. The lawman's expression turned sour as the younger man approached. The other man ignored the marshal's obvious dislike, but it was clear to Birch that the tension was as thick as London fog between the two men.

"Are you Jefferson Birch?" the younger man asked. Birch nodded. "Bartholomew Masterson," he said, "but everyone calls me Bat for short. Arthur Tisdale's waiting for you at The Long Branch."

With a grunt, the marshal got up from his groaning chair and narrowing his eyes, stepped up to Masterson. "You think you're already the sheriff, I see."

Masterson leveled his gaze at the lawman. "The election is a few days away, Marshal. I have no intention of leaving you out of this manhunt. You are welcome to join us at the saloon."

If the marshal's belly hadn't gotten in the way, he might

have looked more intimidating.

As it was, Masterson just looked amused.

"I already caught him," the marshal said with a sneer. "There hasn't been a murder since I put Evans in the pokey."

"At what point did you decide that Charles Evans was guilty?" Masterson held a finger in the air as if he had just come up with a brilliant observation. "As I recall, it was shortly after you went into the saloon business."

The lawman reached up and tugged the brim of his hat. "Charlie's guilty and it has nothing to do with me owning a saloon."

Birch quietly backed away, not quite sure what the two men were talking about, but getting the idea that this had something to do with why he had been called to Dodge. He just hoped this disagreement wouldn't end in gunfire and blood being shed.

Masterson raised his eyebrows. "Oh, then why wasn't your own bartender investigated more closely? Kelly's worked at The Long Branch for close to three years, and the murders began shortly after Jake, your bartender, showed up in town."

It was clear that the marshal had no answer to Masterson's accusation, because he screwed his face up in disgust and spat close to where his rifle stood his ground. "Ah," he said, turned, and waddled toward his office.

"You're running for sheriff, I see," Birch said. He had heard of Bat Masterson's reputation with a gun.

Masterson nodded shortly. "Against Larry Deager, whom you just had the pleasure of meeting."

"From the looks of things, I'd say there is no love lost between you and Marshal Deager. If you win the seat and he stays in the office as marshal, how will you get along with him, then?"

Masterson smiled. "I don't think Deager will stay in his present position after I win the election. I have the mayor's endorsement and the backing of the editor of the local newspaper, and half a dozen more influential men in this town."

Birch thought Masterson was awfully sure of himself, but then he did have a reputation as the deadliest gun west of the Mississippi. And Deager struck Birch as being a man who thought more of his abilities than he was able to display, while Masterson appeared to be more modest.

Masterson indicated that Birch should follow him. "I have some people I'd like you to meet."

When Birch entered The Long Branch Saloon, he was impressed by the décor. Sun filtered through stained glass windows. And the bar was made of fine-grained oak, the front of which was intricately carved. A large beveled mirror in an ornate frame hung behind the bar, and whisky glasses were stacked up on one side of the bar, liquor on the other side. An upright piano stood in the corner of the saloon and a raised platform, meant for other musicians and singers, sat next to it.

It was a quiet afternoon, most of the townspeople being at work, but there were a few patrons scattered around. There didn't seem to be any town drunks in The Long Branch, the men with the sad past who drank because they had no future. The faro table was set up along the back of the room, complete with a dealer and two players. In a corner of the saloon sat five cigar-smoking men who were playing stud poker. One of the men said something as he entered a chip, and the rest of the players roared with laughter.

The bartender, who seemed to be growing mutton chops as compensation for his thinning hair, nodded in Masterson's direction. Masterson led Birch through a door in the back of the saloon. The room appeared to be an office of some sort, and several men looked up from their chairs. Two of the men looked strikingly like Bat Masterson, down to the mustaches. The only difference was that Masterson wore fancier duds.

Tisdale got up and shook Birch's hand. "Good to see you again, Birch. How's your ranch coming along?"

Birch had recently bought a ranch in Oklahoma territory and was planning to buy cattle when the weather warmed up a bit more.

"Birch," Masterson indicated the two men who resembled him, "these are my brothers Ed and Jim. Ed is the assistant marshal and Jim co-owns this saloon." Another older man was standing beside Tisdale. "And that there is our mayor, James Kelly."

"Folks around here call me Dog," the mayor replied.

He said no more in the way of an explanation, clearly wanting Birch to ask.

Birch didn't disappoint him. "Why?"

"His nickname is Dog because he owns a few greyhounds. They're supposed to be good dogs."

Dog Kelly puffed up his chest. "These aren't just any greyhounds. They once belonged to none other than General Custer."

Birch was impressed. "Well, I hope you will allow me to meet your dogs before I leave. It's the closest I'll ever get to meeting him."

Custer had died the year before in a battle at Little Bighorn River in Montana territory. The men roared, Birch along with them.

Lately his mood had begun to lighten. Maybe it had to do with owning land again. Maybe it had something to do with Emma, the woman who was waiting for him back in Oklahoma.

Kelly took the lead. "Mr. Birch, let me thank you for coming here."

"Mr. Tisdale said it was urgent."

"Do you have any idea why you have been sent for?"

Birch glanced at Bat Masterson and was given the nod. "I believe it has something to do with the encounter that we had a moment ago with Marshal Deager."

Kelly and Masterson exchanged glances. Ed looked down and coughed in the uncomfortable silence. Jim blew air through his mustache, ruffling it slightly. Masterson gave the others an account of the exchange.

When he was finished, Kelly nodded, "Yes that's it. The marshal has decided that The Long Branch bartender, Charlie Evans, killed those women."

"If I may interrupt with a question?" Birch said. "I'd like to know what he meant by the fact that the killing had stopped since Evans went to jail."

Ed spoke up. His voice was softer than Bat's and his manner more diplomatic. This was a man who preferred talking to fighting. "Three women have been murdered. The only thing they had in common was that they all worked in saloons."

Birch nodded solemnly. "Were they killed all at once?"

"No, Mary was the first one killed," Jim said. "She worked here at The Long Branch." He looked away as if something had gotten in his eye.

Bat finished for him. "Mary Linder and Jim were close friends. She was murdered on the eleventh of August about three weeks ago on a Saturday night. She was found in her room behind The Long Branch."

Kelly spoke up. "The second woman, Kate Hennington

worked at my saloon, The Lady Gay. She was popular with the customers."

"Where and when was she found?" Birch asked.

"A week later, on a Sunday morning, behind The Lady Gay," Bat replied.

Tisdale spoke, "And the third woman, Evelyn Sandifer, was murdered four days ago."

Another Saturday, Birch thought. The pattern was clear to anyone who cared to look for it. "Where did she work?"

"The Hog's Eye," Tisdale replied. "She was found on Sunday morning, strangled."

"In her room?" Birch asked.

Masterson nodded, a look of distaste crossing his face. "She rented a crib. It was all she could afford."

Cribs were cramped, little huts, usually used by the lowest whores in town, the fallen angels who couldn't afford to rent a room or wouldn't be welcomed in a saloon or dance hall.

Birch turned to Jim and Bat. "Why would the marshal think that your bartender did the killings?"

Jim's expression was one of resignation. "Charlie had been Mary's suitor before I started keeping company with her. There were hard feelings between us for awhile, but then he met Evelyn."

Birch could now understand why Deager had locked up Charlie, but he still didn't see what the connection was between Charlie and Kate and he said as much.

"There wasn't any connection," Bat said with a frown. "And Charlie swears to that. Besides, no one has come forward to say that they have seen Charlie and Kate together at any time."

"Kate liked a good time. She was a little more experienced than Mary or Evelyn," the mayor said, shaking his head.

Ed had taken out some tobacco and paper and was rolling a cigarette.

"You had stepped out with her a few times, hadn't you, Ed?" Jim asked casually.

Ed looked up, a flush creeping up his neck. "Yeah, that's right. Kate was fun to be with."

Birch turned to Tisdale, "Why did you send for me? What can I do that these men, who have law enforcement experience, can't do?"

Tisdale smiled and laid a hand on his agent's shoulder. "You can be impartial. You see, Bat here isn't officially the county sheriff yet, and Ed still works under Marshal Deager and can't officially investigate if a culprit has been caught."

"Besides, Charlie wouldn't hurt a woman. He respects women. He may have had some hard feelings about me and Mary, but he took them out mostly on me. He worshipped Mary," Jim said. "And when he met Evelyn, our friendship resumed."

Birch could see why he had been called in, but he had one more question. "Why don't you just wait until next Saturday night?"

The mayor spoke. "The girls are terrified to work. We promised that they would be escorted home, but Mary was escorted to her room on the night of her death, so it's not much comfort."

"And if we can catch the killer before he strikes again," Bat said, "all the better. We don't want to see any more women hurt."

"Do you have any ideas as to who may be behind the murders?" Birch asked.

All the men fell into an uneasy silence. Finally Jim looked up at Birch and said, "Marshal Deager."

Tisdale took over. "The marshal has business interests in town that conflict with their business."

"The Hog's Eye," Birch guessed.

And from the look on the Masterson brothers' faces, he was right on target. "So Mr. Tisdale and I are here to investigate with no one influencing what we find." The Mayor nodded. "We have all agreed that if you find one of us guilty of murder, no matter who it is, I would rather we had someone asking questions and digging around, instead of the way Marshal Deager went about it."

Which was to take a likely looking suspect and hang the murder charge on him because he had motive in two out of the three killings, Birch thought.

Tisdale took charge. "Thank you, men, I certainly hope we can live up to your expectations."

As they walked out, Bat ended up alongside Birch. "If you don't mind, I'd like to come along with you on your inquiries."

Birch slowed down. "I don't want you to get the wrong idea, but don't you think it would look better if you would stay away from my investigation?"

Bat shrugged. "I've had my run-ins with the marshal, but I haven't been here that long. I didn't know any of the girls, with the exception of Mary. And frankly, with me running for the office of county sheriff, I would like to observe you at work. I need to learn from someone who has done this kind of thing before."

Although Birch liked Bat and liked the idea of teaching investigation to a legend in the West, he wasn't sure if the others would approve. But Mayor Kelly overheard their discussion and put Birch's mind at ease immediately.

"Excuse me, Birch, but Bat has a good idea here. He's not a good suspect, unlike Ed, Jim and me. But he knows the town and can be of help to you."

They began at The Long Branch where Mary had been murdered. Her room in the back of the saloon was small, but well furnished with a goose-down mattress on a brass frame, a rocking chair, a highboy and washstand with a bowl and pitcher on it. Next to the chair was a small crude table with the Old Testament on it, opened to Proverbs 6. Everything was as it had been the night of her murder, even down to the tangled bed sheets.

"How did she die?"

"Strangled," Bat said, "here on her bed. All of the girls were strangled."

"Was Mary's door open or closed?"

Bat frowned. "Her door was closed, but unlocked. Normally she locked it."

"Then whoever killed her must have been let in by her. She knew her killer."

Bat examined the door. "How do you reach that conclusion?"

"She let the killer into her room. She was on her bed when she was strangled, which indicated that she had no reason to be afraid." Birch thought of something else. "Do you know what she was strangled with?"

Bat shook his head. "The bruises on her throat looked like it was something thin and strong, but the killer must have taken it with him."

Birch had finished with her room. There was nothing else that he could glean from what he had seen.

"Bat, I'm wondering," he paused not knowing how to phrase it without insulting Jim. So he went ahead with his question. "Was Mary seeing other men?"

Bat shook his head. His voice was brusque. "I don't think so, she was nice to the customers, but she wasn't a fallen angel, if that's what you are getting at."

"I had to ask."

Bat nodded.

Birch liked the idea of Bat Masterson looking over his shoulder less and less.

"Where do you go now?" Bat asked.

Birch detected almost a challenge in his tone. "To talk to Charlie Evans."

To say that the marshal was not happy to see them was an understatement, but he didn't give them any trouble when Birch asked to see Charlie in the cell. In fact, after they handed him their guns to keep while they talked to his prisoner, he looked downright happy to escort them into the cell area and leave them locked up there.

"Just call when you are ready to leave," he told Birch before locking the outer door to the cells.

Charlie was a nice-looking man in his late twenties. He had a full head of shoulder-length, chestnut hair and a goatee and mustache. But when he stood to greet his visitors, Birch was struck by how short he was, probably no more than five feet five inches in his stocking feet. The women probably liked Charlie, and his demeanor was friendly and respectable to Birch. He smiled when he saw Bat.

"Hey boss, did you come to arrange my bail?"

Surprised to hear Bat called "boss," Birch turned to look at Bat, whose expression was apologetic.

"I'm half owner in The Long Branch," he explained. Being half owner in one of the saloons changed a few things in Birch's mind, but now wasn't the time to go into it. He wondered why Bat hadn't mentioned this fact to him earlier, but he could take a guess. Bat wanted to keep an eye on Birch's progress. That was why the man was sticking so close to Birch during his investigation. Irritation rose in Birch's chest like a river after a thunderstorm, but he pushed the feeling back down. He couldn't lose control now.

He turned to the task at hand, letting Bat introduce him to Charlie and explain why they were there. Charlie looked glum. "I'll do my best to answer your questions, Mr. Birch."

"Where'd you go after you closed up the saloon?"

"I went back to my room to sleep. It had been a rough night. I had to break up at least a half-dozen fights. Jim called the marshal twice when it looked like there was going to be gun play." Charlie paced his cell, hands clasped behind his back.

"Was there anyone who saw you go back to your room?"

Charlie thought about it and then shook his head. "Most nights I have someone with me." He had the grace to blush at having to reveal such an intimate detail of his life.

Birch nodded. "Lately you had been seeing a saloon girl from The Hog's Eye, wasn't it?"

Charlie faced Birch, his hands gripping the bars that separated them. "Evelyn Sandifer. We've kept company. On the night Mary was killed, I was alone. Evelyn told me she was tired and wanted to get some sleep."

Birch wondered if Evelyn had been tired or used it as an excuse to see someone else. He wasn't about to ask Charlie, but he tucked the information away for later. "I know you've been asked this before, but had you given any thought to having met Kate Hennington?"

The prisoner shook his head. "I may have met her, but I don't remember. Why would that be important? Even if I'd known her it doesn't mean I'd kill her."

Birch had encountered cases in which murder had been

committed, but usually there was something that drove the killer to murder. Greed. Passion. A secret to hide. He had never encountered a case in which the motive was so unclear before. Other than the connection between Mary and Evelyn, the murders appeared to be senseless. Birch wondered if the two other victims had known Kate. She hadn't been in town long enough to get acquainted with all of the saloons in town, but she probably knew of or had met the Mastersons at one point, even if they didn't remember her. Kate probably knew the mayor and the marshal by sight and was most likely aware of the rivalry between them.

The marshal reluctantly let Birch and Bat out of the cell area.

"Where to now?" Bat asked.

Birch frowned in thought. "I'd like to see the other places where the women were found, then visit the saloons tonight and talk to some of the customers and bartenders."

Bat led him to where Kate had been found, behind The Lady Gay. It was a small alleyway that led to the street that ran parallel to Front Street. Birch imagined that it was unlit at night. There were no windows in the buildings on either side of the alley that would shine even the faintest light on the passageway. Why would a woman walk alone down a dark street late at night? Dodge City, like most cattle towns, wasn't safe for a woman to walk at night—unless she wasn't alone, Birch thought. But of course she wasn't. She had met her killer here.

Bat stood back and watched Birch walk slowly down the alley until he stopped and walked over to a scrap of paper. He bent over and picked it up to examine it. It was a page from the Bible, Proverbs 6. Maybe there was a connection between the three women, aside from their work. But the connection was written in that passage.

He turned to Bat. "I need to see Evelyn's room. Has anything been moved in it?"

Bat shrugged. "Let's go see."

Evelyn had lived in a crib, a small, unpleasant hut in the bad section of Dodge. Most cribs housed prostitutes, the ones who had fallen so low that they couldn't afford a room in a saloon or hotel. "Was Evelyn a prostitute?"

"I don't know," Bat replied.

Birch could see that the cribs bothered Bat. He wasn't comfortable in this area either, but most of the whores were catching up on their sleep. Although they would be open for business at night when the cowboys were out roaming the streets in search of company.

Evelyn's crib was sparsely furnished, with only a straw mattress. A worn-out carpetbag sat in the corner of the dirt floor. And when Birch went through it, he found only a thin gingham dress, a muslin shift and a crudely carved wooden comb with missing teeth. He looked around for a Bible or a torn page from the Old Testament, but he found nothing.

As if reading Birch's mind, Bat spoke up from the doorway of the crib. "I was here within a few minutes of when she was found. And I remember seeing a book here. Someone must have taken it."

There was nothing to be done until evening. Birch checked in with Tisdale at The Long Branch and explained what he and Bat had found.

"I'll meet with Mayor Kelly and Ed Masterson," Tisdale replied.

Birch kept the page from Proverbs 6 to study. Jim fixed a meal for Bat and Birch and joined them at the table. While they ate, Bat kept Birch entertained with stories of his buffalo hunting exploits on the Kansas range. When they were finished, Birch excused himself and went into the back room to read the page he had found in the alley where Kate had been murdered.

In the light of a kerosene lamp, he found several verses that might pertain to the killer's mind, particularly verse 21. *Bind them continually upon thy heart, and tie them about thy neck.* All three women had been strangled. The killer might be taking the verse too literally, since no binding was found in any of the murder scenes.

Birch mulled over the verse trying to put himself in the killer's place. A chill ran down his spine as the meaning became clear to him. The killer's hate was sated only after he had killed. But why kill these women? It was true that all who worked in saloons, but not all women who worked in drinking and gambling establishments, were prostitutes.

Birch emerged from the back room to find that a few customers had begun to wander in and take the seats at the bar. Bat was nowhere to be seen, but Jim was working behind the bar, pouring whiskey and collecting money.

Birch went over to the bar and took a seat. A man seated three stools down eyed him as Jim placed a whiskey in front of Birch and refused his offer to pay. "You givin' away your liquor tonight, Jim? If so, I'll take some of that." The man shoved his empty glass across the bar and Jim poured without comment.

Jim came back down to Birch's place and said in a low voice, "That's Preacher. He comes in regularly and plays the piano for his drink."

Jim moved away as Preacher approached. "You new here, stranger?"

Birch sipped his whiskey. "Just passing through town."

Preacher eyed him. "Well, you must be someone special, because Jim don't pour the good stuff for just anyone. And then not make them pay."

Birch studied him. He was a skinny man, probably in his forties. Hair slicked back with bear grease and clean-shaven. His nose was crooked and he had a wandering eye.

"I paid in advance." Birch put his glass down. "Jim told me you play the piano here."

The man grinned, showing that he was missing two lower front teeth. "I play the piano at most of the saloons on Front Street."

"Did you know any of the women who were killed?"

Preacher got a sly look in his eye. "Why do you ask?"

"I heard about the killings and wondered what these women had in common?"

"They were all whores, weren't they?"

Birch didn't argue. "I don't know, were they?"

Preacher seemed about to say something else, but instead fell silent.

"Why do they call you Preacher," Birch asked.

A haunted look came into his eyes, and he seemed reluctant to answer. "Used to be a man of God. Preached on Sundays."

"Not now?"

"I fell from grace," he replied shortly. He looked straight ahead and down to his drink, slammed the glass down and left.

Birch watched Preacher weave his way out of the door. He turned to Jim who had been watching the exchange. "When did he show up in town?"

"I don't know. I came here last year and he was already a town fixture."

Birch nodded, finished his drink and left The Long Branch. It was getting dark out when he stepped onto the boardwalk. He walked past the general store, the feed store and came upon The Lady Gay. Kerosene lamps already cast a dusky glow from the saloon windows. The batwing doors were still moving, indicating that someone had just stepped inside.

Birch followed, took a seat in an empty table and located Preacher at the bar. The bartender was handing him a whiskey and leaned over to ask him something. Preacher nodded in agreement and walked over to a piano in the corner. He sat down his whiskey on the piano top and began to play a light, jaunty tune that Birch didn't recognize.

One of the saloon girls walked over and began singing to the piano and Preacher looked up startled. Just as quickly, he looked back down at the keys as if embarrassed by the woman's presence.

While Birch listened to Preacher's music, Mayor Kelly approached. "Will you drink with me, Mr. Birch?"

Birch agreed and the Mayor sat down with him and signaled to the bartender. A moment later, one of the saloon girls brought over two glasses brimming with amber liquid. Birch knew he would have to pace himself if he was going to spend the next few nights in saloons.

"Mr. Tisdale told me what you had found," Kelly said, studying his glass intently. "Why do you think someone would do that to women? I can understand a jealous suitor, but . . ."

Birch glanced at Preacher before answering. "I don't know yet. This is the first experience I've had with a killer whose motive is misleading. I'm trying to put myself in his place and I'm having a hard time with it." He changed the subject. "Can you tell me about your piano player?"

"His name is Preacher." Dog Kelly looked over at the man at the piano and nodded. "He used to be a man of the cloth."

"What's his story?"

The mayor frowned and thought. "Don't know. Never talked to him for long. But he can't have been a preacher since he came here. He drinks and gambles."

"Does he like women too?"

"He's friendly with them, but Preacher is a gentleman around them." He looked sharply at Birch. "You don't think he's the killer, do you?"

Birch shrugged. "He might be. How long since he was the Preacher?"

Kelly shook his head. "A long time. He's been here in Dodge for a couple of years, same as Charlie. He's been playing in saloons since he came here."

Birch's mind began to turn. He was tempted to ask the preacher for help with the Bible verse, but if he was the killer, Birch didn't want to reveal his interest. He had another two days before Saturday night, but he couldn't be sure that the killer wouldn't strike before then. And it was possible that Charlie was the killer after all.

On Friday night the regular customers began coming into town. Birch had run the gamut of saloons and dance halls, but stayed within the area of the three saloons where the women had been killed. He had followed Preacher from one place to the other, watching the way he interacted with women. But there was nothing unusual about his manner. He talked to them, joked with them and got them to sing while he accompanied them on piano. Sometimes he even joined them in harmony. His voice was rough from drink, but he didn't seem at all bitter about his fall from grace.

Birch wondered about Preacher's background. When Preacher got to The Hog's Eye, he looked like he had gotten a spit and shine. He wore a clean shirt and a string tie. He noticed Birch.

Dust and Ashes

"You been following me for the last two nights, and I'm beginning to think I got more than one admirer."

"Well, you do play well," Birch admitted.

Preacher chuckled. "Nice to know there is more than one soul who thinks so. Most folks just come here to drink."

"You have another admirer of your music?"

Preacher drained his whiskey and then nodded. "Young feller. Comes here on the weekends, mostly Saturday nights to listen to me play. Follows me from saloon to saloon. He don't drink though. Told me his daddy was once a preacher too, till he took up with a woman. Killed his mother, he thinks. His daddy started to drink. The woman he took up with worked at a saloon, and his daddy was finally killed in a fight over the woman."

"Tell me, Preacher, who is this admirer of yours?" Birch asked.

"Elijah's all I know him by. I don't know his full name."

Birch's eyes narrowed in thought. "Preacher, did you know any of the women who were murdered?"

He rubbed his chin in thought. "Why, yes I did. Poor things. Mary was a nice woman. Evelyn was a sweet and innocent girl. And Katie was a wild one."

"On each of the nights these women were killed, did you talk to them?"

Preacher brightened. "Yes, they were all possessed of a good, strong singing voice and I accompanied them on the piano." A frown replaced the preacher's pleasant expression. "In fact, Elijah only comes into town on Saturday nights."

"Do you know where he stays the rest of the week?" It was all falling into place.

"I'm afraid not. I don't think anyone knows. He doesn't

work at the ranch, because he rides into town alone and I've never seen anyone with him. I don't think he has any friends." Preacher looked at his empty glass. "I'll have to play something for a refill."

He started to get up, but Birch had one more question. "When did you fall from grace, Preacher?"

The older man got a sad, far away look in his eyes. "In another town, another place. I met a woman, a woman who worked in a saloon. I preached the Lord's word on Sunday in that saloon and she worked there at night. My wife was ill, bedridden, and I would stop to talk to this woman every Sunday. Finally one day she asked me to come and visit the saloon at night. On a Saturday night." A tear slipped down his face. "I did and took the drink. She was my downfall. My wife died on a Saturday night, alone in her bed. We had no children to take care of her. I woke up on Sunday morning in this woman's bed to the sound of the marshal's knock, telling me that my wife had gone. I couldn't face staying there and as soon as I laid my wife's body in the ground, I left. I took up itinerant preaching . . ."

"Until you moved here?"

Preacher nodded. "I still drink. I play hurdy gurdy music. I talk to the women, but I think of Dodge City as my new home." He started to leave, then stopped. "Funny, Elijah keeps asking me when I'm going back to preaching. I keep telling him that it will happen when all of the saloons become churches."

Birch felt the hairs on the back of his neck stand up. "Thank you, sir."

He went back to The Long Branch and talked to Tisdale. A meeting was called of the Masterson brothers and the mayor. Marshal Deager was invited, but Birch was certain that he wouldn't show up.

He surprised everyone by swaggering in late. "What's this all about?" he asked.

Birch told the group of men as concisely as possible. When he was finished, the men looked grim.

All but the marshal. "So you think this Elijah is just killing off saloon girls once a week? That's the most foolish explanation I've heard." Marshal Deager stood up and looked around the room. "This is all just a fabrication to get Charlie out of jail."

Bat spoke up. "But what if it's the truth? What if this Elijah is doing what Birch thinks he's doing?"

The mayor drummed his fingers on the desktop. "The only problem I have is that no Bible or page from the Bible was found in Kate's room."

Ed glanced at the marshal and then said, "Actually there was a Bible there, but after I came back from removing the body, it was gone."

Deager's face turned red. He moved toward his assistant deputy and stuck out a finger in warning. "Are you saying I stole that Bible?"

Ed didn't move a muscle. "I haven't accused anyone of anything yet."

Tisdale smoothed things over. "Marshal, we appreciate your cooperation. If I were in your position, I would have taken the Bible with the intention of showing the mortician which passage was the deceased's favorite, to be read at the service."

Marshall Deager backed off and adjusted his bolo tie. "That could have happened."

"Do you remember what passage the book was open to?" Birch asked mildly.

The lawman took a deep breath as he thought about it.

"Proverbs. It was Proverbs, but I'm not sure what chapter. I didn't look."

Saturday night came quickly. The men had agreed to spread themselves out among the saloons to keep an eye on Preacher. Preacher in turn agreed to point out Elijah when he showed up. "He won't be hard to recognize. He's kind of wild-eyed and looks like he lives on roots and berries, and he's young—under twenty. Doesn't bathe very often either."

Jim stayed in The Long Branch, Kelly at The Lady Gay and Deager at The Hog's Eye. Ed, Tisdale and Birch were free to move from saloon to saloon, changing places all the time. At least one of them in one of the saloons Preacher frequented. The evening dragged on, and there was no sign of a young man named Elijah. Preacher accompanied only one saloon girl that night, Fanny, who worked at The Hog's Eye and had a rough voice that barely hit all the notes. She joked with him and seemed to be familiar with Preacher and he treated her in a good-natured manner.

When evening came to an end, Birch and Tisdale approached Preacher who sheepishly shook his head. "Don't know why he didn't come tonight."

"He may be done with his killing," Tisdale replied. "Maybe he's moved on."

Preacher nodded. "Or he may have heard something about you people looking for him."

Birch said nothing. He was thinking. Tisdale said goodnight and left, Birch following in his wake.

When they got back to The Long Branch Saloon, Birch took the page from Proverbs out of his pocket and studied it. One verse stuck out for him. *My son keep thy father's commandment and forsake not the law of thy mother.*

It led into the next verse, *Bind them continually upon thine heart, and tie them about thy neck.*

Skipping down a passage, Birch felt his stomach knot up. *For the commandment is a lamp and the law is light and reproofs of instruction are the way of life. To keep thee from the evil woman, from the flattery of the tongue of a strange woman, lust not after her beauty in thine heart. Neither let her take thee with her eyelids, for the means of a whorish woman, a man is brought to a piece of bread, and the adulteress will hunt for the precious life.*

He threw the paper down and turned to Tisdale. "Where is Fanny?"

Tisdale looked blank. "Who?"

"Fanny, the woman who sang with Preacher earlier tonight."

Bat had just entered The Long Branch. "Fanny, you say. I saw her leaving The Hog's Eye and heading back to her room. I asked if she wanted me to escort her in the light of the killings, but she told me she was waiting for Preacher."

"Where does she stay?" Birch asked.

"I don't know, but Deager should know." Birch walked quickly to the marshal's saloon, all the time looking for either Fanny or Preacher. As he began to enter The Hog's Eye to ask the man who was sweeping the floor, he heard a scream.

Bat was right behind him as they ran towards the sound. It was coming from the back of the saloon. In the dim light of a half moon, Birch made out two figures—the figure of a woman struggling with a man. He had something around her neck.

Birch drew his gun. "Stop, let her go."

The man didn't seem to hear him. Birch was afraid to shoot for fear of hitting Fanny.

He started toward them, but Bat's voice called out from

behind him. "Duck, Birch."

Birch threw himself to the ground and a shot rang out. The man cried out in pain, released the woman and crumpled to the ground. Birch heard the sound of the woman gasping for breath. And as he got up and dusted himself off, Bat had gone directly to Fanny to make sure she was all right.

Birch went over to the figure that lay still on the ground. Even under the dim light of the moon, he saw the face of Preacher. He clutched his string tie in his hand.

"Elijah?" Birch asked in a low tone.

Preacher nodded. "Name's Elijah Dewey. Make sure they put it on my tombstone."

Birch wasn't sure what had made Preacher, Elijah, suddenly start killing saloon girls after living in Dodge City for over a year. But he suspected that Elijah just started to realize that he had sunk so low, come so far from his calling that he would never get back. And he started to blame the woman who had made him stray so many years ago.

Preacher opened his eyes and Birch thought he could see the tortured look in them finally fade. In a husky whisper, Preacher recited, "Wherefore I abhor myself and repent in dust and ashes." With a peaceful smile, he closed his eyes and took his last breath.

Birch looked up at Bat, who said, "Job 42:6."

Now Angela starts to get dark. This was written for a three-volume tribute to Mickey Spillane. "The Other Woman" was included in Mickey Spillane's Vengeance Is Hers. *I am proud to have been included in it.*

The Other Woman

She had drab, brown hair, big dishwater-colored eyes the kind you see in Keane paintings—and her chin was almost nonexistent. She wore the sort of frou-frou dress a girl from the Midwest would think was the height of sophistication with its full cabbage-rose print skirt, puffy sleeves, and large, square linen-and-lace collar. I'm no Paris fashion plate myself, but I know a silly-looking dress when I see one.

I stopped studying Eleanor Monahan from across my desk and leaned forward. "Just what can I do for you?"

Eleanor shrank into her chair as if I had hit her instead of asking her a reasonable question. But she managed to summon up the courage to tell me why she was there. "Well, Miss Matelli—" she said, lisping slightly.

I winced. "Call me Angela."

She hesitated, then dutifully repeated my first name. "Angela. I want someone followed."

Aha, I thought, the scorned wife. I appraised her again. It was possible, I thought, but she didn't have a ring on her finger. Boyfriend, maybe? I had done background checks on quite a few boyfriends and fiancés for a number of paranoid women.

Normally I don't like to take, as I call 'em, "creep-and-peep" cases. Ever since I was involved in a high profile case that earned me a lot of press about a year ago, my caseload had been full up. But with the recession in full swing, things were slowing down. With next month's office rent in mind, I asked, "Who is he?"

"Not a he," Eleanor replied softly, "a she."

Her lesbian lover? I could feel my eyebrow arching involuntarily. I couldn't picture Eleanor hanging around a gay bar with some biker babe.

She caught my wry expression, blushed, and hurriedly explained, "My lover's wife. I think she's having an affair."

That was a shocker, but I managed not to drop my jaw. She looked to be more the type who attended tent revivals on a regular basis than the kind who would be having a passionate affair with a married man. When I think of the "other woman," the image of a sleek sophisticate comes to mind, not the plain-Jane sitting in front of me. I grabbed a stubby pencil and began scribbling. "Start at the beginning."

Eleanor had met Roger J. Hugo a few months ago. She'd been the costume designer for a summer stock production of *The Taming of the Shrew*. He had played Petruchio and during his costume fittings, he'd seduced her. They had been seeing each other once a week ever since the production ended.

"I'll be thirty years old next week," she said, her voice breaking, "and I'm still single."

"Have you thought about leaving him and taking up with someone already single?" I asked, dismayed. "The odds of him leaving his wife aren't in your favor." The last time I looked, I hadn't seen a sign on my office door that read DIVORCES R US. Despite how nice the money would be, I got a creepy feeling about this job from what little she'd told me.

The Other Woman

Eleanor leaned forward with an imploring look. "He's on the verge of leaving her and he's left her before. I love him. I'd be good for him."

"Aw, gee, I don't know," I replied. "I'm not sure I want to get involved in breaking up a marriage just on that basis—"

"She's *cheating* on him," Eleanor cut in sharply.

I bit my tongue. It would be too easy to point out that Eleanor's main man wasn't exactly Mr. Fidelity.

"How do you know?" I asked, making doodles on my notepad. I resigned myself to the fact that if I didn't look into this matter, some other less scrupulous private eye would take this girl to the cleaners.

"I saw Cynthia, his wife, at a restaurant about a month ago," Eleanor explained. "Roger and I were already seated when she came in. She looked straight at us."

"Didn't he see her?"

"His back was to her. The tables were filled up, but she had walked in as if she were looking for someone. When she saw us, I expected a big scene. Instead, she got this panicked look on her face and left the restaurant in a big hurry."

I had to admit that it was strange behavior for a wife who clearly saw her husband with another woman. Usually a woman who discovers her husband is having an affair will do one of two things: she would let him know she'd caught him in the act, whether at the restaurant or later at home or, if they had an open marriage, she'd have continued doing what she was doing without blinking an eye—she might even stop by the table for a friendly chat with her husband and his mistress. But a woman who turns and walks out with a sheepish expression on her face is not a woman who wants her husband, cheating or not, to know about her affair.

When I asked Eleanor why she had waited so long to do something, she shrugged and dabbed at her swollen, red eyes. "I had only seen her once before. I kept thinking I'd made a mistake, that maybe it hadn't really been her in the restaurant. But just the other day, I saw her again, and it was the same woman. I kept wondering why she hadn't filed for divorce. She must have been meeting a lover when I saw her at the restaurant."

"I suppose he doesn't know any of this," I said, getting a nod of confirmation in return. It was clear to me why she hadn't told him—she was afraid he wouldn't believe her.

"No, he doesn't. And when he finds out, he'll blow his top," Eleanor replied. "Roger has a very bad temper." She sat there, hands folded carefully in her lap like a young girl at church, a look of hope on her face. I could tell she was good at that sort of thing. "Will you take my case?" she asked softly, her eyes lowered. Don't ask me why, but I hate it when someone doesn't look me in the eye.

"I'll look into it." I was half hoping she would back out when she heard what I charged per day. But without batting an eye, she whipped out her checkbook.

As she handed me the check, I asked one more thing that had been bothering me. "Suppose I'm able to confirm that the wife is having an affair, and you present it all to Roger. What if it doesn't work out in your favor?"

She answered simply. "Letting him know will be reward enough." With that, she stood up and thanked me. Before leaving, she handed me a couple of photos of Cynthia Hugo, explaining that she had obtained them from Roger's Mercedes glove compartment.

I spent the next few hours doing a background check on the Hugos. They had bucks, big bucks. Roger Hugo was president of Hugo Manufacturing, a company that made

The Other Woman

plastic containers. Hugo money had not been made with the environment in mind. In fact, Roger had probably never even heard of biodegradable products.

Cynthia, whose maiden name was Bergdorf, was from old Newport stock and her family had a portfolio of Fortune 500 company stock that would make a stockbroker salivate. Since Cynthia's money had been used to build her husband's company into the conglomerate it is today, she owned the controlling share, fifty-one percent, of Hugo Products.

I started surveillance on Cynthia Hugo at six-thirty the next morning.

The Hugos lived near the Chestnut Hill Reservoir, just a few blocks off Chestnut Hill Avenue. Despite being located near a busy intersection, it was about as isolated as a house can get in a Boston suburb. Van Dine Court was an exclusive dead end with only four houses, all authentic Victorian gingerbreads on sprawling landscaped lots. The Hugo house was pale gray with black-and-white trim. Very toney.

Parking my Datsun 510 across from the Hugo residence, I figured my car wouldn't look too out of place in an area where the average annual income of a resident was in the high end of six figures. Residents would probably assume I was the hired help.

There were his and hers Mercedes sports cars in the driveway, one white and one burgundy. One glazed donut and half a thermos of Italian roast coffee later, a small, neatly dressed man with well-cut graying hair left the house and got into the white Mercedes. By my calculations, that had to be Roger Hugo. He wasn't handsome in a classic sense, but there was something attractive about him. Still, it was hard for me to picture him with mousy Eleanor.

When he had driven away, giving my car barely a glance

down his long, thin nose, I had to wait another hour and a half before Cynthia Hugo stepped out the door. Grabbing my binoculars for a better look, I hunkered down so I wouldn't look so much like a spy, which, of course, made me look exactly like one.

Her photo had been unkind, adding about ten years to her face. In person, she looked like she was in her mid-thirties. Dressed in a straight black skirt and scarlet blouse with a black-and-white houndstooth jacket, her pricey little outfit went well with her auburn hair, blunt cut just above the shoulder, and crimson lipstick. I was willing to bet my retainer fee that her blouse was pure silk.

We spent the first part of the morning browsing through Bloomingdale's and Marshal Field. Eventually Cynthia Hugo ducked into Filene's basement sale. Every Boston woman, from Wellesley to welfare, shopped there. Even the wealthy love a bargain. It's the thrill of the hunt, and the triumph you feel when you walk out with a prize. By the time we left Filene's, I was carrying a bag with a leather designer purse and a little black skirt of my own, both marked down to twenty-five percent of the original price.

It was now twelve-thirty and she had bought out all the upscale department stores within walking distance. We headed toward the warehouse district. I was beginning to think that we were going to hit all the factory outlets as well, but she surprised me again by entering a bar and restaurant called The Stronghold. The name was familiar, but I couldn't quite place it. I sat at a small table in the raised part of the restaurant, overlooking Cynthia's table. She seemed to be waiting for someone.

The Stronghold had a rustic theme with exposed brick walls, rough-hewn wooden beams crisscrossing the ceiling, potted plants to give the customer that woodsy feel, and

The Other Woman

waitresses in jeans, flannel shirts, and hiking boots. I usually don't feel weird about eating alone in a restaurant, but I felt a little self-conscious here. The waitress who came over to take my order had light brown hair piled haphazardly on top of her head, wisps of it framing her round face, and wire-rim glasses. I felt like I was back in the early seventies.

"Hi. My name's Flora and I'll be your waitress today. Can I take your order?" she asked.

"I'll have a beer, whatever's on tap, and a pastrami on rye with hot mustard."

She flashed a perky smile. "We have oyster stew today. It's delicious."

"Oh, I think I'll pass," I said, handing her the menu.

"Are you sure?" she asked, wrinkling her forehead and pushing her glasses up the bridge of her nose.

"No, thank you," I replied politely but firmly. I didn't like to eat anything that reminded me of mucus.

She noticed my Filene's bag. "Been shopping today?"

I smiled coolly at her. "Yes," I replied pointedly, "and I'm very thirsty."

She toddled off to get my beer. It occurred to me that my waitress appeared to be flirting with me, but I didn't have time to think on it very much. A thin black woman was approaching Cynthia Hugo's table. She was striking with her upturned nose and dark hair that rippled halfway down her back. Cynthia stood and they kissed—not just a buss in the air, not just a peck on the cheek, but a passionate kiss. I finally took a good, hard look around me and made a brilliant deduction: there was not a single man in the place. I looked back at Cynthia and her friend, their heads close together, their hands touching. Then I looked around the dining area again, and realized there were similar couples all around. Some detective *I* was.

While I was ruminating on all of this, my sandwich and beer arrived. As I ate my meal, a plan formed in my mind. When my waitress came over to give me my check, I smiled at her. While I paid, I racked my brain for her name—was it Fauna? No, Flora.

"Flora," I began, feeling like a rat. She brightened. "Listen, I have a favor to ask."

She carefully counted out change and handed it to me. I waved it away—it was a generous tip. "I'm from the West Coast," I said, lying through my teeth, "and I write for a little publication there called the *Gay Times*. Sometimes we use pieces on the nightlife in other cities. Would it be okay to take a few pictures for an article on this place?"

Flora frowned. "I don't see why not. Why don't I ask my manager?" She gave me a soulful look before departing.

I watched Cynthia out of the corner of my eye. She and her friend were taking their time, pushing their salads around on the plates, touching each other's hands, the occasional kiss, playing footsie under the table.

I hoped my plan would work, but I felt like a heel for what I was about to do. After all, with a husband like Roger, who wouldn't find comfort in the arms of another woman? But I had to keep telling myself that this was no different than working for a wife who had an adulterous husband. Since the Hugos were both having affairs, Eleanor might be right—maybe this would just force the issue of divorce and when the dust settled, everyone would be happier in the long run. At least, that's what I kept telling myself.

Flora came bouncing back. Her manager was really excited that someone wanted to do an article on the restaurant. She didn't think the customers would have a problem because of the restricted circulation of the periodical.

I told Flora to thank her boss for me. She lingered a moment longer. "If you're staying over tonight, maybe I could show you around Boston and Cambridge. We could check out some other places for your article," she suggested in a shy tone.

I now felt about one millimeter high. She really was a sweet kid. Putting on my best disappointed look, I touched her arm. "Gee, I'd love to, but I have a plane to catch. There's a gay rights rally to cover in San Francisco." Flora pushed up her glasses and nodded, her face registering both disappointment and understanding. "But," I added, "the next time I'm in town—"

"Oh, yeah," she replied, brightening visibly. "Come on by and we'll do the town."

When she left, I took my camera out of my bag and began shooting random photos of the place, several with Cynthia and her friend in the frame, having a very cozy conversation. When I was halfway through the roll, I pocketed the camera and left the building. It was drizzling outside. I sprinted to my car and grabbed my new telephoto lens. In Boston, walking is easier than driving, and chances were good that The Stronghold was conveniently located close to Cynthia Hugo and her lover's love-nest.

I was loitering in a doorway across the street from the restaurant, my camera ready for action, when they left together a few minutes later. Like any tourist in Boston, I snapped a few photos and trailed them to a Beacon Street condominium, red brick, fenced in by wrought iron, with lots of character. When they disappeared inside, I entered the foyer and checked the names on the mailboxes. Two boxes listed male occupants, one box listed a married couple, but the name on the fourth box was A. A. Matthews. Most single women think it's clever to put just their initials on their mailbox and in the telephone book to discourage intruders and obscene phone calls, so I reasoned that this A. A. Matthews was Cynthia's friend.

I left the building and crossed the street, taking shelter in the doorway of another old building with character that had gone condo. I was having dismal thoughts about choosing a career that involved standing in the rain when the lights went on in the bay windows to the right of the entrance. The shades were up, and I could clearly see the front room. I fitted the lens to my camera and focused on the window. In the doorway to the living room, I could see the two women kissing intimately, peeling layers of clothing off each other in the heat of passion—until one of them noticed the view of the street. They didn't seem to take notice of me in particular, but a moment later, the shades were drawn. At least I had gotten my shots.

I was drenched by the time I got back to my office. Eleanor Monahan, clutching her purse with the intensity of a mother awaiting word about an injured child, was waiting for me. "I just thought I'd stop by," she explained in a faltering voice. "I was on my way to the subway."

I mustered up a cold smile and led the way into my office, Eleanor trailing the raindrops dripping off my anorak. Inside, the radiator was pinging, a sign that it was working, and my warm office smelled like stale coffee and rancid chicken and mayonnaise. I remembered throwing away half a chicken salad sandwich the other day—apparently the building's janitorial services hadn't bothered to clean my office last night. I made a mental note to have a talk with the building manager.

Once I had shed my damp jacket and was settled in my chair, I gave her a full report. I tapped my camera. "It's all in here."

Eleanor was leaning forward with an eager expression,

and for a moment, I forgot how lackluster she normally appeared. "When can you get the pictures developed?" she asked, blinking. Then she waved her hand as if she were erasing a thought, and her chair creaked from Eleanor practically bouncing up and down in her seat. "No, no, maybe you should just give them to me and I'll get them developed. I know a good place."

I shrugged and handed her the roll. Getting film developed was time-consuming and an extra expense for the client. If she wanted to do the honors, that was fine with me. As she placed the film canister in her handbag, Eleanor's eyes gleamed with the good news.

"This is better than I had hoped," she replied, elation shining in her face. Why shouldn't she be happy? After all, she was about to destroy several people's lives on the very slim chance that Roger Hugo would want her when the dust had settled. More likely, he would despise her for bringing it to his attention. But who was I to pass judgment? I was no better than she was, profiting from someone else's misery.

She stood and shook my hand, then left the office with a determined look on her face. This was a woman who was out to get the man she loved to give up his wife for her—at any cost.

I shook my head, wondering if I'd done the right thing. This was one job I didn't want to repeat.

A few uneventful days had passed when I got the phone call. I had spent the better part of that day playing two-fisted poker—and I wasn't winning.

"Matelli," I said into the phone.

There was no immediate response, but I could hear a man shouting something unintelligible on the other end. "Hello?" I repeated, louder this time.

There was a thunk, as if the caller had dropped the receiver, then I heard heavy breathing. I was beginning to think it was an obscene phone call when a woman lisped, "Miss Matelli? Angela?"

"Who is this?" I asked sharply, not in the mood to play twenty questions.

"Eleanor. Eleanor Monahan. I hired you last Tuesday."

Oh, God, I thought. She's been dumped and now she's going to dump on me. I didn't want to hear this.

"What happened?"

"I showed Roger the photos. I told him about Cynthia and the woman on Beacon Street. He—he got really angry. He hit me and left, saying that he was going to kill her."

I sat up. "What do you want me to do about it?"

"You can probably stop him before he does something stupid. Please," she said with urgency in her tone. "You've got to get down there right away. Roger went to the Beacon Street address."

"I'm on my way," I told her. "Meet me there." I hung up. I wouldn't normally ask a client to go into a dangerous situation, but I figured that by the time he reached his destination, he might listen to Eleanor. And if we both failed, I decided to bring a pal along—my Smith & Wesson .32 automatic.

The condo's security door was propped open. An invisible ice cube ran down my back, sending chills up and down my spine. I took out my weapon and jammed a clip into place.

A. A. Matthews's door was open just enough for me to slip inside. I stood in a small entryway, a full-length mirror on a wide-open closet door reflecting part of the living room. There were no lights on inside the apartment, and the sunlight was no longer hitting the front windows. A

The Other Woman

dim, gray light filtered into the room. I could see a shape on the floor, but I couldn't tell if it was a rug design or something else.

I walked in slowly, my gun preceding me, and took in the scene. The first thing I noticed was the musty smell of death. An end table and a chair had been knocked over in a struggle. There were three people in the room—or should I say, two people and one body. Cynthia Hugo was the rug design I had seen in the mirror. She was sprawled in the center of the room. I was too late. Cynthia Hugo had been strangled. Her lover lay unconscious on the floor near the sofa. There was a trickle of blood from a cut on her temple: It looked like she would be out for a long time.

Roger Hugo stood over his wife's body. A weak light seeped through the window, casting Hugo's ghostly shadow across the grisly scene. The only thing to do now was keep him from handling too much of the crime scene. I slipped my gun back in my purse.

Having seen Hugo only once before outside his home, I wouldn't have recognized him here if I hadn't known the situation. The artfully cut and blow-dried hair from a week ago was now in disarray, as if someone had tried to tear it out. His polo shirt was ripped at the neckline and he had deep scratches on his face and neck.

"What happened?" I asked quietly. I didn't bother to introduce myself.

Hugo didn't seem surprised that a complete stranger was in the room. "I killed the bitch," he replied calmly, his gaze locked on his wife's body. "She was cheating on me. *With another woman.* Can you believe it?"

I choked back my reply. It seemed unnecessary to remind him that he was having an affair as well. The floor creaked and I turned to see Eleanor standing in the doorway. She took in the scene slowly with a sharp intake of breath and her hands fluttering up to her face.

"What are *you* doing here?" Hugo asked from behind me. I couldn't see his expression, but the steely tone of his voice told me he wasn't happy to see her.

"I just came to see if Angela got here in time," Eleanor replied in a strange tone. If I didn't know any better, I'd say that she sounded almost triumphant. I wondered why a woman would be happy about her married lover killing his wife. With the hint of a smile, Eleanor added, "I guess she didn't. Your temper got the better of you this time."

I felt as if I'd walked into the middle of a movie. Before I could ask what was going on, Hugo spoke again. "So you came here to gloat, is that it?" I looked at his flushed face, a muscle in his jaw pulsated.

"Wait a minute," I said. "I thought you two were lovers."

"We were," Hugo said acidly, "but I dumped her about a month ago."

It took me only a moment to put it together. I turned to stare at Eleanor. She no longer looked like the shrinking violet who had come into my office a week ago. The narrowed, glittering eyes, the sly cat smile told me that she had engineered all of this. And I'd been the sucker who put it all into motion.

"You told me about his temper," I said to her, "but you didn't tell me the affair was ended. I would never have taken the job if I'd known that."

"Of course you wouldn't," she replied lightly. She crossed her arms, a satisfied smirk on her face. "But you're the detective. You should have checked out my facts."

It took two seconds to get to her. I hauled her up by her coat lapels until she was nose to nose with me. "You *used*

The Other Woman

me," I said, angry at her, angry at myself. She was right, of course. I had been sloppy. I was just as much to blame for Cynthia Hugo's death as Roger Hugo and Eleanor. Roger would go to prison. My license might be in jeopardy if the police felt inclined to pursue the matter. But Eleanor would be able to walk away from this without a blemish on her record. She had orchestrated it all, but had done nothing that could be construed as illegal.

She pulled away from my grasp and straightened her collar, her expression betraying no emotion. "Roger taught me that everyone gets used at one time or another," Eleanor replied in a hard voice. Then with a giggle, she addressed Hugo. "I got you good, you son of a bitch. You're going to spend the rest of your sorry life in prison. This is better than I'd hoped for."

Hugo was behind me, so I was caught off guard, thrown against a wall of bookshelves. Several books rained down on my head. Hugo launched himself at Eleanor. In the feeble light, I could see that although Hugo was small, he was powerfully built. His face was red with fury, making him look almost demonic. Eleanor struggled in his grip, her eyes wild with panic, her nails tearing at the grip he had on her shoulders.

I tried to get up, but my ankle had twisted when Hugo shoved me, and I collapsed back against the shelves. I tried again. Taking it slowly, I pulled myself up. Hugo was sitting on Eleanor's prone figure, strangling her with his bare hands. I thought he was going to succeed, but Eleanor reached into her coat pocket and pulled out a gun. I tried to warn Hugo, but the blast covered up my yell. His body jerked once, then hung suspended for a moment, his hands still tight around her neck. Gasping for breath, she managed to shoot him again. Hugo collapsed on top of her in a heap.

Sobbing and coughing, she tried to push him off, but her gun hand was pinned under his body.

Eleanor threw me a weary, pleading look. "Help me get him off."

I tested my ankle. It felt all right, but I knew it was sprained and I'd pay later if I didn't get some ice on it soon.

Eleanor started to whimper and struggle. "Angela, please. Help me."

I limped over and looked down at her. Hugo's blood was soaking the floor around them. "I'll go call the police," I said before I turned and hobbled out, leaving her pinned under the dead man.

"The Right Thing to Do" was written for a noir *gaming company called Archon Gaming. I wrote five* noir *stories for them. This story, a twist on the "James Cain love triangle" was published in the two volumes of stories about Archon's* noir *crime world that were never released.*

The Right Thing to Do

I was working for Goldman Insurance as a secretary to Hiram Goldman. I was married, but not very happily. My husband, Joe, was a good man, but after the war, he was never the same. He had been a demolitions expert, and he must have seen some awful things. In any case, he never talked about it. He just drank to forget.

My job was our security. Joe worked sometimes when he was called to demolish a building. But his reputation was damaged by the fact that he drank, and everyone in town knew it. I had inherited my parents' house and furnishings, even a bit of money to save toward our retirement. But I was unhappy. I tried to make our marriage work, but after a time, we settled into the role of roommates.

Then I met Peter. I was sitting by the duck pond in the park one day, about to eat an apple when he stopped beside me and asked if he could share the park bench to feed the birds. His full name was Peter Allen O'Connell and he was handsome, debonair, and rich. I recognized him from photos I'd seen in the sports pages—he was the manager of the Bulldogs, the city's baseball team.

"You must be on your lunch break," Peter said. "Do you get an hour or only half an hour?"

I hesitated. Was he talking to me? I was dazzled, flattered. "I only get half an hour. On a beautiful day like this, I wish I could take the entire day off."

The sun scurried behind the clouds and the day darkened. We looked at each other, then at the sky, then laughed at the same time. "Well, I guess I won't feel so bad about going back to work now," I added as I stuck the uneaten apple in my purse, crumpled my paper lunch sack and tossed it into the trash can nearby. I stood up and stretched, watching him toss breadcrumbs into the pond, watching the ducks waddle after the food, flapping their wings.

I could feel his eyes on me and I knew I was blushing. "Well, good luck with the ducks," I said as I started to walk away.

He stood up suddenly, spilling breadcrumbs all over the sidewalk. "Are you free for dinner tonight?"

I didn't know what to say. I stood there, dumbfounded. Why would a handsome, wealthy man ask me out? I wasn't bad looking, but I always thought of myself as kind of average—average hair, average face, average figure. Nothing remarkable.

"Oh, I'm sorry," he said, looking flustered. "It's just, you remind me of—"

I knew he was going to say "my sister," or "my mother" or "my favorite aunt." Instead, he surprised me by saying, "—an old girlfriend from high school." He looked unhappy for a moment, then seemed to remember that I was there. He extended his hand and introduced himself. "Peter O'Connell."

After a moment's hesitation, I took his hand. "Emma. Emma Price. Pleased to meet you."

"Well, will you?"

The Right Thing to Do

"Will I what?" I was still amazed that this handsome man was talking to me, seemed interested in me. Okay, interested in the fact that I reminded him of a lost love, but still—

"Have dinner with me. It would mean so much."

I gave Joe some thought, but it didn't take long to decide that since my husband never took me anywhere, I would do this favor for this nice stranger, and get a free dinner out of the deal. I found all of this very exciting. I normally led a very dull, predictable life.

"All right." There. I said it. I was going to have dinner with a handsome, wealthy man for once in my life. I tried to feel guilty about Joe, but it was hard to feel anything anymore. God knows that ever since Joe came back from the war, our marriage hadn't been the same.

Peter broke into a radiant smile, a smile that almost made my heart melt. My knees were definitely shaking. "That's wonderful. Really, you don't know how much this means to me. We'll do up the town. Do you have a nice dress?"

I wracked my brain, trying to remember what was in my closet. "I'm sure I can find something," I assured him.

His smile faltered for a moment, then he nodded. "I'll pick you up at eight, is that too late?"

I blinked. I usually was in bed by nine, but not tonight. "No, that's fine. Eight o'clock is just fine."

"I want to take you to the Harbor Grill, then the Parisian for jazz. Would you like that?"

I had never been to either place, but I knew both the Harbor Grill and the Parisian were places that only the elite could afford. I didn't want to give Peter my address, so we agreed to meet down the street from my house at a small corner bar. I went back to work, wondering where I was going to find an appropriate dress.

After work, I went shopping for a dress and had my hair done. The dress I bought was dark blue chiffon with a draped Grecian neckline that hung low in back to show off my shoulder blades. The shop girl told me that I had nice shoulder blades and that men would find them very sexy. I wouldn't know a sexy shoulder blade from a hole in the wall, and I didn't think it was appropriate for a married woman who was doing a man a favor, but I held my tongue. I wanted to look like I belonged there.

Back at my place, I got dressed with minutes to spare. Joe was still in some bar, soaking up his gin. I knew he wouldn't be home for hours.

I turned to look in the mirror. A different person stared back at me. Her mousy brown hair had been darkened and styled, make-up defined her cheekbones and generous mouth, and the dress set off the ivory tone of her skin.

"This can't be me," I said in wonder. "Am I really this beautiful?"

I walked down to the corner bar, Denny's Den, and stood outside. It would never do for Joe's cronies to see me. I reminded myself that most times, they couldn't remember their own names, so even if they saw me, the chances of remembering that they saw me this dressed up were slim. But the timing must have been right because Peter pulled up in a red convertible and got out. He opened my door and stood there, a white gardenia corsage in one hand.

"Hello," I said, breaking into a smile that probably looked more confident than I felt.

He stared at me, not saying a word. I cleared my throat and looked down. "Is anything wrong?"

"Wrong?" he repeated. "No. You look ravishing. I just

The Right Thing to Do

didn't—" he gestured to the corsage, a wrist corsage, then tossed it in the bushes and held out his arm. "No, you deserve something better." We walked to his shiny red sports car.

Peter drove expertly to our destinations, caressed every curve as if the car was his hand and the road, a woman's body. The car's top was down and the wind whipped my hair freely around my face. I loved the feeling and vowed that if I ever came into some money, I would buy myself a shiny red sports car just to have the feeling of wind through my hair.

We talked through dinner, and listened quietly to jazz at the Parisian, and Peter ordered champagne, which I sipped slowly, savoring the bubbles that tickled my nose, burst on my tongue, and skittered down my throat.

Maybe it was the champagne, maybe it was the powerful freedom I felt with this night, maybe it was how grateful I felt for Peter asking me to dinner. Whatever it was, I felt comfortable with him.

He finally slowed down on the outskirts of the city, near a beach. I heard the waves crashing down on the sand, smelled the tang in the air, and felt the salt in the wind as it lovingly caressed my face. I got out of the car, and almost stumbled. The sand was soft and my heels sank into them. I took my shoes off, not caring that I would ruin the hosiery I wore.

"This is wonderful," I shouted. Peter watched me quietly, a slow smile forming. I giggled. I'd never giggled before. He brought something out in me, a free spirit that had never been there before. I tossed the shoes in the car and raced toward the waves, then leaped and screamed as the cold water hit my ankles. Peter came up behind me and grabbed me around my waist, pulling me close. I turned around and our lips met.

Later, much later, we lay in the sand, away from the waves, listening to the surf pound its watery fist against the shore. Peter stroked my hair.

"I have to say, Emma, you surprised me."

I closed my eyes, enjoying the feel of a man's fingers running through my hair. "I think I surprised myself."

He propped himself up on one elbow and looked down at me. I settled down in the sand, smiling up at him. A part of me, detached, wondered what I thought I was doing, making love to a man the first time we went to dinner. Committing adultery. I tried to feel guilty about Joe, but nothing happened. But another part, a stronger, newer part of me pushed those thoughts right out of my head: This was *my* night. Probably my *only* night.

"I want to see you again, Emma."

The surprise must have shown on my face. "But I'm married."

He shook his head. "I-I thought we'd just have dinner, listen to jazz at a nightclub, and maybe a chaste kiss by the end of the night."

"In memory of your first love?" I asked, trying to keep the bitterness out of my tone. I couldn't help feeling a bit possessive, a bit envious of this nameless woman who had been part of his life years ago.

Peter pulled himself up and hugged his knees, looking out at the moonlight that settled gently on the shining water. "Jennifer was very special to me. We were going to be married after we graduated from high school. But her father wouldn't allow it. I went on to college, and Jennifer ended up marrying a man her father approved of. She was an unhappy woman. She committed suicide. I just keep thinking that if we had been together, stood up to her father—"

I sat up and touched his shoulder. "You couldn't have

The Right Thing to Do

known. Besides, she was probably unhappy about a lot of things, not just her marriage. Usually it's more than one thing that drives a person to want to die."

Peter looked at me now, a strange, intense look. "You sound as if you know that feeling."

I hesitated. "Yes, I've felt that way for a long time." I told him about Joe, about his drinking, about our loveless marriage. "When there's nothing left for you, it's hard to find a reason to keep on living," I concluded, smiling bravely. The tears were hot and heavy behind my eyes.

Peter's eyes were troubled, and he put an arm around my shoulder, giving me a light kiss on the lips. "I hope you consider me a reason for living."

My breath caught in my throat for a moment, then we kissed again, a lingering kiss this time, as a tear rolled down my cheek. Peter gently brushed it away.

Things between us progressed at a fast pace. Peter bought gifts for me, took me out to dinner, a concert or play, or a nightclub, almost every night. The gifts became more expensive. I gradually became used to the lavish way he treated me. But underneath it all, I wondered when it would end, when I would wake up from this dream, my reading glasses slipped between the pages of a romance novel. I wish I could say that I felt guilty, but I felt the excitement of reawakening passions.

Joe didn't even seem to notice. He was usually passed out in front of the radio when I came home, or I would get a call from the police that they'd picked him up again, sleeping on a park bench, or worse.

Up until the day Peter dropped the bomb.

We were in a motel room, lounging around in bed after a long lovemaking session. Then, in a sheepish voice, he told me.

I leapt out of bed. "You're *what?*"

"Married." He avoided looking at me. I pulled the sheet off the bed and wrapped it around my body, then marched into the bathroom. I turned on the shower and stood under it for what seemed like an hour.

When I finally got out and dried off, I expected Peter to be gone. Instead, he was dressed and waiting for me, looking like a puppy that had just been kicked by its owner. I remained silent as I gathered up my things.

"Emma, *you're* married. What's the difference?"

I whirled around. "I *told* you the first night. You knew from the beginning. I *didn't*." I stalked over to the nightstand where a coffeemaker sat. I felt stupid. I'd known he was the owner of the town's baseball team, but I hadn't dug any deeper than that. I'd never paid much attention to the society pages.

"You don't understand." He followed me into the bathroom as I got the coffee ready for the percolator, my movements brisk and uninviting. "I don't *love* her. At first, I only wanted companionship from you." I turned away from him to plug in the machine. He grabbed my elbow and spun me around. "I didn't expect to fall in love with you."

I cried. He held me and stroked my wet hair and told me about his wife, Karen. "I married her on the rebound from Jennifer. A few years later, her father died. I had no idea how rich Karen was until after she inherited the estate."

I sipped my coffee and looked away. "I really don't see what the problem is."

Peter sighed. "Things changed. She became, I don't know, demanding, difficult, different. Maybe it was the fact that we couldn't have children. Maybe it was the death of her father, or a combination of both. She started to gain weight. Stopped doing the things we both loved to do.

Started treating me badly. I fell out of love with her."

I knew all about that. I wasn't sure I was out of love with Joe, but I knew that things would never be the same between us.

I continued to see Peter for the next two months, and sometimes he talked about his unhappy marriage. One day, we were in a restaurant, eating breakfast, when he said, "Sometimes I wish Karen was dead so we could get married."

I put my fork down slowly and looked up at him. "You don't mean that."

"Yes, I do," Peter replied, fiddling with a knife. He had lowered his eyes. "Don't you sometimes feel that way about your husband?"

I looked around, suddenly uncomfortable. I felt as if there was an unasked question that hung in the air. I waited. When he didn't say anything, I leaned forward. "Why don't you just divorce her, Peter?"

When he looked at me, his eyes were full of misery. "She's Catholic. She wouldn't stand for it. For better or worse. And it's gotten beyond worse."

"You can't take—" I stopped. I felt as if I'd spin out of control at any moment. I leaned toward him, lowering my voice. "You can't just take someone's life because she's become an *inconvenience*."

He stopped toying with the knife and looked up at me with sad eyes. Then he reached over and touched my hand. "You're right. I don't know what I was thinking, Emma. At least we have this time together." He squeezed my hand. "You're such a good person. You have enough of a burden in your own life." I wish I'd taken notice of the calculating look in his eyes.

★ ★ ★ ★ ★

I spent the next few days thinking over what he'd said. I can't say I wanted to think about it—his words haunted me. One night, I got home to find Joe still awake. Something about him was different.

"So, you're finally home, Emma." He got up and I noticed that his eyes were red and swollen from crying, not drinking. "I know all about it. You're seeing someone, aren't you? Is he better than me?"

I didn't answer. Joe gave a ragged sigh and answered his own question with surprising candor. "Probably. Look at me. I'm a drunk. A goddamn sot." He sat down and covered his face with his hands. "All because of the goddamned war."

Something reached in and tugged at my stomach. I sank into a nearby chair before the pounding in my heart made me faint. "What happened to you over there, Joe?" A tear rolled down my cheek as I thought back to those happy days when we had plans for the future, when we wanted children, when Joe was going to grab the world by the tail and tame it.

Joe touched my cheek and when our eyes met, for a moment, I saw the Joe I had fallen in love with. He wasn't handsome or wealthy, but he loved me. He'd always loved me, not some made-up version of me that Peter loved—the *me* who looked like Jennifer, the me who gave him the attention he craved. "You couldn't handle it if I told you," he said softly, tentatively.

"Try me," I replied calmly.

And he told me, told me about the horrors of what bombs did to human beings, told me about picking up the pieces. By the time he was finished, we were both crying.

"You've got to get help, Joe," I said. "There are groups—"

The Right Thing to Do

"I've already joined one," he said in a quite tone. "I went to my first meeting today. They're going to help me get off the sauce."

"Why now?"

He closed his eyes. "I don't want to lose you. I love you."

I thought about Peter, about how close I'd come to giving up my marriage. I still didn't know if I loved Joe the way that I used to—it would take time. But I would have to break it off with Peter and give our marriage a chance to work. I told Joe it was his imagination—I wasn't seeing anyone else.

"You can't leave me," Peter said to me when I told him. He was clutching my hand as if it were a lifeline.

"Peter, my *marriage* is at stake. It was stupid of me to start an affair in the first place."

He looked so miserable, I added, "You can make your marriage work again, I know you can. If I can do it, so can you."

He pleaded with me. "Emma, you have to help me get out of this marriage. You have to help me kill her."

With a sharp intake of breath, I withdrew my hand. "I can't help you, Peter." I stood up. "I have to go now. Goodbye."

He grabbed my hand and I turned back around to him, catching a nasty flash in his eyes. "Don't walk out on me, Emma. I chose *you*. Don't do something you'll regret."

I stumbled backwards, then turned and walked away as fast as possible.

That wasn't the end of it. I hadn't told Joe the truth about my affair because I was afraid it would destroy him.

During the next few months, there were times when he backslid, having a drink, but he'd wake up from his drunk and start all over again. But soon he went off the wagon less and less. Joe was determined to do well, but I could see how fragile his newfound self-worth was.

One day, I got a phone call. "Emma, it's Peter." His voice sounded ragged, as if he wasn't sleeping well.

I wanted to ask him how he was doing, but instead, I kept my voice neutral, remembering our last conversation. "How are you, Peter?"

"I tried to be nice about this, Emma, I truly did. But now I'm desperate. If you won't help me get rid of Karen, I'll tell Joe about us. Meet me at our usual spot in an hour." He hung up. I knew he meant the duck pond, where we met sometimes.

I arrived first. My throat constricted at the sight of him and I found it hard to breathe. "I thought you loved me once," I managed to say.

His eyes narrowed. "Do you think I could ever love someone like you?"

I was finally seeing the true Peter. I had done a little checking between his phone call and our meeting. Peter was a gambler and was into the Mob for lots of money. Apparently his wife kept the purse strings relatively tight.

It was meant to hurt me. I could see that, but I laughed and told him the truth. "I don't think you love anyone but yourself, Peter. You think because you're handsome and rich, I fell in love with you?" I stopped laughing and gave him a withering look. "I could never love anyone like you." I could see that I'd struck home. His confidence faltered and his smile wavered slightly. I continued, "I used you as much as you used me. Besides, how would I be of any help to you?" I drew myself up and started to leave.

The Right Thing to Do

But Peter had to have the last word. "Joe worked with bombs. He knows about building them."

I stopped and stared at him. "How on earth would I get Joe to make a bomb without telling him the truth?"

Peter clutched my arm eagerly. "You could tell him a story. You're good at lying." I struck out, but he caught my arm and squeezed so hard I knew I'd have bruises there tomorrow morning. "Remember, with just a few words from me, I could put Joe right back where he was."

I tugged at his grip, trying to get away. But he held me fast. "And just as a little incentive, if you convince Joe to make a bomb, I'll make sure you get a bonus, sweetheart." Then he whispered a figure to me that was half my salary for a year.

Before I could get away, Peter turned my face toward his and kissed me hard. It wasn't a nice kiss. I could feel the desperation and ruthlessness behind it. He was trying to break me. I stomped on his foot, which made him draw back and howl. Then I slapped him and left without another word.

On my way home, I thought about what to do. It seemed that I didn't have a choice. I wanted Joe to be all right. I didn't know how desperately I loved him until he clawed his way back to sobriety because he was afraid of losing me. Now I was afraid of losing him again.

I thought about Karen. Once Peter told me he was married, I began to take an interest in the society pages, combing the news for pictures and information about his wife Karen. I'd wanted to know what Karen looked like, what type of woman she was. She was a little plump, but I thought she looked like a nice, caring person. And most of the news about Karen involved charity balls, dinners with the mayor and long trips to Europe. The photos rarely showed Peter escorting her—she was usually by herself or with a friend. Of course, that was all surface. Peter had told me stories about their life behind closed doors, away from the charity balls.

But for all his confessions to me, Peter turned out to be less of a man than Joe. What was I going to do? I thought long and hard about my predicament before it came to me clearly: Joe was more of a man than Peter. Telling Joe the truth was the right thing to do.

When I got home, Joe started to put on his coat. "Glad you got home. I was beginning to worry about you. It's early enough for us to take in a movie tonight."

I was still shaky from my meeting with Peter and I must have looked like hell. Joe frowned. "What's wrong, honey?"

Tears began to roll down my cheeks. He reached out and brushed them aside. I told him the truth. It was the hardest thing I've ever done. It was hard for me to see Joe hurt like that. To be the one hurting him. We were both crying by the time I was done. He took out his handkerchief and wiped my eyes, then his own. He looked at his hands. "I think I knew all along. It was just much easier for me to believe that you weren't having an affair."

We both sniffled a bit, and talked it out.

"Now that I know the truth, Peter has no hold over you," Joe said after I'd told him all the gory details.

"You won't go back on the sauce?"

"No." Joe looked sincere.

"And you won't divorce me?"

"Honey, I love you. I'm not happy that you had an affair, but you stuck by me when I was down, and I'm doing the same." He brushed back a tendril of my hair that had escaped. "He has no hold over you now."

I frowned. "But he'll still kill his wife. He'll sucker some

The Right Thing to Do

other poor woman, or he'll go the conventional route and hire a killer. Do we want that on our consciences?"

Joe fell silent for a moment. He pulled out his cigarettes and lit one, offering me one, which I waved away. "He *did* offer us a lot of money," Joe finally said.

"With that money," I said, "we could get out of this city, get a little place elsewhere. Maybe start our own business."

"On the other hand, we could take this information to the police. We don't have to leave our names."

We looked at each other, talked a little more about what other possibilities were available to us, then we finally agreed on what to do. Then I made the phone call. It was the right thing to do.

A week later, I awoke at the same time I'd been getting up for years. But then I remembered that I didn't have to go in to work. I'd quit the day before, giving Hiram Goldman my resignation without any notice. He didn't seem to care. I'd just been a secretary, and he could find another one from his secretarial pool. Besides, I knew there wouldn't be a gold watch or even a bouquet of flowers for me if I'd given him two weeks' notice. Mr. Goldman hadn't been a very nice man to work for.

I padded to the front door just as the newspaper hit our stoop. Unrolling the paper, the headlines leaped out at me: *Car Bombing Shakes City.*

I felt nothing as I read about the death in the paper. Peter had been in debt for hundreds of thousands of dollars, and now he was free of it all.

I'd also done a little detecting on my own and learned a few things to my advantage. While working for Goldman Insurance, I was able to get into the files pretty easily, and I dug up an insurance policy on Karen that had been useful when I made my phone call the other week.

I looked at the time and realized that I'd have to get dressed if I wanted to get to my meeting on time.

Joe was stirring in bed. He'd quit his job, too. Our things were packed and we were ready to move away from here, away from the city and from the greed and crime and everyday drudgery. We'd already made a down payment on a little house in another state.

"What time is it?" Joe asked me as I slipped into a blouse and a skirt. He was squinting and his hair was flat on the side he'd slept on. It was endearing, now that he wasn't drinking.

"Almost time for my meeting."

He blinked several times and looked a little more awake. "Want me to come with you?"

I smiled fondly at him and bent over to kiss his forehead. "No, darling. You go ahead and get the car packed up. I won't be long. There's some coffee on the stove."

I left and walked briskly to the park, to the duck pond. She was sitting on the bench already, throwing crusts of bread to the ducks. I sat down next to her.

She wore designer sunglasses. "You're on time. I like that."

"I'm sorry about your husband."

She turned and pulled her dark glasses down, a humorless smile on her face. "I'm not. The shit. I've gotten over it and moved on with my life. I suggest you do the same."

We sat in silence for a few minutes.

"Oh, hell, I guess I kind of miss Peter," Karen O'Connell said with a sigh. "I suppose I should play the part of the grieving widow."

"It hasn't been easy for you," I said. She'd put the bag of

The Right Thing to Do

crusts between us and I dipped my hand into the bag to feed the ducks.

"When you called me, at first, I was angry with you, then with him. I'd known he was cheating on me for years, but to have the Other Woman call me up—"

"The *former* Other Woman," I reminded her.

She nodded. "Then I got to thinking, the bastard's lied and cheated on me over and over, and what have I gotten out of it but a lot of debts. His salary as the manager of the Bulldogs wasn't enough to satisfy his gambling or his women." She inspected me closely. "You're not what I expected. He usually liked his women—" she stopped, seeming to be afraid of saying anything insulting.

It was my turn to smile. "He was using me. It was almost too late by the time I realized that. And it was wrecking my marriage."

She kept eyeing me. "Yes, you told me about your husband. How's he doing after—?"

She didn't have to finish the question, we both knew it had been difficult for Joe to make a bomb to kill someone, but I'd talked to Joe about it. Eventually he began to see that Peter was the enemy: the only way to stop him was to kill him.

Besides, Karen had offered us three times what Peter had offered us. But even if she hadn't offered to pay us, we probably would have killed Peter just on principle. I'd originally called Karen to let her know what was going on, but when she pressed me for details, I gave them to her. And I'd been a little reluctant—she could have taken what she'd known to the police, or maybe confronted Peter, who could have lied and turned on us.

But Karen was a shrewd woman. It didn't take long for her to see things my way. We talked again, and it eventually came out that she'd stopped loving him a long time ago. She was just a bank account to him now. And to find out that he wanted to kill her, well, at first, she didn't believe me. In fact, when we had our first meeting, I'd taken a copy of the insurance policy with me. There was no corresponding policy on file in case Peter died. I'd been guessing that Karen didn't know about this policy. And I was right.

Karen now stood up and shook my hand, then hugged me, slipping a fat envelope into my shoulder bag. "I hope you and your husband are going to be very happy in your new home."

"I'm glad you're satisfied with our services. We've decided to expand."

She raised her plucked eyebrows in surprise and a faint, pleased smile crept over her face. "I'm glad you've thought about my suggestion. I have plenty of friends who could use your—unique services. I'll be sure to tell them."

"You know how to get in contact with us."

She raised a hand and we parted.

I was looking forward to getting home with the money, driving our new car this afternoon out on the highway, heading toward our new home.

Joe and I had bought a red convertible so I could feel the wind whipping through my hair.

This is the last of the three Jefferson Birch stories, published in The Fatal Frontier, *edited by Martin Greenberg and Robert Randisi. There is a bittersweet tone for this one. I enjoy writing about Birch and hope for more opportunities in the future.*

Winston's Wife

Jefferson Birch had been reluctant to take this case, especially when Annabel Winston asked him to look into her husband's disappearance, then proceeded to offer him her entire savings. Birch should have saved himself the trouble of looking for Joe Winston by explaining to her that men who disappear into the night, with a packed bag and all the savings, usually didn't want to be found. But he hadn't had the heart to turn her down when she began to cry in his presence.

Birch had been working at a ranch near Sacramento the day Annabel Winston came knocking on his bunkhouse door. Except for Birch, the bunkhouse was empty, his bunkmates having already gotten up with the sun and gone. Birch and the other cowhands had just come in off the trail the day before. During the last ten miles of the trail, Birch had gone after a stray calf and twisted his ankle while rescuing it from a ravine. On orders from the trail boss, Birch was resting up.

Whoever was timidly knocking at the door would not go away, and Birch finally limped over to answer it, expecting the ranch wife to be standing there, asking if his ankle felt good enough to do a little saddle repair. Instead, he opened the door to find a woman he'd never seen before.

"Mr. Birch? Jefferson Birch?" she had asked. Her eyes widened at the sight of him in his longjohns.

Birch had the presence of mind to shut the door quickly. "I apologize, ma'am," he called out through the door as he reached for his denims and stepped into them. "I'll step outside when I'm respectable."

Inside the bunkhouse, Birch hobbled over to a tin mirror nailed to a wall above a beat-up basin with a few inches of water in it. He ran a hand over his whiskers, deciding not to take the time to shave, splashed water on his face, and combed his wet fingers through his hair. Grabbing his least dirty shirt, he paused to test his ankle. The swelling had gone down and he was able to slip both his boots on.

Birch wondered if he had really seen an attractive lady outside the bunkhouse or if maybe it had all been a dream. Shrugging, he opened the door and stepped outside.

She was still there, wearing a gray traveling dress now thick with dust, a little indigo bonnet perched on her fair hair. Two spots of color were fading from her cheeks, remnants of the embarrassment she must have felt when she saw Birch standing before her in all his longjohn glory.

"I apologize again, ma'am," he said.

"Nonsense," she replied, her slender hands twisting her thin, dark blue gloves. "It was my fault. I should have allowed someone to accompany me out here, but I was so eager to find you that I . . ." She stopped, lowering her eyes and smiling slightly. "I didn't think," she finished.

"What's so urgent?"

She looked up at him, gazing directly into his eyes and introduced herself as Mrs. Annabel Winston. "I heard about you through Arthur Tisdale, who is acquainted with my parents and who is currently back east on business. I want to hire you to find my husband. He's been gone almost a year, and I haven't heard from him in almost six months."

After leaving the Texas Rangers several years ago, Birch worked for Tisdale's investigations agency from time to time.

Mrs. Winston gave Birch the details: One year ago, they had been living on a small farm outside of Redding. One day, her husband came back from town, very excited. He had run into an old friend who had been living up north, panning gold on Oregon's Rogue River. Winston wanted to go up there himself to pan a little gold. When Annabel expressed her concern about pulling up stakes to pursue a dream, her husband had decided it would be better if he went alone.

"I begged him to think about it for a few days, but he was packed and ready to go the next morning," Mrs. Winston said, blinking rapidly. She turned and paced a bit in front of Birch to collect her thoughts. "I received a wire from him a few weeks later, telling me that he'd bought a stake on the Rogue River not far from Klamath Falls. He wrote about once a month, telling me that the claim was almost worthless. Then three months ago, he stopped writing."

"Are you afraid something's happened to him?" Birch asked.

She nodded, small frown lines marring her smooth forehead. "I just hope I'm not too late."

"Why did you wait so long?"

She lowered her eyes, a hesitant look on her face. "Well, I waited about two months for a letter, hoping that he might be disheartened, or out of money and ashamed of telling me. About three weeks ago I contacted the marshal of the nearby town of Gold Hill. He was very kind, making inquiries on my behalf. Unfortunately, Marshal Stanley learned next to nothing. There were a few miners who recalled my husband, but Joe hadn't stayed around long enough for anyone to get to know him. It was as if one day he was there, and the next day he was gone."

So Birch had taken the money she offered, along with a photograph of her husband that had been taken just before he left for Oregon. Joe Winston had a stern nose and small, fierce eyes. He had a look about him as if life had disappointed him one too many times. Birch gave notice to his ranch boss and saddled up his horse, Cactus. When he left the ranch, the weather was sunny, warm, and dry. When he reached Oregon two days later, the rain was dripping off his hat and Cactus was restless to find shelter.

Gold Hill was a small but growing town, built by men who wanted to profit from the gold miners who populated the banks of the Rogue River. Restaurants offered outrageously priced meals; general stores stocked supplies that cost twice the going rate; and saloons, with working girls who insisted on miners buying a drink before sitting down, advertised over-priced, watered-down drinks. All of these businesses ate away at the greenhorn miners' hard-earned gold. If a man lasted long enough, he learned to avoid Gold Hill like a poisonous snake.

Despite the abundance of businesses intent on parting a miner's gold dust from his pouch while providing a good time, Gold Hill didn't look like a very inviting place. The rainy season had churned up the main street, and the air was chilly with the promise of another deluge. Birch huddled deeper into his whitewashed canvas coat, glad that he was wearing his thick wool shirt underneath.

It was late afternoon when he dismounted and tethered

Winston's Wife

Cactus to the hitching post outside Marshal Stanley's office. Inside, Birch was grateful for the warmth of a potbellied stove. A rangy man in his mid-forties sat in a chair with his boots propped up against the lip of the stove, a steaming tin mug in his hand.

Birch took off his hat. "Marshal?"

The man bobbed his head to acknowledge that he was, indeed, Bill Stanley. "State your business, stranger."

Birch introduced himself and explained why he was in town. Stanley straightened his chair and stood up, placing his mug on the stove's surface.

"You want some coffee?" he asked, already reaching for an empty mug on his desk. Birch wrapped his fingers around the full mug. Stanley pulled up another chair and indicated that Birch should sit. "I'm sorry that Mrs. Winston hired you. I've already talked to the other miners who had stakes near Joe Winston, and they said that he left after six months. No one knows where he went."

"I'm sure you did the best you could, Marshal," Birch said, "but it must be hard for you to devote much time to a missing miner when you have to keep order in this town."

"Well, I can't stop her from throwing her money away," the marshal said with a shrug.

Birch was curious. "What do you think happened?"

Stanley sighed. "Probably what happens to most of the men who come here to mine. They give up."

"So why didn't he go back to his wife?"

"Ashamed of failing. They either go off to make a new life or they kill themselves."

Birch digested the information. He had had some dealings with miners a few years ago, and he knew that they could also be very jealous if a fellow miner struck it rich. "Is there any possibility that he may have been killed?"

"It's unlikely. I already looked into it," Stanley explained. "Most miners aren't very bright. I think the fever makes 'em stupid. If another miner had killed him for his stake, he would have moved right onto it. No one was mining his stake. The miners I talked to said that Winston was barely eking out a living." Stanley leaned back in his chair and stretched. "No, I think he just packed up and moved on."

When Birch finished his coffee, he thanked the lawman and got directions to the river. It was almost dark when he arrived at the first claim. A dubiously makeshift shack with a ragged blanket for a door sat about twenty-five feet from the riverbank. Birch stayed on Cactus and called out. A moment later, a large hand pulled the blanket aside and a bear-sized man shambled out, shotgun resting easily in his hand.

"I'm looking for information on a fellow named Joe Winston. He disappeared from his land a few months ago."

The miner sullenly squinted up at Birch. "Don't know anything."

Birch looked around the site, noting the beat-up gold pan and the rusted coffeepot on the campfire. He took a silver dollar from his pouch, casually flipping it in the air and catching it. "That's too bad. I was hoping to find someone who could give me some information."

The miner licked his lips, his eyes darting from the coin to the riverbed, which was, no doubt, played out. He ran his forearm across his mouth. "Look, stranger, I don't know much. Honest. I hardly knew the man. He didn't spend much time with the rest of us miners. But I can tell you that someone's working Winston's claim now."

Birch was surprised. "Marshal Stanley was here just the other week and was told that no one wanted it."

The miner gave a short laugh. "None of us wants it,

that's for sure. No, this is some greenhorn from down South who took it over. Claims Winston sold it to him and he has the papers to prove it."

"You think he got a bad deal?"

"Depends on what he came up here for," the miner replied, amusement evident in his eyes. "If he's here for his health, that's one thing. If he's here to get rich from panning that sorry lot, he's out of luck. When Winston left, a few of the other miners snuck onto his claim to try it out. But they left the poorer for it."

Birch tossed the silver coin to the miner. "Where's this claim?"

"About three miles downstream. Just follow the Rogue."

It was full dark when Birch came to a dying campfire.

The sound of a rifle being cocked brought Cactus to a standstill.

A man's voice called out, "This is my claim, stranger. I hope you're just moving on." There was a quaver to the voice, betraying how young and inexperienced the owner of the voice must be.

"I'm just looking for information on Joe Winston," Birch said.

There was a silence, then the sound of the rifle being uncocked. A black man stepped into the light of the campfire, rifle at his side. He was no more than twenty, his face ravaged by smallpox, and his prominent Adam's apple bobbing up and down. "I only met him three times."

"Where?" Birch asked.

"Bodie. I was working at a saloon, cleaning tables and sweeping up at night. Saved me enough to buy a stake."

"Bodie's a pretty good mining town," Birch said.

The young miner's shoulders slumped. "You have to have a lot of money to buy a stake near Bodie. And it's a rough area. Didn't like all the shootin' goin' on. So when Winston came through town and offered to sell his stake, I took him up on it."

"Any luck?" Birch asked.

The question brought a hooded expression to the miner's eyes. "Winston didn't warn me that it was played out. I thought I knew everything I needed to know about mining. I'd overheard lots of miners talk in Bodie when they'd had a few too many whiskies and I stored up the knowledge." He rubbed the back of his neck with a grubby, calloused hand. "But I guess learnin' and doin' are two different things."

"I'm sure things'll get better for you. You happen to remember where Winston was staying in Bodie?"

"Far as I know, he's still there," the miner replied. "Place called the Nugget Hotel."

Birch thanked him and rode off.

He was a day's ride from Bodie, but he pushed himself and Cactus to ride on into the night. As the dawn lit the sky, Birch found himself at the edge of the boomtown.

With a population of ten thousand and more than fifty saloons, Bodie had a reputation as a dangerous town. Newspapers back East reported more killings per week in Bodie than in any other gold rush town in the West. Knowing that violence could erupt at any moment, in any place, Birch kept his eyes open for signs of trouble. He wasn't long finding it. As he passed by the Gold Stake Saloon and Gambling Parlor, he heard the crack of gunshots from inside. Birch spurred Cactus to a trot in time to see two men stagger outside and fall face down onto the dusty street, smoking guns in their hands. A third man walked out of the saloon to examine the two dead men. Then he wadded up a handkerchief and pressed it to a bullet wound in his upper arm.

Winston's Wife

In the center of Bodie, most of the gambling parlors were clustered on one side of the main street, and the hotels on the other side. The Nugget overshadowed the rest of the buildings; it was not only a hotel, but a restaurant, saloon, and gambling parlor as well. The façade was a bright red and blue that looked freshly painted.

The inside was a different story. Birch took time to glance around the lobby. The faded elegance of its imported blue wallpaper and worn, polished hardwood floors were second to the crystal chandelier, with several prisms missing, that hung just above and beyond the registration desk. Birch walked up to the registration desk, where a clerk looked at him expectantly.

"I'm looking for Joseph Winston."

The clerk shook his head, disappointment and suspicion replacing his previous expression. "No one here by that name."

Birch frowned. "May I see the registration book? He may be listed under another name."

"I'm afraid I can't help you, sir," the clerk replied, now with his nose in the air.

Before Birch could explain why he was here and maybe offer a small bribe for a look at the book, a bell rang. Room 10 needed assistance. With an irritated glance in Birch's direction, the clerk left his station unattended. The book sat on a swivel stand to the far left of the counter. Birch quickly looked through the signatures for the past few days. One set of names stood out: Mr. and Mrs. J. Swinton registered in room 7. It was the only name that was entered day after day.

Before Birch started toward room 7, a man walked into the lobby. He was dressed like a gambler, with a dark suit coat over a fine linen shirt and brocade vest. When the man doffed his bowler at a passing woman, Birch recognized him as Mrs. Winston's prodigal husband. He approached.

"Mr. Winston."

The man's eyes widened in recognition of his name. "I'm afraid you have the wrong man," he said, glancing around the lobby to make sure no one overheard their conversation. "My name is Swinton." He began to walk toward his room.

"No, I'm sure I have the right man," Birch replied, lengthening his stride to catch up. Winston quickened his pace, trying to ignore Birch. "In fact, I have a photograph right here." Birch reached into his vest pocket to draw out the portrait.

Winston stopped in front of his room and grabbed Birch's arm to stop him. "Not here," he said with a hiss, opening the door and drawing Birch into the room.

Inside, gray daylight filtered into the room through grimy windows. It was actually two small rooms. The one in which Birch stood was a sitting room shabbily furnished with a small sofa, a wingback chair, and a desk and chair in the corner. There was barely enough space to take three strides from the door to the opposite wall.

A second chamber, presumably the bedroom, could be seen through an open doorway. Birch guessed that it had a separate entrance. He remembered passing a door in the hallway that was only a few steps away from the doorway through which Winston and he had just entered.

A young woman appeared in the doorway between the two rooms, dressed in an ivory silk robe, her heavy, dark hair tumbling all around a lace shawl collar. Birch took off his hat in her presence. Her best features were her translucent blue eyes, accentuated by slender dark brows that arched delicately above.

Winston's Wife

She moved farther into the room, the robe swirling around her like silken water, and looked at Birch with open curiosity. From her expression, it was clear that the couple rarely had visitors. "John?" she asked.

"Grace," Winston said nervously. He cleared his throat. "Grace, why don't you get dressed. I bet you haven't eaten a thing all day." Grace lowered her eyes and went into the other room. Winston strode over to the desk, opened a drawer, and brought out a half-empty bottle of whisky and a none-too-clean glass. Not bothering to offer a drink to Birch, he poured himself a generous amount and gulped it down. "How did you find me?"

"The man who works your claim."

Winston's laugh was bitter. "I didn't think he'd still be there. Seemed too soft for that sort of work. Besides, the stake's played out."

Birch wisely refrained from contradicting him. "He seems to enjoy the role of miner right now."

The woman called Grace came into the room again, this time dressed in lace-trimmed muslin. Her hair was pinned up with tortoiseshell combs and her cheeks were lightly rouged.

"Where are your manners, John?" she said sternly. "Aren't you going to introduce us?"

Winston grunted. "This is my wife, Grace. Gracie, this is . . ."

"Jefferson Birch, ma'am."

"We have some . . . business to take care of." Birch met Winston's eyes and caught the warning in them. "Why don't you go down to the lobby and wait for me. I'll take you out to a nice restaurant in a little while." His eyes had softened as he watched her leave, then hardened again when the door closed.

"All right," he said to Birch. "I'm Joe Winston. What do you want?"

"It's not what I want," Birch replied mildly. "It's what your wife wants. Your first wife, that is. I take it that girl thinks she's married to you."

"As far as I'm concerned, she is my wife." Winston took a tobacco pouch out of his coat pocket and began to roll a cigarette. He shook his head. "I have nothing to give Annabel. What does she want, money?"

"She was concerned about you. She's taking in sewing and laundry to make a living, and she spent her hard-earned money hiring me to find you." Birch watched Winston's impassive face.

Winston lit his cigarette and inhaled deeply. "I don't want to go back to Redding and the farm. I want to stay here. I was a terrible miner, but I'm a good gambler." He withdrew a fat poke from his inside vest pocket and shook it to drive home his point. "I took the little gold I came away with from the claim and turned it into a decent living. Now I play poker and Monte, occasionally roulette."

"So you don't feel any obligation to either woman, not even to get a divorce from Annabel in order to make Grace an honest woman."

Winston laughed cruelly. "Grace hasn't been honest since the day she set foot in Bodie. And as far as Annabel is concerned, I don't feel anything anymore for her. I stopped loving her the day she told me she wouldn't sell the farm to pay for my gold claim."

Birch was having a hard time listening to Winston. Clenching his jaw to keep from saying anything he might regret, Birch jammed his hat on his head and stood.

As he made his way to the door, Winston asked, "You won't tell Annabel where I am, will you?"

Birch paused, then turned. "You won't object to a divorce, will you?"

Winston shrugged. "If she can find me, I'll happily consent to a divorce."

Birch couldn't contain himself any longer. He strode over and grabbed Winston by his lapels, hauling him to his feet. An uppercut to the chin knocked Winston across the sofa, head over heels.

The knuckles of his right hand smarting, Birch departed without another word. He was halfway down the hall when he heard the shot. Racing back to the room, he found the bedroom door partially open. Through the open door to the sitting room, he could see Winston slumped in the sofa, blood staining his brocade vest. He heard a sound behind him.

"Don't turn around, Mr. Birch," she said. Her voice was shaking.

"Mrs. Swinton—" he began.

She cut him short. "No, call me Grace. I came back to the room to get my evening bag and I heard most of your conversation." Birch could hear the sorrow seeping into her voice.

"I'm sorry, Grace."

She hesitated. "You were only doing what you had to do. The person for whom I grieve is his wife. No matter what he told you about me, Mr. Birch, I would never . . ." Her voice broke and he could hear the sob caught in her throat.

"But why did you kill him?" he asked, wanting to turn around and look at her again. "Why not just leave him?"

"John, I mean Joe, wasn't an easy person to leave. I don't know what life with him was like for his wife, but he didn't always treat me well. Maybe that's why it was so easy—" She trailed off again, then added in a stronger voice, "I'm sorry, Mr. Birch. But I had to do it."

He felt the blow to the back of his head before he sank into unconsciousness.

Birch wasn't sure how long he was out. When he opened his eyes, the room was almost dark. Standing up cautiously, Birch staggered into the sitting room. Winston was still there, still dead. Grace was gone.

He was surprised that there hadn't been more of an uproar when the shot had been fired earlier. Then he remembered he was in Bodie, where a person was killed just about every hour. People had probably gotten used to minding their own business.

Birch pondered what to do. Grace was obviously gone. He thought about sending for the law, but he didn't much like the idea of putting them on the trail of a woman betrayed. In a fit of passion, Grace had killed a human being. Then again, Winston wasn't much of a human being, having lied to one woman and hidden from another.

If she was caught, there was a chance that she would be found not guilty. But justice was a tricky thing. She might also be sentenced to life or even hanged.

Birch touched the back of his head and winced. He squinted at his fingers, but he couldn't see blood. She hadn't broken the skin, but he would have a nice-sized goose egg for a few days. Birch closed the hotel room door and walked down the hall. The registration desk was empty. He crossed the quiet lobby and left the hotel.

It wasn't until he was heading out of Bodie that he realized he'd made his decision. He hoped Grace left Bodie to start a new life. Meanwhile, it was difficult to know what to tell Annabel Winston. He finally decided to tell a small lie, that he had come to Bodie a day late, that Joe Winston had been shot by a person or persons unknown. He wanted to spare Mrs. Winston the sordid details. She didn't deserve what had happened to her.

Birch reached into his vest pocket for his bandanna, but it was missing. In its place was a poke. He pulled it out and examined it. Although it was not as full as the one he had seen earlier on the dead man, it was definitely Winston's bag. It was filled with gold and silver coins.

Birch could only guess that Grace had taken a few coins for her escape, but had left the rest with Birch to give to the new widow.

Dying was probably the only unselfish thing Winston had ever done. The money would enable two women to have a better life than when he was alive.

It was a better legacy than Joe Winston deserved.

I lived in Ireland for two years and it left an imprint on me, and when I began fishing around for another series character, DI Maggie O'Malley of the Rathcoole Garda was a natural.

Feis

It was a slow day for Maggie. In fact, it had been a slow week for the Rathcoole Garda. She had finished her paperwork, done her court duty by testifying in the case of Seamus Brophy, who had been caught stealing milk from the cows in his neighbor's pasture. The weather had stayed nice, never dipping below fifty, and it was early summer—prime time for soft days, rainy weather.

Maggie was doodling to keep her hands busy so she wouldn't pick up a fag. She'd been trying to quit, and hadn't lit up in over four days. Of course, she was as irritable as a cow who hadn't been milked in the same amount of time.

There were two other detectives and three constables at various desks, talking on the phone, writing up reports or smoking. The urge to light up became so overwhelming for Maggie that she abruptly shoved away from her desk and stood up. The other detectives and constables looked up, and she walked over to the small electric pot of hot water to make a strong cup of tea. It was either that or a fag.

Inspector Riordan took out his pack of cigarettes and walked over to Maggie as she poured hot water into a mug with a moose on it. He waved the pack under her nose and she took a deep breath of rich tobacco.

"Just one, Maggie girl . . . What would it hurt?"

Maggie steeled herself, turned around and grabbed the pack, throwing it across the room. "Feck off, Colin."

A roar of laughter rose from the room as she flipped them off, then went back to doctoring her tea. As she was adding milk and sugar to her mug, DCI O'Rourke, Maggie's supervisor, strode into the small station. Every conversation stopped and every face turned toward him.

Aidan O'Rourke had that effect on his staff. He was fifty-one, tall and austere. He was a former Christian brother. But not one constable or inspector could say O'Rourke wasn't fair. Maggie liked him. He had been there to push her career along, making her the first female detective in Rathcoole.

"I've got a favor to ask of you all," O'Rourke announced. "My sister is involved in organizing the Naas Feis on Saturday night. They're light on security and asked if a few of my men," he eyed Maggie and added, "and women, would be interested in signing on. You get to listen to some good music, watch some good step dancing competition. And there'll be free meals for those who sign on. Clannad and Christie Moore are to play a concert. My sister, Riona, and her band are opening for them. Rumor has it that the rest of Planxty might reunite with Moore for a few songs."

Maggie enjoyed *feisanna*—pronounced fesh-anna—and had planned to go anyway. She liked the festival atmosphere, the booths filled with art and jewelry, food and drink, the *seanachies*—storytellers—poets, and musicians. *Feisanna* often combined step dance competition with performances of all kinds—music, plays, games and athletic competitions, and dance programs. It didn't hurt that Christie Moore and Clannad were playing there. Maggie had grown up on their music and always tried to attend a concert where one or the other performed.

Several constables had already volunteered. The other inspectors grumbled and made excuses involving family plans. O'Rourke turned to Riordan. "What about you, Colin? You don't have a wife and kids."

Riordan's eyes slid sideways as he stubbed out his cigarette. "Oh, uh, sorry, sir, I've already got plans for the weekend."

"Yeah," DI Flanagan piped up. "Plans for drinking and womanizing." A roar of laughter rose up from the room.

Riordan gave the room the finger, then seemed to realize that his supervisor was still there. He looked sheepish. "Ah, sorry, sir."

"Ah, the wit and wisdom of a good retort," O'Rourke replied, then looked over at Maggie. "What about you, O'Malley? Are you willing to give up a night at the pub to do a little security and listen to some good music?"

The room hushed. Maggie shrugged. "I'll be glad to do it, sir. I have no plans for the weekend." She'd recently broken it off with the bloke with whom she'd been stepping out. She'd caught him one night with another girl, who turned out to be his wife. Maggie didn't even have to exact revenge—she could tell that the wife, who looked like a nice girl, was shocked and hurt at first, but after Maggie got done explaining who she was, she could see the wife's mouth tighten and the bloke's face pale. But it wasn't anyone else's business and she kept her romantic life out of the workplace.

O'Rourke nodded. "I'll see you there then. Thanks. My sister will appreciate it." He turned and marched into his office and shut the door.

Riordan came up and whispered in Maggie's ear. "Brown-noser."

"Slacker," was her reply.

*****

On Saturday early afternoon, Maggie got into her Mini and drove the fifteen miles to Naas. In the heart of County Kildare where people often came on holiday, Naas was a town renowned for its racetracks and golf courses. The Naas *Feis* was just one more way to bring revenue into the county.

O'Rourke had suggested that she be there early to see the layout of the concert area. The festival was located on the grounds of a donated mansion on the edge of town. The stage area had been built and the scaffolding had speakers secured to either side. There was plenty of seating as well.

Maggie stood in the back and watched the action on stage—people moving lights and adjusting props. Suddenly a man strode onto stage. He was slender, slight, wavy ginger hair and close-cut beard under a sharp nose and clear blue eyes. Maggie could see his blue eyes even from where she stood. He looked vaguely familiar to her.

"Jesus, Mary and Joseph!" he said, waving his hands at a couple of stagehands who were positioning chairs and microphones. "Is it our heads you t'ink we use to dance? We're *dancers*, the audience wants to see our legs and feet."

"Caoilte Callaghan," she murmured. He'd been in her class in Catholic school back in Rathcoole.

The stagehands began taking the chairs down. Another man, taller than Caoilte, handsome, muscular and stocky with a restless energy, came on stage. "What the hell are you doing?" he asked the stagehands. The two men stopped and looked confused. The man seemed to notice Caoilte for the first time, but Maggie could tell that he had been quite aware of the other man the entire time. "Can I help you?"

Caoilte stepped up. "What the feck are ye doing? This is my troupe's dress rehearsal time."

The American's expression sharpened. "You must be Caoilte Callaghan." He pronounced it *keel-tcha,* not as soft as the brogue would allow. "I'm Stephan Shandy, director of the South Boston High Steppers." He announced this as if everyone should know of him. In fact, Maggie had heard something of the Boston dance troupe—in the wake of *Riverdance* and *Lord of the Dance,* this troupe performed the story of Grainne, daughter of high king Cormac Mac Art, and Dermot, the soldier Grainne eloped with to avoid marrying the aging hero, Finn Mac Cool.

Caoilte eyed the American director. "Pleased to meet you, but my question is still, what the feck are you doin' here during my stage time?"

"I asked to change rehearsal times last night. One of my dancers needed to rest after a minor injury. Someone was supposed to contact you about it. Your dress rehearsal time was," Shandy looked at his watch, "about an hour ago." He had an American accent, east coast, Maggie thought.

"No one contacted me about this change," Caoilte replied with exaggerated patience.

"Well, maybe you can squeeze in some time after—" Shandy noticed someone or something to the side of the stage and trailed off. "Well, since you're here, we might as well let you know—" He turned and gestured to someone offstage. A young woman slowly walked onto the stage. Her swan-like neck and wavy coppery reddish hair were the two things about her that Maggie first noticed. "Aoishe, go ahead. Tell him," Shandy said encouraging her by taking her hand. But Maggie got the impression that Aoishe was a bit reluctant.

"Tell me what?" Caoilte stepped forward, crossing his arms against the bad news.

Suddenly the American director noticed Maggie. She

was startled to realize that she'd slowly been creeping forward as she'd been witnessing this drama.

"What are you, a reporter?" the man said with a snarl. A light in his eyes and a slow smile appeared. "Well, I can give you a story for your paper."

Maggie started to protest. "I'm not—"

Caoilte stared at her, his frown turning to recognition—relief and delight evident in his face. "Maggie O'Malley!"

At the same time, the American said, "Aoishe Killian has consented to be my wife." He turned to the suddenly speechless Caoilte and added, "I suppose that means she'll be dancing with my troupe from now on. Sorry, old man." He turned to leave, Aoishe staring at Caoilte, who seemed to have forgotten Maggie's presence. For a moment, Aoishe and Caoilte seemed suspended in a look that crossed the stage—Maggie noted the look of regret and pain that Aoishe gave Caoilte.

"*Aoishe!*" The American accent was harsh on the soft syllables of her name and she jumped slightly, turned quickly to Caoilte and mouthed the word "Sorry," then flitted across the stage to disappear.

A hand touched Maggie's shoulder and she jumped. Turning around, she came face to face with a younger, female version of Aidan O'Rourke. "Hi, I'm Riona O'Rourke. You must be Maggie O'Malley." She was almost as tall as her brother, thin to the point of bony, sparkling eyes and dark Irish looks. She was also much younger than Maggie's superior, by at least twenty years if not more, which wasn't unusual in Catholic families. Riona was clearly the baby, and only a few years older than Maggie herself. "Aidan described yourself to me." Her wide grin was catching, and Maggie found herself grinning back. Riona's eyes strayed to the stage where Caoilte still stood.

"Caoilte," Riona called, bringing him out of his preoccupation, "meet our security chief for tonight."

Maggie turned to her, startled at the thought that she was being put in charge.

Riona noticed and laughed. "Let me guess—Aidan didn't mention it to you. We can pay you a paltry sum for your services, plus all the free food you can eat. We need to compensate you and the others in some small way."

Caoilte joined them. He looked worried and distracted, which wasn't unusual considering what Maggie had just witnessed.

Caoilte snapped out of his troubled state and really looked at Maggie. "Maggie, what are you doin' here? I haven't seen you in an age."

"It has been a long time," she acknowledged. "I'd heard of the Naas Dance Troupe but I didn't realize you were the director."

"We're a small troupe, still looking for dancers. That's why we're holding this *feis*."

"If you don't mind me asking, how did that other dance troupe end up here?" she asked.

Caoilte turned to Riona, who looked regretful. "I'm afraid I'm the one who brought the South Boston High Steppers here. I play pennywhistle and fiddle in a band, and Stephan is a client of my manager. I was pressed into inviting him." She turned to Caoilte. "I heard about Aoishe, Caoilte. I can't believe she's marrying that creep."

He rubbed the back of his neck and scrunched up his face. "Ah, her da must have pressed her into the union. He's wanted to emigrate for ages. Now he sees a golden opportunity to make his daughter miserable so he can see the States."

"Was she your girlfriend?" Maggie asked.

Caoilte shook his head, appearing amused by the thought. "Aoishe is a talented step dancer. She'll be a great one with the right training." His tone suggested that Stephan Shandy was *not* the right trainer.

"But her fella Aengus won't be too happy to learn of her betrothal," Riona added.

"I expect it's a sudden t'ing for her as well," Caoilte eyed Maggie critically. "So you're security for tonight?"

"She's an inspector with the Rathcoole Garda, Caoilte," Riona chided him. Maggie felt distinctly uncomfortable. "Don't you keep up wit' the local news?"

Maggie interrupted. "Well, I'm sure you need to get back to your troupe, Caoilte. Riona needs to show me around."

As they walked and Riona pointed out the areas to be watched more carefully, Maggie's thoughts kept drifting back to the argument on stage, which seemed to be about more than who got the stage for dress rehearsal. She conjured up the image of the dancer, Aoishe, and how beautiful she was. The way the brash American boasted that she was going to be his wife, Maggie suspected he thought there was more to the relationship between Caoilte and Aoishe.

"Inspector O'Malley!" Sergeant Donal Leary loped toward Maggie. He wore blue jeans and a white pullover cotton shirt, which was the uniform DCI O'Rourke had told them was required by the *feis*. Maggie had also complied by donning a pair of dark blue jeans and a white short-sleeved polo shirt.

"Call me Maggie, Donal. We're not on duty as the garda today." He hadn't been on duty the day DCI O'Rourke asked for security volunteers, so their superior must have called him later.

He was a tall red-haired man of twenty-four, slightly

younger than Maggie herself. She usually ended up working with him when she went on a call.

She introduced Donal to Riona, then excused herself to inspect the fairgrounds.

Maggie strolled along the fairway, admiring the booths with cases of silver and gold earrings, bracelets and necklaces, inhaling the sweet bakery aroma and observing the young step dancers in their Irish dresses, hair perfectly curled, walking along ahead of her, whispering secrets to each other and giggling. Her eyes swept the area for potential problems, entrances and exits, but she couldn't get her mind off of the scene she had witnessed between Caoilte, Aoishe, and Shandy earlier.

Maggie came to the end of the *feis* grounds. She began to head back toward the stage area when she caught sight of Aoishe and a young man slipping behind a booth. On impulse, Maggie followed, staying close enough to hear their exchange, but out of sight.

"I don't know what else to do, Aengus. Me da is pressing for this."

"But ye don't love him, do ye, Aoishe?" Maggie peeked around the corner of the booth and studied the dark-haired boy who held Aoishe in his arms. He was lean and muscular, with strong features. His face was still pimply with only a few stray dark red chin hairs. A thin mustache lined his upper lip.

Aoishe put her head against his shoulder and held on tightly to him in answer. Feeling like an intruder, Maggie slipped away to find Riona and her security staff.

After Riona introduced the staff to Maggie, she left to rehearse with her band. Maggie briefed her crew of twenty and handed out assignments. She kept Leary by her side and they covered the stage area with three others from security.

Caoilte's troupe was dancing onstage, and Maggie admired the quick footwork of the dancers. The music turned into a lively jig then suddenly Aoishe was front and center, leading the ladies in a graceful slip jig, her black ghillies flying, tapping, and kicking. Maggie knew only the basics of step dancing, but even she could see that Aoishe was special.

The American stalked out onto the stage and interrupted the rehearsal. "Caoilte!"

Aoishe stopped dancing. Someone turned the music off. Caoilte had been watching from the seats and he stepped forward now.

"What can I do for you, Stephan?" he asked.

The man was trembling. He looked from Caoilte to Aoishe and back. "I don't know how you did it, but Aoishe's broken off our engagement and has told me she wants to stay with your troupe."

"Wouldn't that be her decision?" Caoilte asked. He fumbled with a pack of fags, put one between his lips, and lit it. Maggie watched, fascinated by the way he inhaled, held it and exhaled.

"Aoishe—"

"Leave me alone!" The girl's eyes brimmed with unshed tears. "I was only after marrying you for me da's sake. But I can't go t'rough with it." She turned and fled the stage.

The American watched, apparently stunned by his ex-fiancée's behavior, then seemed to recover and turn back to Caoilte. "This is all your fault. You put her up to this."

Caoilte shook his head. "I have no sway over Aoishe. If she made such a decision, she did so without my knowl-

Feis

edge. You heard her—she said she was after marryin' you for her da."

Stephan jumped off the stage and headed for Caoilte, his fists clenched, his face contorted with fury. Maggie caught Leary's eye and they headed toward the angry man.

"Is there a problem?" Maggie called out as they approached.

Caoilte tossed his half-smoked fag, Stephan turned sullen. "I guess your friends are here to back you up. You Irish stick together."

"I'm only here to keep the peace," Maggie responded.

Stephan stepped up to face her, his intention clear. Maggie held her ground. Leary and Caoilte started toward them to come to her aid, but she gestured them to stay back. "You'll not intimidate me, sir."

Stephan leaned in further until he was nose to nose with her. Maggie had to fight to keep from flinching. "That may be, but you stay out of my way."

She leaned in. "And you listen to me. You may be American but that gives you no right to throw your weight around or intimidate that young girl. You stay away from her and from Caoilte. Your dance troupe may perform as long as there is no more trouble from yourself."

He stepped back, his eyes widening. "Yeah, I guess we can do that. But after this, my troupe will never set foot in Ireland again." He spun on his heel and left.

Maggie rolled her eyes as he turned to leave. "What a loss!" she said dryly. "I'm cryin' in me pint."

She really could have used a fag about then.

The *feis* dance competition began right after mid-day dinner. The beginner category went smoothly, as did the novice category, but it was during the open category that a scream went up. Maggie was prowling the perimeters of the audience when she heard it. It had come from backstage and she broke into a loping run.

Leary was leaning over the body backstage when Maggie arrived. He stepped back to let her inspect the crime scene. It was the boy who had been with Aoishe earlier. He was curled up, a large tarp having been thrown over him.

"Who found him?" she asked.

"One of the dancers stumbled over the tarp," Leary explained. "She kicked it to get it out of the way, and when it didn't move, she pulled a corner free."

Maggie crouched over the body and examined the body. She noticed a ragged hole in his sweater near his heart.

"Look around for the murder weapon, Sergeant." Murder had brought them back to inspector and sergeant. She leaned over the body to examine the hole in the sweater without touching the body and caught a whiff of the familiar smell of Guinness. The victim had been drinking before he was stabbed. She turned her attention back to the ragged hole. The thread had been cut, not just worn away like a hole made from age. "This looks like it was made by a knife."

Maggie turned to the other three members of her security staff who had come running. "Eamonn, call the Naas Garda. Finn, Liam, secure the area, make the rest of the security staff aware of the problem." Liam and Eamonn worked with her in Rathcoole—she knew they would be efficient.

Riona came onto the scene. "What's happened?" Her eyes widened when she saw the young man on the ground and she gasped.

"Can you identify this victim?" Maggie asked.

"That's Aoishe's fella, Aengus."

"Last name?" Leary asked. He'd somehow found a notebook and pencil in all this chaos.

"O'Mahoney."

A keening sound rose up behind Riona. Aoishe stood there, her hands on either side of her head. Both Caoilte and Stephan appeared, took in the situation and started toward the grief-stricken young girl at the same time. Riona had the presence of mind to grab the girl by her shoulders and pull her away from the rivals. "You two have done enough damage, wouldn't you say?"

Caoilte had the decency to look ashamed. Stephan just looked furious.

"Da! Da! Where is he?" Aoishe bleated.

Riona held her and patted her shoulder. "She's asking for her da. Someone go find him," she ordered sharply to Caoilte and Stephan. "Is it that he's after drinking pints at one of the pub booths?"

Caoilte stirred. He glanced at Maggie for permission to leave and she nodded. The security staff wouldn't be much help if they didn't have a description of Aoishe's father. "Go find him."

The Naas Garda showed up within ten minutes—two constables and a detective named Hanratty. Maggie gave Hanratty an account of what had happened. Hanratty, a man in his forties with a pointed chin and Roman nose, nodded. "You'll be staying on here, won't you, Inspector O'Malley?"

Maggie was surprised and pleased. "Only if you approve, Inspector. These are your stomping grounds."

"You caught the case, you should be allowed to work it, even if it's outside your area. We'll start with inquiries of the witnesses in the immediate area."

The forensics team had arrived and started taking photos and samples of the crime scene.

"My men will help your staff search the area for the weapon," Hanratty said.

The medical examiner finished his initial examination of the body and approached the detectives. "Knife wound. Approximately twelve and a half centimeters long. An upward thrust between the ribs. He's been dead less than an hour." He shook his head. "Terrible waste of a good young man."

Hanratty nodded his thanks and turned back to Maggie. "Who do you favor?"

She frowned. "Well, this American, Stephan, is brash and not a terribly nice person. I think he's the favorite around here. But I can't rule out Caoilte Callaghan. And Aoishe Killian, to a lesser extent." A knife killing wasn't usually a woman's choice. Maggie couldn't help but think that she was missing something. It was difficult for Maggie to consider Aoishe seriously. She seemed more the victim than the killer, and she didn't appear to have the strength or the height to carry off the killing. But Maggie knew that Aengus' death was a crime of passion, and Aoishe was connected to it.

The most likely scenario was that the spurned American had tried to convince Aengus to step aside, they had gotten into it, and a knife had been produced. Aengus had been stabbed. She couldn't come up with a convincing scenario for Caoilte to kill Aengus, unless the dance director harbored a secret love for Aoishe. From Maggie's observation, Caoilte seemed to be more in the role of Aoishe's protector. Still, wouldn't that be enough motive?

Maggie walked the grounds around the crime scene. The ground was still soft from a recent rain, and there were indistinct footprints where a scuffle had occurred. Maggie tried to picture the scuffle from the angle at which Aengus had fallen. She recalled that Aengus had been a tall youth. Stephan and Caoilte were shorter. An upward thrust might have been the way a shorter man would stab at a taller man.

"We'll start with that American," Detective Hanratty announced. Two Naas garda moved away to find the dance director.

Leary sidled up to Maggie and said in a low voice, "Caoilte Callaghan has asked to talk to you."

"Can it wait?" she asked. She wanted to be in on the grilling of Stephan Shandy.

He shook his head. "He says it's very important."

Maggie nodded and followed Leary out to the front of the stage where the audience and dancers milled around restlessly. Caoilte was near the stage, smoking again. Maggie had to tear her eyes away from him to watch Stephan Shandy pass by, escorted by a Naas garda. He stopped and addressed her. "Going to help your friend rehearse what to say to those other cops?"

She eyed the American with displeasure. "Is it something you want to accuse me of, Mr. Shandy?"

"He's your friend, and if he's guilty, you're too close to the case to be unbiased."

She smiled. "For your information, Caoilte and I haven't been in each other's company in nearly seven years. For another, I resent the implication that I would cover up any information that might point to him as the killer." She turned and left him to be interrogated by Hanratty.

"Maggie," Caoilte said when she arrived.

"What can I do for you, Caoilte?"

He looked away, swiping a hand over the back of his neck and sighing. "It's not what you can do for me, Mag—

Inspector. It's me who's after doin' a favor for you." His eyes met hers. "Was Aengus stabbed?"

She closed her eyes. "Are you just guessing or is there a reason for this inquiry?"

He sighed again. "Then I guess I killed him, Inspector. It was my knife that was used, wasn't it?"

This was too easy and both Maggie and Leary, who was in earshot, knew it. They accompanied Caoilte to Inspector Hanratty, taking care that their suspect didn't get another look at the crime scene.

Hanratty noticed the new suspect and, leaving Shandy in the care of a garda, came over. "What's going on here?"

Leary took Caoilte over to the Naas garda car while Maggie explained Caoilte's confession.

"Do you believe it?" Hanratty asked.

She thought. "I believe his knife may be the murder weapon, but the confession seems contrived, as if he's protecting someone. Maybe Aioshe had access to the knife and he's afraid she killed Aengus." Maggie followed Hanratty back to where Caoilte was being guarded.

"How did ye stab him, Caoilte?" Hanratty asked.

"Like this." Caoilte showed how he raised the knife above his head and thrust downward.

"Why did ye kill him?"

Caoilte's eyes slid to the side. "He was standing in Aoishe's way. She should go to America with Shandy and become a star. She has the potential. Aengus didn't agree."

"Caoilte!" Aoishe stood not far away, having slipped through the garda. Tears slid down her face. "Is it true that ye killed my Aengus?" She covered her face with her hands.

He looked away. "I want the best for ye. Shandy could do that, giving you a wider venue to dance over in America, and he seems to love you."

Maggie spoke up. "What did you do with the knife, Caoilte?"

"I—er, I t'rew it away."

Hanratty followed her lead. "Where?"

"I don't remember."

Hanratty studied him for a moment, then motioned to Maggie. They walked a little ways away. "What's your impression of his confession, Inspector?" Hanratty asked.

She was a little surprised that he wanted to hear from her. He must have read it in her expression. "Don't think we haven't heard your name before. Everyone knows how you handled the murder at St. Jude's last month. Fine work. Even with one murder case under your belt, you've had more experience with homicide than the average country garda. I've only caught a few in my fifteen years with the Garda, and the murderer has always been obvious. Often, we've caught 'em with the murder weapon in hand. This one is different for me, and any help you can offer will be appreciated."

"Well, thank you, Inspector," she replied. "I'm just here to assist in any way I can. As for Callaghan's confession, it strikes me as more of a sacrifice. His demonstration of how he killed the victim was quite wrong, and he's too coy about the knife's whereabouts. I'd say he hasn't any idea. I'm willing to bet that the only truth in his story is the fact that it was his knife." She frowned. "The other theory is that Callaghan is telling us this story in order to make himself look innocent. It seems too contrived, but—" She trailed off with a shrug.

Hanratty nodded. "I'll wager he's covering up for that lovely young thing."

Maggie blinked. "You think *she* did it?"

He shrugged. "It isn't the American. He has an alibi—he

was on stage at the time of the attack, in front of hundreds of witnesses. Although if I could arrest him on nasty personality alone, I'd have locked him up a long time ago."

She nodded.

"Let go o' me, ye bleedin' bastards," a loud, drunken voice called out. Two garda escorted a short compact man with a ruddy lived-in face and white hair. The man wore a sweat and Guinness-stained short-sleeved T-shirt, an ill-fitting black jacket and baggy black trousers. "Where's my girl? Aoishe!"

The young girl seemed to shrink back, her cheeks flaming with embarrassment. Then she seemed to steel herself and stepped forward. "Da! Where's the pullover I made for ye? Don't tell me you've lost it."

"Ach! It was too hot to wear." He was having trouble standing and one of the garda led him over to a chair. The reek of Guinness emanated from him.

Maggie took in his grimy hands, powerful hands for a drunk. She sidled over to Hanratty. "Aoishe's da?"

Hanratty nodded. "Well-known in Naas. Ainfeach Killian." He pronounced it the old way, *awn-fawch*.

Something about the way Aoishe's response to Aengus' murder bothered Maggie. "Do you mind if I do a little canvassing of the pub booths?" she asked. "I've got an idea. I need to borrow your camera as well."

The Naas detective gave her an odd look. "Whatever will solve this case. I don't fancy arresting the director of our dance troupe, especially when his story makes no sense."

She nodded and walked over to the garda with the Polaroid camera. "May I borrow that? Are there pictures left?"

The garda had been staring dully into space when Maggie approached. Now he gave the detective a startled look. "A-a few left."

Maggie showed the badge she always carried with her and smiled at him reassuringly. The garda's eyes widened as he fumbled to get the camera strap over his head.

She took the camera and snapped a couple of pictures, startling one of her subjects. The other subject, Aengus, was beyond reaction as his body was carried out on a stretcher by two garda.

Maggie returned the camera with a smile and nodded her thanks.

A few minutes later, she was making the rounds of booths that served pints of ale, questioning the barkeeps. She finally found a bartender who recognized both photos.

"They were in here," the man said as he polished a just-washed glass. A customer came up and ordered a pint. The barkeep poured the pint, collected the money, then returned to Maggie.

"How long ago?"

He squinted in thought. "About an hour and a half. De young one was talking in earnest to the older man. Den the older man pounded his fist on dat table over there—upset de young man's half pint—and said, 'I'll have none of your nonsense talk, boy! She's headed for America and dat's all there is to it.' Den he got up and walked out." The publican paused, then added, "Well, actually he wobbled a bit. De young man stayed a few minutes, mopped up his table, and den left."

Maggie thanked him and left the booth. She wandered behind the booths and poked in the trashcans until she found the items she was looking for. Careful to wrap them in discarded newspaper, she headed back to Hanratty and the crime scene.

Aoishe was tending to her father, and Caoilte was being handcuffed by a garda. Hanratty nodded to her. She brought the wrapped items over and with Leary's help, laid them on a nearby table that had originally been set up for the dancers, now cleared off for use by the garda.

"Have you found anything useful, Inspector O'Malley?" Hanratty asked.

Maggie carefully unwrapped the item, the ratty tan sweater with bloodstains apparent, then unwrapped the sweater to reveal the knife.

"Da, that's your sweater . . ." Aoishe began, then clapped her hand over her mouth. Tears squeezed out of closed eyes. "Oh, Da—" she breathed. "Tell me you didn't kill Aengus."

Her father wiped his hand over his face. "Ah, Aoishe, I didna mean to kill him. He wouldna back off and let you go to America to dance. I told him this was your one chance, that makin' you stay here an' keepin' your talents to this area was a sin against God and the Mother Mary." He shook his head as a garda handcuffed him.

Maggie stepped up. "Mr. Killian—"

He had sobered up a bit and was mustering up a bit of his dignity, even with his hands cuffed in front of him. "Ainfeach, lass. Call me Ainfeach."

Leary had opened his mouth, most likely to correct the old sot that he was addressing an inspector. She held up her hand to stop him, and gave him a small smile of thanks as well. "How did you end up with Caoilte's knife?"

Ainfeach Killian's shoulders caved in. "I took it. From Caoilte."

Caoilte spoke up. "I lent it to him. He was having trouble eating an apple."

Ainfeach Killian sighed. "Me choppers. False. I'd forgotten me penknife."

Hanratty spoke up. "So Mr. Callaghan is off the hook."

Barely, Maggie thought. He'd tried to cover up his suspicions that Aoishe's father had killed Aengus.

Hanratty addressed Killian. "You have the right to an attorney, or you can make your statement now."

Killian closed his eyes. "I didna mean to stab Aengus. I only meant to threaten him to stay away from Aoishe. But he kept coming toward me, I kept backing away, and he stumbled. Onto the knife." He looked down at his cuffed hands. "I have blood on me hands and I must atone for my sins." A tear slipped down his whiskered cheek and Aoishe embraced him gently.

"It's all right, Da. I'm sure Aengus knew it wasn't on purpose." She buried her face in his shoulder and sobbed.

Maggie didn't think she'd ever seen a man as sad as Ainfeach Killian at that moment. Even drunk, he must have realized, she was sure, that he had killed Aoishe's chances of emigrating to America now just as surely as he had stabbed Aengus with malicious intent. From the position of Aengus' body and the angle of the knife wound, Ainfeach Killian had stabbed Aengus intentionally. Probably not a planned killing, but a killing nevertheless.

Leary was at her side. "What do ye think he'll get for time?" he asked in a low voice.

She took a deep breath as they watched Killian being led away, Caoilte and Riona coming to Aoishe as she collapsed. "If his attorney is any good, he'll manage to get his client a charge of accidental death."

"Not much comfort for the victim's family," Leary muttered.

"I need a fag, Donal," Maggie sighed.

He dug in his pocket and handed her his pack and a light.

This story is set during the Clinton administration, during the troubles in Bosnia. Published in the fourth volume of Cat Crimes, *entitled* Cat Crimes in D.C., *I was told to please refrain from using Socks, the Clinton cat, in my story because the editors had been inundated with requests to do a Socks story. So I used a cathouse instead, which is pretty common in D.C., I'm sure. And I used my cat, Karma, who has since passed away.*

Indiscreet

Dolores Mendez must have been watching from a window because the door was open before Louise reached the bottom step that led to the Georgian-style home. Eyes red and cheeks streaked with dried tears, Dolores's iron gray hair was not in its usual neat bun, but instead hung in careless strands around her maternal face.

"I'm so sorry," Louise said, giving her friend a gentle hug. "I'm going to miss Celeste."

"First Celeste, then Miss Kitty."

"Miss Kitty's died as well?" Louise asked as she followed Dolores down the hall that whispered its elegance in dark wood and muted wallpaper. For some reason, this news alarmed her more. Maybe it was the idea that the murderer had gone to the trouble of killing Celeste's pet as well as Celeste.

Dolores led her into the kitchen. Two cups of hot tea were waiting for them at the table. "No, she disappeared."

"For how long?" Louise caught sight of her reflection in the shiny chrome finish of the refrigerator. Although she was tall, model-thin, and black, she was just a caramel-colored blur dressed in black and gray to the indifferent appliance.

Dolores stirred sugar in her tea. "It's funny, but ever since I found Celeste's body, I didn't think about Miss Kitty. Until this morning when I called you. But I don't recall seeing Miss Kitty since the murder."

Louise didn't have to ask for details. As soon as she heard that Celeste Knapp had been found dead in her bed yesterday morning, she called in a favor with an old Georgetown University classmate who was now a sergeant in Homicide. He had provided information that Louise would not have otherwise been able to get—Celeste had been strangled in her bed with a garrote. "Sounds premeditated," Louise had said. "Probably a pro," the sergeant had speculated.

Louise brought her mind back to the current problem—Miss Kitty "So she could have disappeared at any time, starting when Celeste was found yesterday morning."

Dolores nodded, a tear sliding down her weathered face.

Celeste Knapp had been the madam of a high-class brothel well known for its high-powered clientele and hush-hush discretion. Louise had been introduced to Celeste when she was assigned to do a series of articles for her paper on prostitution in the nation's capital. As a journalist, she knew she would have to put aside her preconceptions and prejudices to write an unbiased look at the profession. It had been difficult at first, but Celeste Knapp had proven to be an eloquent interviewee, revealing the human side to prostitution. Louise became more comfortable in the presence of Celeste, Dolores, and their prima-donna cat, Miss Kitty, and the friendship had continued long after the series of articles ran in the *Washington Sun*.

"Have you talked to any of the girls?" Louise asked.

"Rachel's still sedated and Holly's with her boyfriend at Georgetown University, but Sarah's been here for me. She's gone to the drugstore to get a prescription for me." Dolores ran out of breath. Her face scrunched up in pain.

Reaching across the table, Louise gave Dolores's hand a squeeze. "What do you want me to do?"

"Help me find Miss Kitty." Miss Kitty was a Maine coon feline weighing in at a massive eighteen pounds. She had a beautiful tortoiseshell coat with white legs and underbelly. In a certain light, she looked a bit like a crazed raccoon. She had probably slipped outside during the commotion right after Celeste's death. Despite Miss Kitty's size, Louise wondered if the pampered pet would take care of herself.

She had no doubt that if the feline could find her way back home, Miss Kitty would be found on the back doorstep, begging for that canned gourmet cat food.

Louise sat back in her chair and crossed her legs. "You might as well ask me to find Celeste's killer." The moment it left her lips, she knew it was the wrong thing to say. Now that it was said, she decided to pursue the subject. "By the way, have the police narrowed it down to a single suspect?"

"You know how it is with us working girls," a voice drawled from behind Louise. Tall, lithe, blond Sarah joined them, a mug of coffee in her hand. "We don't rate a thorough investigation."

As cool and elegant as she appeared with her clients, they rarely got a glimpse of Sarah when she was angry. Louise found Sarah's icy anger frightening and refrained from contradicting her. She knew that the D.C. police were overworked, especially in the homicide division. If the suspect wasn't immediately apparent when the witnesses' statements were taken and the evidence was gathered at the scene of the crime, chances were good that the case wouldn't warrant much attention. There were too many people being murdered in their beds every day to try to solve every case.

Louise changed the subject. "So what's going to happen to the house?"

Sarah and Dolores looked at each other, then back to Louise.

"For the moment, business will go on as usual," Dolores said. Behind Dolores's back, Sarah made a face at Louise to show just how thrilled she was about working so soon after Celeste's death. Louise recalled that during an interview with Celeste, the madam had affectionately said that Dolores had eyes in the back of her head. In this case, Dolores turned slightly toward Sarah and pointedly said, "We have to keep clients happy in order to pay the bills, you know."

"Who did Celeste leave the house to?"

Sarah spoke this time. "Celeste's will was interesting, to say the least."

"And very generous," Dolores added.

"She had specified that those girls who had been with her for five years or more would share in the profits as equal partners with Dolores, who will continue to run things."

Louise raised her eyebrows in surprise. It was an unusual way to dispose of a business, but then it was an unusual business. This clause meant that Sarah and Rachel would share in the partnership, since they were the only girls who had been with Celeste for over five years. Louise wondered briefly if one of the two women might have offed Celeste in order to gain the profits of the brothel, but it didn't seem likely. Both women were close to Celeste and shared her serious approach to the business. And as far as Louise knew, Sarah and Rachel had no bad feelings toward Celeste. Besides, they would have had plenty of opportunity over the years, and better ways of orchestrating Celeste's death without raising suspicion.

Dolores spoke up again. "So will you do it?"

In her pensive mood, Louise had lost the thread of the conversation. "Do what?"

"Find Miss Kitty."

Even Sarah's forehead puckered a bit. "That's right. I haven't seen the little monster all day. Come to think of it, I don't recall seeing her yesterday, either."

Dolores recounted the saga of the missing cat to Sarah.

"I wouldn't worry too much about Miss Kitty, Dolores," Louise said. "She'll find her way home. You have much bigger problems right now."

The three women drank their tea and coffee in companionable silence. "This must be hard on everyone in the house," Louise finally said. "Where was everyone when Celeste's body was discovered?"

"I was sleeping in," Sarah replied distractedly. "I hadn't been feeling well the night before and Celeste let me off work early."

The door opened once more and Holly slipped into the kitchen. "Hi, guys."

Even with Celeste's death, Holly could not be subdued. She wore sloppy grape-colored sweats and had made an effort to tie back her untamable red hair. Louise figured she was grieving in her own special way, the way young girls do when they think they're immortal. Although she looked barely eighteen, Holly had been with Celeste for three years. The older customers preferred the less flamboyant and more sophisticated call girls, but Holly was very popular with the younger customers, especially those in the foreign embassies.

The door opened once again and Rachel entered, her usually sleek, dark hair plastered against her skull on one side. Her patrician nose was red from crying and her blue eyes were still glazed over from sedatives. She made no attempt to hide her grief. Dolores got up and went over to her, one motherly arm sliding over Rachel's thin shoulders. She guided Rachel into a chair and sat next to her, one hand protectively covering Rachel's right hand.

Louise turned to Holly, who had just sat down at the table with a can of Coke. "So, it must have been a shock," she said.

The youngest prostitute slouched in her chair and slurped some soda before answering. "It was awful. I mean, I didn't discover the body or anything, but after the detective took my statement this morning, I had to go over to my boyfriend's apartment just to get away. It still gives me the creeps to think that Celeste was killed in this very house." She shuddered visibly for effect, then turned to Dolores with an imploring look. "Dolores, do we have to work tonight? Can't we take a night off? You know, out of respect or something!"

Dolores stiffened, then let her shoulders slump. She shook her head. "I wish we could, Holly, but there are some customers who have standing appointments and they won't understand why we've closed down." Louise realized that Dolores was referring to men from foreign embassies who couldn't be reached by phone. If Dolores turned them away tonight, they might take their business elsewhere.

Holly turned back to her Coke and pouted.

"Holly, where were you when Celeste was killed?"

She turned to Louise and widened her eyes. "I'm not even sure when she was killed."

"The coroner has estimated the time of death to be between three and five this morning."

Holly rolled her eyes. "I was sound asleep, silly."

Rachel spoke up for the first time. "You weren't sound asleep, Holly. I heard you walk past my door about three-thirty."

Holly's amiable manner evaporated and she suddenly looked nervous. "Well, I . . . I guess I had trouble sleeping, so I came down to the kitchen for a glass of milk." She finished off her soda and abruptly stood up, tossing her empty can into the trash. Louise noticed that Holly's face had closed down like shutters over a window. "Well, it's been nice talking to you all. I've got to take a shower." She left quickly.

Silence settled in once again.

Rachel finally spoke. "For what it's worth, Louise, I'm an insomniac, so I spent the night reading in bed."

"How did you know it was Holly who walked past your door?"

Rachel fought a glimmer of a smile. "My room is next to Holly's, and her room is the last one in the east wing."

It was no secret that the two women were opposites in every way. Serious Rachel had little patience with flighty Holly and the feeling was mutual. When Celeste was alive, she had managed to keep them in balance. With the madam gone, Louise wondered what would happen to the cathouse. Dolores was a good woman, but she didn't have the necessary diplomatic skills that Celeste had picked up from her work with the embassies.

Dolores stood up, her face troubled. Signaling Louise to follow her, they went out into the hall.

"It slipped my mind when the detective was taking my statement," Dolores began in a low voice. "I can't tell you what time it was because I was just drifting off to sleep, but

I'm certain I heard the front door opening and closing. I made a mental note to oil the hinges in the morning."

"You'd better call the detective," Louise said. The missing Miss Kitty crossed her mind and she wondered if that was how the cat had gotten outside. It almost certainly was when Celeste's killer had slipped in or out.

Dolores hesitated, then shook her head. "I'm not sure what good it will do."

"Does Holly's behavior strike you as odd lately?"

Dolores frowned. "Well, she seemed a little nervous, but we're all a little on edge."

"Has she done anything out of the ordinary?" An idea was beginning to form in Louise's mind, but there were too many pieces of the puzzle missing.

Dolores thought. "She visits her boyfriend an awful lot, sometimes for only an hour or two, like she did today. But that's not unusual for a young girl who's in love." Louise went back into the kitchen, leaving Dolores to make her call. The phone rang a few minutes later, then Dolores came into the room, a puzzled look on her face.

"Are you okay?" Sarah asked.

"It's probably nothing."

"What?" Louise prompted.

"I just talked to Holly's boyfriend, Tom. I told him she was in the shower and I'd have her call him back. Then I teased him about not being able to live without her for more than an hour." She paused and sipped her cold tea.

Rachel prompted her. "And?"

"He asked me what I was talking about and I said, 'Well, wasn't she just over to your apartment this morning?' He said he hadn't seen her for two days."

"What did you tell him?" Louise asked, leaning forward.

"That I had probably jumped to conclusions. He was

upset, probably thought she was cheating on him. I had to calm him down."

Louise's eyes narrowed. "Dolores, how often does Holly go to Tom's place?"

She pushed back a strand of gray hair and shrugged. "Quite often. Several times a week. She stays overnight on her days off, but will usually visit him for just a couple of hours at least once during her work week."

Sarah jumped in. "Louise, you surely don't suspect Holly of anything like murdering Miss Celeste. She doesn't have enough brains to pull off something like that."

"Maybe she's not guilty of murder," Louise said, "but she might be involved."

Two pieces of the puzzle were beginning to fit, but Louise still couldn't see the whole picture. She knew she was onto something, but it was nothing that could be brought to the police yet. There was no evidence, nothing concrete. Still she had a plan. Leaning over the table, she talked to the other three women.

It was close to a week later, Louise heard from Dolores. She was in her office and it was a few minutes before noon. "Louise? She told me that she's going over to see her boyfriend."

"See if you can delay her for five minutes. Ten minutes would be better. I'll be there as soon as I can." Louise hung up, grabbed a camera from the bottom drawer of her desk, and left.

It was a lucky coincidence that the brothel wasn't far from Louise's office. Five minutes later, she was standing across the street watching the front door when Holly walked out, bouncing down the steps two at a time. Dolores stood in the doorway, barely glancing in Louise's direction.

"Be back here by five," she called after the retreating Holly. "You have an appointment at six."

"Yeah, yeah." Holly's voice bordered on irritation. Louise followed at a discreet distance until Holly got into a taxi. There was a moment of dismay when Louise thought she might lose her, but she was able to flag down a cab almost immediately and say what every driver longs to hear: "Follow that cab."

The driver grinned and complied, keeping a car length behind Holly's cab until they reached Jefferson Drive on the Mall. Throwing a few bills at the cabby, Louise climbed out in time to watch her quarry disappear into the Hirshhorn Museum and Sculpture Garden. Holly had never struck Louise as an art lover. She remembered once mentioning Manet in passing and Holly had asked if he had invented mayonnaise.

After paying the entrance fee, she caught sight of Holly across the room, passing into the sculpture garden. Louise walked over to the windows that faced the court and kept her quarry in sight. With so many magnificent sculptures surrounding her, Holly sat on a stone bench and stared blandly into the reflecting pool. A short, swarthy man with a large mustache sat down on the other end of the bench. He wore the muddy green short-sleeved polyester shirt and brown pants of a tourist. Louise raised her camera and began taking pictures.

They didn't talk to each other. In fact, it was all over in a few seconds. The man got up, leaving behind a small, white envelope. Holly sat there for another few moments, then casually slid the envelope into her purse and made a beeline for the exit. Unlike Holly, the man was a professional. He spent a few minutes pretending to study the garden sculptures before departing the museum. Louise followed him.

Indiscreet

There was no doubt about it—this man was good at what he did, whatever that was. Instead of hailing a taxi, he caught a bus. Public transportation was the best way to get lost in D.C. Louise sat in the front of the bus and surreptitiously watched him until he got off on 22nd Street. From there, he walked to R Street. She walked on the other side of the street, occasionally snapping a picture here or there, trying to look like a tourist, not someone who was interested in swarthy little men with bad taste in clothes. When he turned into the walkway of a large white Federal-style building, she focused her camera and began clicking. Crossing the street, Louise got a look at the sign on the front gate: Embassy of the Socialist Federal Republic of Yugoslavia. Her fingertips started to tingle. All her newshound instincts told her that this was very important material. But Holly, a spy? At first it was difficult to believe, but as Louise started to think about it, things began to make sense.

On her way back to the office, Louise began to wonder what the connection might be. As Celeste told Louise in their interview, she had always considered her establishment as neutral territory, much like Switzerland. She considered herself and her girls to be like priests. Whatever a client told a working girl was never to be repeated or discussed with anyone. Even among themselves.

Yugoslavia was in the midst of civil upheaval and there were a number of things that an unscrupulous spy for the Bosnians might want to get from the United States—things that couldn't be gotten through the normal channels. Besides, the Bosnians weren't in favor with the United States—in fact, they weren't much in favor with anyone at the moment.

Although Holly wasn't a call girl with the older, more

powerful client base, she was a favorite among the younger men, many of whom were assistants to men in power such as senators, cabinet members, and diplomats. And they were usually in their bosses' confidences. Maybe Holly had cut a deal with someone here at the embassy to sell information that she had acquired from her clients.

When Louise got back to the office, she put a rush order on developing her film. While she waited, her editor called her into his office for another assignment.

"I can't go to a press conference right now," Louise said.

"That's what we pay you for." Carl Ringwald, the editor, leaned back in his office chair, folded his hands behind his head, and stretched. "Hillary Clinton may make an appearance. Bring your camera."

"I'd be happy to, but I really can't. I think I'm onto something big." She proceeded to tell him what had occurred, giving him just enough information about the events and how they might tie into Celeste's death to whet his appetite.

Ringwald relented. "You're not going to do anything stupid, are you?" He had returned his chair to its proper upright position and was straightening papers on his desk, belying the fact that he was excited about the prospect of breaking a hard-hitting news story about blackmail and politics. "You could be in danger. I'd like the story, but I don't want a dead reporter on my conscience."

"I've taken a defense class," Louise said lightly, although butterflies were doing a dance in her stomach. She was aware that there might be some risk involved. Investigating a murder was one thing, investigating a murder with possible political intrigue was a whole new experience for her.

"You're going to the police with this, right?"

"Eventually," was all Louise would promise. She left his office and picked up the photos.

Fifteen minutes later, she was sitting in the parlor with Dolores and the other girls, the photos spread on the coffee table in front of them. "Have you ever seen this man with Holly?"

Dolores picked up one of the pictures and frowned. "He doesn't look like one of our clients. I don't think so."

The doorbell rang and she got up to answer it.

Sarah examined a photo and shrugged. "It's hard to imagine Holly with this guy."

"He's certainly not her boyfriend," was Rachel's observation. Louise was feeling slightly disappointed, but she still had another place to show her photos. It just might be more dangerous, though.

Dolores returned with a tall black man. Louise thought he looked a little like Wesley Snipes, the actor. He wore a crisply pressed gray suit and his small goatee was neatly trimmed.

"This is Detective Sergeant Dean Griffith from Homicide," Dolores said.

His smile was serious, and he studied her as if he were wondering if she was a working girl. Suddenly she was self-conscious about her association with Dolores and Celeste.

"Uh, I'm a reporter for the *Washington Sun*," she said, much to her shame. Then she straightened up and added, "And a friend of Dolores here, and the deceased."

When he shook her hand, Louise found herself looking for a wedding ring, which made her blush. Dolores told Griffith that Louise was trying to help them find their missing cat. Griffith's eye strayed to the photos that Louise had tossed onto the coffee table. He picked one up and studied it.

"Where did you get these?" he asked in a sharp tone.

Louise explained where and why she had taken them. She couldn't help asking, "Does that man look familiar?"

Griffith smiled enigmatically without answering. She noticed that he didn't put one of the photos back down on the table; instead, he slipped the photo of Holly and the mysterious stranger sitting together in the museum courtyard into his inner jacket pocket.

When the homicide detective pulled out prepared statements for Dolores and the girls to sign, it was a good time for Louise to leave. Although she started to drive back to her office, she decided to turn around and head for the embassy. She had the pictures, maybe she would get lucky and be able to attach a name to the face. Showing the photo around the Yugoslavian embassy was risky, but she had a cover story prepared.

Louise entered the embassy only to discover that the guard was away from his window. A plate-glass wall separated the lobby from the cramped vestibule where the security guard questioned visitors about their intent. Louise peered into the embassy's lobby, which appeared impressive at first glance, but upon closer examination it had a shabby elegance. The red velvet upholstered chairs looked lumpy and gold paint was flaking off the chair legs and arms. The chandelier was missing a few crystals and some of the bulbs were burned out.

"Yes? What can I do for you?" The man's voice was laced with a heavy Slavic accent. She turned to face a solemn man in a guard's uniform. He laid a clipboard down on his desk and gave her his full attention.

"I was looking for this man—" Louise was interrupted by a high-pitched meow. A plumed tortoise-shell tail floated across the line of the guard's desk, seemingly of its own accord. The guard turned.

Indiscreet

"Excuse me," he said, stooping to pick up a large cat that resembled a raccoon.

Louise managed to choke back her surprise and recognition, and forced herself to smile. "What a beautiful cat!"

The guard smiled back, the first sign that he was human after all. "She appeared at our embassy the other day," he explained. "I had come on duty at eight o'clock yesterday morning and she was inside the lobby."

"You've never seen her before?" He shook his head. Louise chose her next question carefully, not wanting to raise suspicions. "Is it possible that she belongs to someone here at the embassy?"

"No, I've asked and no one has ever seen her before." He shrugged and scratched her ear. Miss Kitty complied with a loud purr of contentment. "She is probably a stray." The guard paused. "For a moment, it looked to me as if you recognized her." He was sharper than she had given him credit for.

"I'm not sure," Louise put just enough doubt in her voice, "but she does look an awful lot like an acquaintance's cat."

The guard put Miss Kitty down and brought the conversation back to business. "What did you come here for? You said something about a man?"

"Oh, yes," Louise said, trying to sound as if she was distracted. She fished the photo of the man out of her purse. "I'm a reporter and I was taking pictures of the Hirshhorn for my newspaper earlier today. This man was in some of the photos and I thought it would be an interesting sidebar to get his impression of the museum. A foreigner's view and all." She hoped the story sounded plausible.

The guard frowned as he studied the photo. "Why did you not ask him at the museum?"

"I lost him when I ducked into the ladies' room, but he had dropped a calling card with this embassy's name on it." Louise knew that embassies sometimes gave their low-level employees generic business cards because the turnover rate was so high. She hoped this guy wasn't high-level. Studying the guard's face while he examined the photo, she didn't see any flicker of recognition.

"May I see the card?" the guard asked, looking up at her.

Louise made a pretense of looking for it in her purse. "I'm sorry. I seem to have misplaced it. But I was certain it was this embassy."

The guard shrugged. "He does not look familiar. We have so many people working here. Sometimes I only look at the badges and not the faces. If he is from our embassy, he may not wish to be interviewed. Some of our officials speak very poor English."

"Then this would be a chance for him to practice," Louise said brightly. She took the photo back and handed the guard her business card. "If you find him, please give him my name and number."

She left the building. It was hard to leave Miss Kitty there, but she seemed content enough.

Louise went back to the office for another hour of work, then stopped at a takeout Vietnamese restaurant around the corner from her apartment. It was after six when she opened her door and entered the vestibule; there was something ominous about the quiet of her dark apartment. Before she could flip the light on, a strong arm dragged her away from the entry and the door slammed shut. Although she was frightened for a moment, anger took over and so did her self-defense lessons. She jabbed her elbow into the intruder's ribs. He gasped and staggered back a step, but maintained his hold on her.

Indiscreet

She stepped back with him and brought her heel down on what she hoped was his instep. He grunted and she felt his hold on her weaken momentarily. By now, her eyes had adjusted to the dark and she could make out the outline of her attacker's free arm in front of her, a knife in his hand. She bit the wrist of his constraining arm. He yelped, drawing his arm away. Louise took advantage of the moment and yelled to startle him and maybe summon help, then she dropped to the ground and used her legs, aiming vicious kicks at his knees. She could hear him muttering unintelligible curses when her kicks connected with his legs. When she felt him grab one of her ankles, she screamed again.

Suddenly, there was the sound of cracking wood. Light spilled in from the hall and men were shouting. Someone turned on the overhead lights, causing Louise to squint and blink. She fell back onto the floor, exhausted, and watched as plainclothes cops surrounded the intruder. It was the man from the museum, Holly's contact.

A firm hand helped her off the floor. "You!" was all Louise could say as she stared into the dark handsome face of Detective Sergeant Griffith. "How did you—?" But she already knew the answer.

"After you left, Dolores told me that she was worried that you might do something foolish," he replied, a mixture of amusement and annoyance in his voice.

"So you had me followed to the embassy. You did know who this guy was, didn't you?" Louise said, rubbing her throat where her attacker had a choke hold on her.

"Well, it didn't hit me until I showed the photo to my supervisor. His name is Yevgeny Medjovic and he's a Bosnian sympathizer who has been suspected of trying to find an arms dealer now that the Russians are no longer a reliable source. I think he was hoping to make a deal with someone in the Pentagon. Holly was being paid for information that would lead Medjovic to a contact."

Louise watched with some satisfaction as one of the undercover cops clapped handcuffs on her attacker. She grabbed her camera, hoping she had enough film left in the camera, and snapped a couple of shots.

"Hope you don't mind, detective, but it's my job."

Griffith nodded. "I wish we could tie him in to Celeste Knapp's murder."

"You can." As Louise explained Miss Kitty's disappearance, Griffith's eyes mirrored growing admiration for her.

When she was finished, he shook his head. "My, that's some story."

"Are you going to have any problems putting Celeste's murderer behind bars because of his diplomatic status?"

"My guess is that the embassy will deny any knowledge of his actions and throw him to us as a gesture of good will."

Several days later, Louise sat in the kitchen of the cathouse with Dolores. This time, she was there for dinner. The smell of chicken and wine permeated the room.

"Imagine," Dolores said as she took the roasting pan out and basted the simmering chicken with the wine sauce. "You not only found Miss Kitty, but you caught Celeste's murderer as well." She put the pan back in the oven and straightened up to face Louise. "How can I ever thank you?"

Louise grinned. "I think you already have. That chicken smells wonderful. And the one who really deserves the attention is Miss Kitty. If she hadn't followed Medjovic back to the Yugoslavian embassy, Detective Griffith would never have been able to link him to Celeste's murder." She felt a small regret that after her statement had been taken, she hadn't seen the handsome detective again. "I have to say, Detective Griffith has been very much the gentleman with this case."

Dolores agreed. "I'm used to being treated with contempt by the police. He told me that he didn't have anything against places like ours. He said he's strictly homicide and doesn't meddle in the other departments." She opened the lid of a pot and stiffed something fragrant. "It's too bad about Holly," Dolores added gently.

"She's in for a long stretch, if she's convicted. Don't feel too sorry for her," Louise replied. "She was passing along sensitive information to anyone who would buy. Medjovic was just one in a long line. When Celeste found out, she was about to throw Holly out on her ear and go tell one of her more powerful clients. Medjovic couldn't have that happen because Holly was close to handing him an arms contact in the Pentagon. It was easier to kill Celeste than to find another cathouse and another call girl who was willing to become a traitor." Louise poured two glasses of wine and handed one to Dolores. The kitchen door opened and Dean Griffith walked in.

Louise's eyes widened, then she looked back at Dolores, who was beaming. "I forgot to mention that he's been invited to dinner as well." Dolores handed her glass to him, poured herself another glass, then raised it. Louise and Griffith followed suit.

"To Miss Kitty," Griffith said. Their glasses clinked.

"To Miss Kitty," Dolores and Louise solemnly intoned.

An insistent meow could be heard from a corner of the kitchen. Three pairs of eyes turned to watch Miss Kitty march back and forth in front of the oven, guarding the chicken.

Another cat story that was published in Murder Most Irish *and my name was on the front cover, sandwiched between James Joyce (my hero) and Edmond Crispin. Of course, a $9.99 sticker price conveniently covered up my name, but I'm still thrilled to have been included. It didn't hurt that I spent 2 years in Ireland and seven months of those years as a houseparent for the Killary Harbor hostel in County Galway.*

Soft Day

The morning came too early for Rachel. She felt as if she might be coming down with Michael's cold and wondered whether they would have to stay at the Ballygesh hostel for another day while she recovered. She staggered out of bed and splashed cold water on her face. As she was getting dressed, she noticed that Hazel, the British woman whom she had met late last night, was still asleep in one of the bunks. She looked at her watch and wondered whether she should wake her. The hostel liked to close to hostellers at 10 a.m.

"Hazel," Rachel called softly, going over to shake the woman's shoulder. "It's nine-thirty—" Hazel flopped over, her face blue, her sightless eyes staring at nothing in particular. Rachel yelped and stepped back, her thoughts still a blur from waking up. Something under Hazel's sheets moved. At first Rachel thought maybe Hazel wasn't dead after all. But when Eddie the cat emerged, Rachel screamed and jumped. The cat purred and rubbed its face on Hazel's cold cheek.

The dorm door opened and Maire, the houseparent, took in the scene. "What in heaven's name—?" Maire turned pale at the sight that greeted her.

"She's dead," Rachel said numbly. "I-I found her that way. The cat—"

Maire brusquely grasped Rachel by the shoulders and guided her out of the dorm. "We must call the constable."

"It'll be fun, Rach," her boyfriend, Michael, had said when they started planning their trip to Ireland. "Just the two of us, walking Ireland's roads from one coast to the other. Jim and Helen did it last year and Jim told me it only took them two days to walk from Dublin to County Galway. What do you say?"

It had taken five days for Rachel and Michael to get to County Galway. Rachel had originally suggested they plan the trip with bed-and-breakfast inns in mind. But it wasn't rustic enough for Michael, a college linebacker and health nut who wanted to camp out the entire way. The only problem with camping out was that it rained practically the entire time and weighed them down with soggy camping gear.

Then Michael caught a bad cold. When they went in search of a warm, dry hotel where he could recover, they discovered that flashing Jim's American Express card didn't get them a room. At the height of tourist season, even the little B & Bs along the way were filled to capacity.

Finally, the owner of a small B & B took pity on them and called ahead to a nearby *An Oige* hostel in Ballygesh—*An Oige* being the Irish equivalent of the American Youth Hostel—and reserved beds for them. Fortunately, Rachel had had the foresight to pack her hostel card.

The Ballygesh hostel was a series of small, whitewashed cottages. One cottage served as the common room and

Soft Day

kitchen area with an attached peat shed. Two served as dorm rooms, one for men and one for women. The fourth cottage served as the residence of the caretakers, a young Irish couple, Maire and Dennis. When they arrived, Maire noticed Michael's cold and sent him packing off to bed with a hot whiskey and water—"It'll take away the chill"—and several blankets. Dennis signed them in.

"It's a soft day today," he said to Rachel, "and on days like this, we leave the common area open for the hostelers."

Rachel had heard the term "soft day" often enough during the last week to know it meant that it was gray and rainy. It was a pleasant surprise to learn that the hostel was open during the day—most hostels were not required to stay open between ten in the morning and five in the evening. But the Irish hostels out in the country tended to bend that rule, considering how many soft days Ireland had and how few places there could be to take shelter.

After claiming one of the bunks in the women's dorm, she went to check on Michael. Calling out to make certain that the men's dorm was empty, Rachel received no reply, so she sneaked in and found Michael sound asleep, the empty whiskey glass by his bed. An orange and gray cat with green eyes sat nearby, looking up at Rachel with curiosity.

"Don't mind me," Rachel told the cat as she picked up the empty glass to take back to the houseparents. The cat blinked slowly once, then stood up and arched its body in a long stretch before padding over to a red backpack that was propped precariously against the bunk next to Michael's. Emitting a loud purr, the cat rubbed its face hard against the material, causing the backpack to fall onto the rough plank flooring. The cat rolled over on its back, grabbing the backpack with its claws and trying to pull it closer.

"You careless rascal," Rachel said with a chuckle as she crossed the room to right the backpack and swat the cat away.

"What are you doing here?" a sharp, German-accented voice demanded.

Rachel straightened up quickly. She turned around to face a large man with a red face, blond hair, and a beard. He was standing on the other side of the bunk, where the red backpack had been propped. She noticed an open pack of Gauloise cigarettes on the mattress. Without taking his eyes off Rachel, he picked up the pack and slid it in his T-shirt pocket.

"I, uh, the cat—" she looked around, but the cat was smarter than Rachel and had taken off at the first sign of a confrontation. "I was checking on my boyfriend, and the cat knocked over your backpack." Rachel held up the empty whiskey glass as proof that she had legitimate business in the men's dorm. She could feel her face growing hot as the silent German fellow continued to glare at her.

"It's the truth," she said loudly, glancing at Michael, who snorted peacefully in his sleep. He would be of no help if she needed to defend herself. The whiskey concoction must have knocked him out.

The German strode around the bunk toward her. Rachel shrank back as he brushed brusquely by her to check the pack. Rachel slunk out of the dorm and went over to the common room.

Three other people occupied the common room: a young French couple and an older American man who looked like a businessman on vacation. Rachel wondered whether he'd brought his whole family.

The French couple were oohing and aahing over a pot of boiling water. They introduced themselves to Rachel as

Soft Day

Francoise and Jean-Marc. She promptly forgot their last names, but she figured she probably wouldn't see them after tomorrow. Jean-Marc took a cigarette from his Gauloise pack and lit it. The pungent tobacco cut through the clean Irish air. Jean-Marc offered one to Rachel, which she politely declined.

"See what we bought from a fisherman down by the Ballygesh wharf," Francoise said, proudly holding up a limp lobster with one claw. "He told us that he couldn't sell it to a restaurant."

"Mmmm", Rachel murmured, wondering what she was going to eat for dinner. She hadn't stopped to get supplies. "It looks wonderful."

Francoise grinned and turned away to check the salted boiling water. Rachel wondered who would get the claw.

The American had been watching her. "I'm Bob from Chicago." They shook hands. Without much prompting, Bob began to tell her about his mail-order business back home, and his divorce, and the revelation he had that he had missed so much of life by marrying early.

"So now I'm doing what I never had the chance to do when I was young; hiking around Europe."

"Why aren't you staying in hotels and B & Bs?" Rachel asked. "You can certainly afford it."

Bob scowled. "What makes you think I can afford more than this?"

Rachel averted her eyes. "Well, I just thought, with your business and everything—"

He sneered and stood up. "Well, I can't afford even this, but I'm doing it anyway."

Rachel stared blankly at his retreating back, puzzled by how touchy he'd been over an innocent comment.

"Don't pay any attention to him," Jean-Marc said with a

laugh. "He's done nothing but complain since he got here this morning. I just wish he'd get back in his little Fiat and go find a hotel."

"What about the German fellow?" Rachel asked.

"Wolfgang?" Francoise had joined them. The lobster was nowhere to be seen. Rachel assumed it had met its fate. "He just got here. What about him?"

Rachel explained about her visit to the men's dorm to check on Michael. Jean-Marc and Francoise frowned.

"Well," Francoise began, "it is not common practice to allow women to visit the men's dormitory. But we are in Ireland, and rules have been broken here many times. He is a German—" Francoise and Jean-Marc exchanged a knowing look, "—so I suppose he was startled to find you breaking the rules."

Rachel shrugged it off and continued to talk to the young French couple until the lobster was ready to eat. Then she left the common room to take the empty glass back to Maire and Dennis.

"I met your cat," she said. "He was in the men's dorm."

Maire tilted her head and raised her eyebrows. "That's rare. Eddie doesn't usually stray too far from our cottage. She's very territorial." Rachel noted that Eddie was a she.

Rachel's stomach growled, reminding her that she hadn't eaten since that morning. Dennis suggested a pub called the Black Swan, which was located half a mile down the road. "They serve a very nice oxtail soup and a good *colcannon* with bacon."

Rachel thanked them and went down the road to the Black Swan. Inside, it was warm and smoky and smelled of stale Guinness. Seated in a corner of the pub, a young man played the tinwhistle while an older man accompanied him on fiddle. Rachel enjoyed the quick airs and slow laments, even recognizing one contemplative lament as "Brian Boru's March." She felt a little out of place in a pub that seemed to cater mostly to local men. Still, it was nice to sit by a warm peat fire and relax over a half-pint of Guinness.

By the time her meal arrived, she was sleepy with Guinness and the warmth emanating from the fireplace. She had ordered the *colcannon,* which turned out to be steamed cabbage and potatoes with lots of salt and a little pepper. Rachel found herself picking out the limp bacon, which seemed to be there mostly for flavor.

On her way out, Rachel spied Bob and Wolfgang huddled in a booth by the entrance, both smoking. Realizing that she would have to pass by them, Rachel found no reason to be cordial to them since they had both acted rudely in her presence.

"We can make the trade tomorrow morning—" Bob was saying before he caught sight of her. He motioned to Wolfgang, who craned his neck to glare at her, then started to get up. Rachel turned away from them and quickly left the pub, her heart beating rapidly. Was it her imagination or had there been a menacing look in both Bob's and Wolfgang's faces? She wondered what they were planning to trade in the morning.

The walk was brisk, erasing the sluggishness that had overcome her during the meal and the Guinness. But when she got back to the dorm, the day's activities caught up with her and she decided to crawl into her bed after checking the common room one more time for Michael. Jean-Marc and Francoise were gone, which meant they were either out walking or had retired to the dorms, but there was a new hosteler, a woman about Rachel's age.

"Hi," she said with a British accent, looking up from a steaming mug. "Want some tea? I just made a pot."

Rachel smiled and shook her head. "I'm afraid I'm ready to retire."

"You wouldn't happen to be Rachel, would you?" the woman continued.

"Yes, I am," Rachel replied, caught by surprise.

"A man recovering from a very bad cold shared some of my dinner and asked about you." The woman poured a cup of tea for Rachel despite her protests. "That nice young French couple told him they thought you had gone out to the pub."

"I suppose he went back to bed." Rachel sipped the strong, bitter tea.

The woman smiled. "Yes, I expect he did. He didn't eat very much, but he seemed as if he were on the other side of a cold. My name is Hazel, by the way."

They sipped tea in silence for a minute, then Hazel spoke again. "God, I'm dying for a fag and I'm all out. You wouldn't happen to have one on you, would you?"

Rachel shook her head, congratulating herself on knowing that the term "fag" meant cigarette in England. "I'm afraid I don't smoke."

Hazel waved away Rachel's apology. "Well, there's nothing for it, is there? You've got your health, and I've got a filthy habit." Then she grinned and Rachel relaxed. They talked pleasantly for a few more minutes before Rachel made her excuses and went back to her dorm room to crawl into her bunk in the dark.

Now it was morning and Hazel was dead. Rachel stood in the doorway, looking around the common room. Jean-Marc and Francoise were doing their chores—Francoise was sweeping the floor and Jean-Marc was wiping down the tables. A bleary-eyed Michael was wrapped in a blanket, seated by the fireplace, warming his hands over a mug of

Soft Day

tea. Wolfgang was seated at one of the tables, hunched over a breakfast of eggs and toast. Bob was missing. Remembering what Jean-Marc had said the night before, Rachel glanced out the window. The Fiat was gone.

Maire had gone back to her cottage to call the constable. Michael was looking up at her. "What's wrong, Rachel?"

"I-I found one of the hostelers this morning, dead."

Jean-Marc and Francoise stopped their chores. Wolfgang stopped eating. "The American, Bob?" Wolfgang asked.

"N-n-no," Rachel replied, realizing that her teeth were chattering—not from the chill of a soft day, but from the chill of death. "It was a British woman. I met her briefly last night." She wondered why Wolfgang would think Bob was dead—did he think she had stolen into the men's dorm again for some illicit activity that involved his backpack? And why was Eddie the cat hanging around the men's dorm? She turned her attention back to Wolfgang. "I don't see Bob's Fiat outside. He must have left already."

Wolfgang jumped up, upsetting the table and his breakfast, and sprinted to the door to peer out. "Why that two-timing, double-dealing—" He switched from English to German, spouting a stream of bitter invectives that made Rachel wince, even though she didn't understand a word of it.

From Rachel's vantage point by the window, she could see Dennis coming up the walk with the village constable, a tall young man in uniform. Wolfgang had calmed down and was cleaning up the mess he had created, when Dennis introduced the constable to the hostelers.

"I'd like you all to remain here while the doctor makes his examination of the young woman," Constable Barnes said. "Is there anyone missing?"

Wolfgang was quick to point out the missing Bob. A

second constable was dispatched to search for the American.

Barnes started his questioning with Rachel. "I understand that you found her."

Rachel launched into her story, trying not to leave anything out. The constable listened with great interest, interrupting her only to ask one or two pertinent questions. When she was finished, he leaned forward and asked, "Tell me, do you recall anything unusual happening yesterday?"

She bit her lip. "Well, actually, when I went to the men's dorm to check on Michael, who was asleep, Eddie the cat was in the dorm. As I was leaving, Eddie went over to a red backpack and rubbed her face against it, and it fell over. The housemother told me that Eddie never goes into the dorms. She thought that was unusual." Rachel told the rest of the story, lowering her voice slightly and glancing at Wolfgang occasionally. The truculent German sat across the room, his sullen face red, his arms crossed in a defensive position.

The constable frowned and looked at Wolfgang briefly. "Well, Miss Birney, I've always trusted in cats' behavior. Let's go have a look at that backpack."

As they stood up, the constable casually told the room, "Miss Birney and I are going to take a look at some of the backpacks in the men's dorm to see if she can identify one. Does anyone have any objections?"

The white-faced group shook their heads uncertainly. Michael looked pale and drawn, and Rachel just wanted to get them both back to Dublin, although she would settle for Galway City or Limerick.

She got up and followed the constable to the men's dorm, which he surveyed with a critical eye. "Which backpack was it?"

There were only two backpacks in view—Michael's tan pack and a green one. Rachel poked around, looking for the red backpack. She shook her head. "I don't see it. I wonder if it was that other American's pack."

Barnes frowned, grabbed both packs, and escorted her back to the common area. He approached Wolfgang. "Show me your pack."

Wolfgang smiled and pointed to the green pack. Rachel half-stood. "B-b-but, that can't be yours—" she started to say.

Wolfgang's smile was triumphant. "Ah, but it is. I only went over to the red backpack yesterday to make sure you had not tampered with it."

It was Rachel's turn to glare.

An hour later, an official-looking car drove up with Bob in the back. He was taken out of the backseat, as was his backpack. Barnes brought Rachel out to look at the backpack, which was red. She shook her head. "That isn't it. The pack I saw yesterday was smaller. Eddie knocked it over and acted all goofy as if he were smelling catnip. Maybe if Eddie were here, I bet she could find it."

Constable Barnes called Maire and Dennis out of their house. "Is Eddie about?" he asked.

Maire smiled and nodded, ducking back inside, and soon returning with a sleepy orange and gray cat. "She was catching a few winks on our bed."

Rachel cradled the sleepy, warm cat in her arms and followed the constable back to the dorms. They let Eddie into the men's dorm, but after a perfunctory look around, Eddie seemed inclined to leave. Barnes picked the cat up and they went into the women's dorm, where Eddie took another apathetic turn.

"I wonder what made Eddie so crazy the other day," Rachel said as they took Eddie into the common room. Wolfgang had lit a cigarette that, Rachel noted, smelled stronger than the Gauloise he had been smoking the day before. Bob looked morose. Francoise and Jean-Marc looked pale and worried. Michael just looked exhausted.

Constable Barnes turned Eddie loose. The cat sniffed the air, then made a beeline for Wolfgang, who looked down at Eddie with scorn.

Eddie rubbed her face against Wolfgang's pants leg and the German tried to move his leg. Eddie followed, flopping down on Wolfgang's shoe and grabbing it with her paws.

Rachel blinked. The thick smoke stung her eyes and the heavy smell made it hard for her to breathe. Wolfgang was staring at Eddie as if she were an alien creature. "Get it off my leg!" He stood up suddenly and tried to move away. Eddie seemed to be attached to Wolfgang's leg, however. "Keep the damn monster away from me!" Wolfgang's eyes were wide with panic. Rachel thought it was a strange reaction for a cat.

"Open the window," Constable Barnes ordered. Rachel quickly opened a window, wondering what was going on. Barnes strode over to Wolfgang and confiscated the half-smoked cigarette.

"Hey! Why do you take my cigarette?" Wolfgang asked, standing and blinking furiously. "I—I—" He collapsed back in the chair, his eyelids drooping. Then he shook his head. "I—I think I need to lie down." The constable helped the German to the window and ordered him to breathe the clean air.

"What happened to him?" Rachel asked. Michael was half standing. Bob had leaned forward. The French couple had moved to a corner of the room, cringing.

Constable Barnes ignored her question, continuing to

Soft Day

frown. "There were only two backpacks in the men's dorm. And the American had his with him. Someone's pack is missing."

Rachel turned to the group. "Wolfgang's and Michael's packs have been accounted for. So has Bob's." Everyone looked at Jean-Marc and Francoise. "The red backpack has to be yours, Jean-Marc."

"What's going on, Rachel?" Michael asked. He looked uncertainty at her and then at the French couple, who had suddenly become morose. She glanced at her boyfriend. "I'm not sure, Michael, but I think we're about to find out."

A loud, plaintive meow came from the open door of the peat shed next to the kitchen. The constable and Rachel rushed there to find Eddie pawing desperately at the pile of dried peat.

"It looks as if it's been rearranged in the middle here," Barnes noted. They removed bricks of peat to reveal a red backpack. Constable Barnes opened the flap and inspected the contents. Sure enough, he pulled out several bricks of cocaine from among the clothes, books, toiletry items, and cigarette packs.

Rachel thought it was odd that most of the cigarette packs were open. She picked one up and sniffed it. "This smells sort of like marijuana, only—" she thought for a moment, "—different."

Constable Barnes took the pack from her and inhaled deeply. "Catnip," he said. "This is laced with catnip."

"Whatever for?" Rachel asked, amused at the thought of catnip being brought in illegally to sell to cats like Eddie.

A racket in the other room brought the constable and Rachel running into the common room. Michael was sprawled on top of Jean-Marc, who struggled to get out from under. A bleary-eyed Wolfgang held a sullen Francoise, who was halfheartedly trying to get away.

Michael looked up and grinned at Rachel. "It's a good thing I know how to tackle. This guy almost got away."

Rachel smiled. "My hero."

It was later in the day, after Jean-Marc and Francoise had been taken away, that Bob got up, ready to leave. Rachel was heating some canned chicken soup for Michael when Wolfgang's heavy hand came down on Bob's shoulder.

"And now we complete our business transaction," Wolfgang said.

Bob turned pale and started to sweat. "Er, the fact is, Wolfgang, um—"

Rachel saw Wolfgang's hand squeeze Bob's shoulder until pain registered on Bob's face. "I don't have them. I lied. I took your money and was planning on getting away."

"What don't you have?" Michael asked. He stood next to Rachel.

Wolfgang regarded them. "Blue jeans. He promised to sell me two-dozen blue jeans cheaply. I could take them back to Germany and sell them for a profit. He took my money and left." He suddenly let go of Bob, who sagged into a nearby chair.

"I lost my job back in Chicago and I'm going through a divorce. I couldn't face the fact that I couldn't pay my child support, so I took off for Europe, thinking I could hide out, avoid my responsibilities for a while. Then I discovered that Germans frequent Ireland and they love anything American. So I've been going around the country, to hostels, selling nonexistent blue jeans to Germans."

Wolfgang's hands had turned into fists, but instead of going for Bob, the German turned away and hit the table.

Then he turned back and gave Bob a look of contempt. "Get out of here before I break every bone in your body."

Bob threw the pound notes on the table, backed out of the common room, and hurried to his car, then took off.

Rachel and Michael went back to the dorms and packed their things, then stopped by the caretakers' cottage. Maire answered the door, a sad smile on her face, Eddie twining herself around Maire's ankles.

"It looks like Eddie saved the day," Rachel told her.

She brightened and gathered Eddie in her arms. "She has, at that."

Dennis came up behind his wife. "You're leaving now?"

"We have to get back to Dublin," Rachel said.

Just then, Constable Barnes pulled up in his car. "You look like you're both ready to go. Don't you want to find out what happened?" he asked with a twinkle in his eye. "After all, you were instrumental in solving the murder."

Rachel nodded. "Who killed Hazel and why?"

"It was an accident. Jean-Marc and Francoise came into the common room not far behind you and offered Hazel a cigarette. Unfortunately, it was one laced with catnip oil."

"Catnip oil?" Michael asked dubiously.

"It was discovered in an experiment in the 1960s that tobacco laced with catnip oil can cause hallucinations similar to LSD," the constable told them. "It's not common, but some people still like to smoke catnip-laced cigarettes. Apparently Jean-Marc opened the wrong cigarette pack. Hazel began hallucinating, much like Wolfgang did earlier today. Francoise quieted her down and brought her into the dorm, intending to tuck her in. Hazel panicked and Francoise covered her face with a pillow."

Rachel winced. "And I was asleep the whole time? How could I steep through that?"

"It was done quietly," Constable Barnes explained. "And the Irish air has been known to make even insomniacs sleep like newborns. I don't think Francoise intended to kill her; she just wanted Hazel to pass out. But it doesn't take long to smother someone who's in an hallucinogenic panic."

Rachel had an inspiration. "So that's why Wolfgang acted so strange earlier. I saw him take a pack of open cigarettes off a bunk yesterday. That's the cigarette you confiscated from him."

"That's right," the constable nodded. "Fortunately, he didn't smoke much of it, and I think it was lightly laced with catnip, so his reaction was mild." Constable Barnes thanked them again for their help and bade them good-bye before taking his leave.

Rachel leaned against Michael. "Let's go home," she suggested. "I don't think I'm in the mood for traveling anymore."

This is the story I am most proud of writing. First nationally published in Murderous Intent, *I had originally written it for a local writers' group zine. I was editor of the zine at the time and had made it a policy not to publish my work in it because it was a place for aspiring writers' work. Receiving a panicked late-night phone call from the editor in charge of printing, I was asked to write a 1500-word story, PLEASE. I had all of three hours to write it, and again, used the humorous Hitchcock plot. I've only changed one line, the last line, once—when it was to be published in* Murderous Intent. *An editor asked that I use an active voice and it worked much better.*

Miami

Joey leaned against the lockers, scanning the bus terminal from his vantage point. This wasn't his usual crowd, a little too lowbrow for what he needed, but he was in a fix, he needed cash fast, he had to get out of town. If he hadn't been so careless, he'd be taking the next plane south, first class all the way. But now the cops were after him, and his partner had gotten away with all the money.

When he and Lenny had decided to rob the jewelry store, all Joey had to do was get a car and be the getaway man. The problem was that he'd liberated one from an auto repair shop the night before, but it must have needed a lot of work because while he waited outside the store during the heist, it died. He started it. The car died again. So he cranked it a third time. That's when Lenny came out, running, the wrinkled brown paper bag full of cash in his fist. A short, fat man with a sweaty, balding head, Joey figured to be the owner, came out then, brandishing a Magnum .357.

Lenny paused by the dead car, then looked up the street. Joey looked up the street, too, and saw the downtown bus stopped at the corner, half a block away. Joey cranked the ignition again and the engine wheezed. "Geez, Joey," was all Lenny said before sprinting down the block and hopping on the bus.

The storeowner hesitated, watching Lenny and his money disappear in a puff of bus exhaust, then he turned to Joey in the car. The engine finally caught, and just in time. The angry storeowner had taken careful aim at Joey's head. The car jumped forward just as the back windshield was blown to smithereens. The back of Joey's head tingled all the way down the street.

Joey waited for three hours at the meeting place that he and Lenny had agreed on before the robbery—in case something went wrong—but Lenny never showed. Finally Joey ditched the car near an abandoned warehouse and caught a bus uptown. He went by Lenny's flophouse, but had enough sense to keep walking when he saw a cop car drive by. Joey wasn't sure if the black-and-white just happened to be there or if the jewelry store owner had identified him and Lenny that quickly in the books down at the police station, but he didn't want to do anything else as stupid as lifting a car from a garage. It wasn't as if the police didn't already know Lenny and Joey's MO. Joey wasn't even sure if it was safe for him to go back to his place to get the emergency money stashed under his mattress, so he didn't even try.

Now here he was, loitering in a bus terminal, looking over his shoulder every few minutes.

"Excuse me, young man," said an elderly lady. She wore

Miami

a battered hat with a fake flower stuck in the crown and carried a clear plastic shopping bag. Her old-fashioned handbag dangled from her left arm. "Can you help me with this newfangled locker system?" Through the bag, Joey could see a bus ticket. If only . . .

Joey saw a computer terminal on each side of a bank of lockers. He watched a man throw his backpack into a locker, slam the door, and deposit coins. A slot spit out a slip of paper with a secret code written on it that only the owner could use. Spying a discarded ticket on the floor near an empty locker, Joey had an idea.

"Sure, I can help you." Joey crouched to open the locker of his choice, palming the discarded ticket as the old lady slid her bag inside. He gave the door a good, hard shove.

"Well, aren't you nice, young man." Dipping her hand into the depths of her purse, she counted out four quarters. Putting the coins in the slot, he punched in the locker number on the pad. A slip of paper slid out and Joey tore it off, then handed her the bum ticket.

"Now, all you have to do," Joey explained, "is when you're ready, punch in the code." He indicated the number pad. "It only opens your locker."

"I wouldn't have been able to do it without your help." She beamed at him and patted his forearm. Joey felt like a real heel, but what could he do? Cops weren't on the lookout for a little old lady.

While she hobbled over to a bank of hard, plastic chairs, Joey opened the real ticket and punched in the numbers. The locker popped open.

Five minutes later, Joey was settled in a private stall in the men's room, rifling through the bag full of yarn and knitting needles. He hit the jackpot when he found a roll of twenties, fifties and hundreds, big enough to choke a dinosaur, tucked in among the pink and yellow yarn balls.

"Geez," Joey muttered as he stared at the windfall, "where'd a little old lady get such a big bankroll?" He pulled out the bus ticket. Miami. "Yeah, I could go for Florida this time of year."

Stuffing the bag into a trashcan, he went back to the main terminal. It wasn't hard to avoid his victim in such a large bus station, but he also had to stay away from two uniforms who were undoubtedly looking for him.

Joey made sure he was first in line for Miami when the announcement came. He snuck a look at the lockers and saw the old woman approaching them, the fake flower on her hat tilting crazily. She peered at the ticket he'd given her, then at the number pad.

The bus driver opened the door and surveyed the line.

"All those passengers with their names on their tickets should come forward," he announced. "Those with reservations get on the express to Miami first."

Everyone groaned. The last time Joey had taken a bus across country, to attend his mother's funeral, it had been first come, first serve. Reservations were for plane tickets.

"Hey, what is this?" Joey asked the driver. "Since when did you start this reservation thing?"

The driver, a tall, humorless man, glared at Joey like he was stupid or something. "Since about a year ago."

Joey was so close to getting out of town, and with a bundle of dough too, that he decided to keep his mouth shut. So he watched people shuffle forward with their reservation tickets.

Joey could feel the sweat break out on his forehead. He needed to get on that bus. Whenever the "reservations only" tickets appeared to slow down, one more elderly person came forward, waving their ticket. A light bulb went

Miami

on over Joey's head. He looked at his ticket.

"Hey, I got a name on my ticket," he said.

The driver took his ticket and studied it. "Your name's Evelyn Winters?"

Joey felt his face flush. "Yeah, uh, my mom named me after her sister."

"Yeah, right," the driver replied, like he'd heard it all before. Still, he took the ticket.

With a big sigh, Joey pushed past the man and got on the bus.

During the trip south, he'd decided to go straight, maybe use some of the money left, about five grand, to buy into some business, maybe a snack stand. No more jewelry stores for Joey.

In Miami, outside the terminal, the sun seemed to wash everything clean. Joey felt as clean as a freshly wiped slate. A dazzling white limo pulled up in the no parking zone in front of the terminal.

Hey, Joey thought, I'm gonna ride in one of those someday.

A man got out of the driver's seat, tall and dark with sunglasses that hid his eyes. He came around to the curbside and opened the back door of the limo. Another man, shorter and better dressed, climbed out. He helped a third passenger, an elderly woman with a battered hat, a fake flower stuck in the crown.

Joey didn't move. When she straightened up, the well-dressed man looked at Joey and asked her, "Is that him, Granny? Is this the man who ripped you off?"

She nodded, her mouth set in a grim line, as she looked Joey up and down like she was really disappointed in him. "Shame on you, taking my knitting bag like that. I was making a baby blanket for my granddaughter's baby shower."

"I-I'm sor—" Joey croaked. He recognized the well-dressed man from pictures in the papers back home. The guy was Dominic Winters, a well-known drug kingpin. Joey started to back away, but the chauffeur was right behind him, helping Joey into the limo's front seat.

"Let's just get your bags, Granny, then we'll take care of him," Dominic Winters was saying. "I'm just glad I was able to get you on the train down here. I wish you weren't afraid of flying. There'd've been less chance of you being taken advantage of."

"I think that punk has my money, too," Granny replied, adjusting her hat.

The chauffeur closed the door in Joey's face.

Last Angela Matelli story, last story in this collection, and the title story. That's a lot to shoulder, but I went back to using humor with this one. It was published in Lethal Ladies, *the first volume. I wanted to explore the world of decoys, attractive men and women who tempt their prey in order to discover for the client whether the wife/husband/main squeeze is being faithful. But I added a twist.*

Check Up

Sometimes you have to do things you really don't want to do. And sometimes, you get the feeling that something's not going to work out right, but you can't help it—you are drawn to disaster.

That was my instinct the minute Chuck Eddy called, asking me to do him a favor. Eddy was a private investigator, but until recently, not a very successful one. About a year ago, Eddy discovered that the lucrative decoy market hadn't been tapped here in Boston.

When he first decided to specialize, Eddy had given me a call. He figured it would be good for business to have a broad as a partner. But it was an area of investigation that didn't interest me, and since I was doing well enough in my own line of investigation—mostly repos and investigating insurance scams with an occasional truly interesting case thrown in the mix—I passed on the partnership.

The way it works is, a husband or wife comes into an agency because they want to find out if their spouse is capable of cheating on them. The private investigator turns a decoy with a tape recorder, sometimes even a hidden camera, loose on the spouse. The decoy, an attractive young man or woman, strikes up a conversation with the mark. Sometimes the sucker takes the bait, sometimes he or she doesn't.

When the phone rang, I was hammering a nail into the wall behind the desk, intending to hang a print I'd recently bought of a duck sitting in a beach chair, a cool drink in his feathered hand, with two bullet holes in the wall behind him. It was by some French artist and I just liked it. So sue me for bad taste.

I answered the phone with my usual, "Angela Matelli Investigations. May I help you?" and heard, "Angela, I need a small favor." I recognized Chuck Eddy's voice and immediately got the feeling that the favor wasn't going to be so small.

"Okay, Chuck. I'll bite," I replied, swinging around to lean against the wall. Unfortunately, the hammer was old and the head was loose enough to fall off and onto my foot. "Ow!" I said.

"Angie? Are you okay?" Eddy asked.

"Uh, yeah. So what's the favor, Chuck?"

"Well, see, I know you don't like this kind of work, but, see, I'm in a bind. I promised this client, see, that I'd get a decoy on her hubby."

I groaned.

Eddy paused and asked, "Are you sure you're all right?"

"Yeah, Chuck. You're short one decoy."

"Well, see, I had one all lined up," he said apologetically, "but she called a few minutes ago to tell me she's got an impacted wisdom tooth and is having emergency oral surgery tonight."

"You don't have a list of alternate decoys?"

Check Up

"Sorry, Angie. Val was the last one. It's been so busy around here," Eddy said, his voice smug, "even the decoys on the alternate list have been working steadily." He couldn't resist adding, "You should have partnered with me when you had the chance. So, would you do me a favor and play decoy tonight?"

I closed my eyes. I didn't need the money, but it would be a good excuse to cruise the bar scene. My latest love interest, Joe, had unceremoniously dumped me when he made the decision to go back to his wife. I hadn't had much luck with men since I left the Marines. Joe had been my longest relationship—almost two months. Before Joe, I'd had a series of month-long relationships. It got to the point where I was forgetting their names and, in the company of my sisters, would call them by the month in which we were dating. Bob had been Mr. May, Rick had been Mr. July, and Joe had been Mr. August, until I realized that we were still going out in September.

It wasn't like I'd started picking out a china pattern or anything like that, but I'd had hopes for Joe. He was ex-military like me—a lieutenant commander in the Navy—and was working as an insurance investigator. So we had a lot in common. He was a little older—forty, to be exact—and legally separated, with two kids. I had enjoyed his company, he was a good lover, and Ma was happy for a change.

"Angie! I'm so relieved you found someone who would make a good husband," she told me last Sunday at dinner. "So he's a little older and not Italian. At least he's Catholic." She conveniently forgot the divorce thing and, by the end of dinner, she had us married and living nearby in Malden with two kids of our own.

"Ma. Give me a chance to get to know him before we throw the net over him," I replied.

My younger sister Rosa covered her mouth and giggled while Sophia and my three brothers just rolled their eyes.

"Angie?" Eddy's voice sounded tinny on the phone. "Angie? You still there?" Eddy always did that to me—he could talk and talk and I'd just drift off, thinking about something completely different.

"Yeah, I'll do it, Chuck. When and where?"

It was a hotel lounge, of all places, called L'Aubergine, which is French for eggplant. Don't ask me why they called it that. Some bozo in the head office probably decided that it had a worldly ring to it.

I sprinted home to change into something resembling sophisticated. Decoys are usually coed material. I was, well, a little long in the tooth to pass for a coed, but Chuck assured me that the mark was in his mid-forties and would probably be flattered that a woman my age (a little over twenty-nine) would show interest in him.

Most of my work is done in jeans and T-shirts, so I had to borrow something to wear from Rosa. I went downstairs—Rosa has the apartment on the second floor—and knocked on her door. When I explained what I needed and why, Rosa immediately went to her closet and started tossing dresses out on her bed.

"It's about time you went out."

"It's a *job*, Rosa, not a date."

She threw me a look over her shoulder. "Yeah, maybe a job, but you've got to look nice and maybe after you get what you're after, you'll stick around and meet a nice guy."

I laughed. "At a bar? I don't think so."

"L'Aubergine is not *just* a bar. It's a bar in a five-star hotel where rich businessmen stay."

"Rich, *married* businessmen," I reminded her as I sorted through the dresses on the bed. I started to hold up one to

Check Up

see if the color was right when Rosa stopped me. "I think you should try this one on first." She was holding a little electric blue number. "Little" is the operative word here.

"You've got to be kidding. I couldn't slither into that with a can of Crisco and a shoehorn." I took it from her and held it up, but it didn't even cover ten percent of me.

"Try it on," my younger sister said.

Half an hour later, Rosa stepped back from my face, mascara brush in her hand. "There. You're done. And if I do say so myself, you look fabulous."

I turned to inspect the finished product and gasped. "I look like a high-class hooker." My hair was fluffed up and sprayed so high, I thought I'd have trouble walking through doorways without taking a little off the top. My body was encased in what amounted to be a shocking blue sausage casing that barely covered my tush, and my make-up was courtesy of Barnum & Bailey.

"You look like most upper-class women these days. The hooker look is still in," Rosa replied, unruffled by my reaction.

I tottered to the doorway in the matching three-inch blue stiletto heels.

"You have to work on your walk," Rosa added. "Try to thrust your hips forward and slink."

"You've got to be kidding," I replied for the second time in an hour. I managed to make it to the car and drive away with some dignity intact.

Thirty minutes later, I was sitting in Chuck Eddy's black van, waiting for Mr. Wrong to show up.

"I gotta tell you, Angie," Eddy said, "you look hot."

"I am hot. Turn the air-conditioning on, Chuck," I replied.

"No, I mean you look really good. I don't suppose when this case is through, you'd wanna go out to dinner with me?"

233

It didn't surprise me that a guy like Eddy would think this was what a real woman should look like. I scanned Chuck Eddy's puffy body, sparse beard, and mashed-in nose. "Uh, thanks for the offer, Chuck, but we really don't have anything in common. Besides, I was just dumped and I'm trying to get over it."

He shrugged as if it was my loss. "Well, if you ever change your mind—" He turned the binoculars on a dark Mercedes sports coupe that was pulling into the lot. "Well, there's our boy. Your recorder's on?"

Eddy had actually invested in small video recorders and mine fit in a small evening bag. After testing it, I clambered out of the van and wobbled to the entrance, promising myself that as soon as I got into the bar, I'd find a seat and stay there all evening. Lover Boy would have to come to me. His name was Dick MacAfee and his wife suspected him of cheating on her. She thought it was just one-night stands, and that was where I came in. As soon as he picked me up and voiced his intentions, I could make an excuse and leave.

The man who got out of the Mercedes was good-looking in a middle-aged, receding hairline, "I got the money, baby, if you got the time" kind of way. I maneuvered myself into his path and bumped into him. Actually, the bumping into him part was not planned, but it got his attention.

"Well, excuse me," he said with a smile, one hand lightly on my elbow. "Are you going in here?"

I returned the smile. "Yes, I've heard the band is good here."

He looked a bit puzzled. "I didn't know there was a band tonight."

The bar was upscale with lots of blond oak trim surrounding dark green walls and frosted glass. In the kind of

Check Up

bar I frequent, the assorted barflies wear Timexes, drink Michelob, and talk about the latest sure bet. These barflies wore fake Rolexes, drank Stoli on the rocks, and talked about the latest sure bet. The difference was that in my bar, Santarpio's, the sure bet is at Suffolk Down and in L'Aubergine, it's on Wall Street.

He escorted me to an unoccupied table in a corner. Fortunately, there was a small jazz band playing. Apparently on Thursday nights, there's usually canned music. I ordered a black Russian and he went up to the bar to get my drink and his own, a whiskey neat. We exchanged names—I lied and said my name was Sherri and made small talk. He asked what I did for a living—I lied and said I was a secretary and when he asked me where I grew up, I lied again, mostly because I was enjoying being another person.

He told me his name was Dick, he was head of a large sportswear corporation, and he was single. Truth, truth, lie. I batted my eyelashes. The atmosphere was humid and I hoped my mascara hadn't melted, which would make me look like a raccoon. Several times, I had to lean toward him so I could furtively sneak a look at the recorder, just to make sure it was still running. I noticed that every time I did this, Dick's eyes zeroed in on my cleavage. He didn't even pretend to look elsewhere.

As I leaned over for the fourth time, I noticed a man on the far side of the room who looked an awful lot like my current ex, Joe. In fact, I realized it was Joe. He was sitting at a table with a girl who looked to be about thirteen. Upon closer inspection, I decided she was probably in her early twenties, but she had that beautiful anorexic Kate Moss body and large Oxfam eyes: I knew it wasn't his wife, and I knew he didn't have any daughters that age.

"Sherri?" I felt Dick's hand touch mine. I smiled again. I

knew I'd wake up tomorrow with sore facial muscles. I never smiled this much.

"Oh, uh, sorry. I saw someone across the room who looked like my, uh, brother." I was seething inside. Joe hadn't even had the decency to tell me he wanted someone younger, the son of a bitch. Well, as soon as this little job of mine was finished, I'd damn well go over and give him a piece of my mind. I looked at Dick and turned my smile up a notch. "You were telling me that last quarter's returns were enough for a bonus that allowed you to buy that beautiful sports car I saw out in the lot, right?"

He beamed at me and nodded. "I have my own helicopter, too."

"Ooooh," I cooed. *Liar,* I thought. I'd seen his sheet in Eddy's van and it didn't say anything about his own helicopter.

"Maybe I can take you for a ride in it tonight." He leaned toward me, his eyes still fixed on my cleavage, his voice suddenly husky with desire. I must have leaned over the table once too much.

"Gosh," I replied in a squeaky voice, "that sounds like fun." I glanced over at Joe and wondered if Dick would suspect anything if I requested that we buzz the Burlingame area where Joe lived and put a spotlight on his apartment.

Whack! The sound came out of nowhere. Dick's head hit the table with the force of a tsunami. At first, I thought it was gunfire and I jumped up, ready for action—until I remembered that I didn't have my gun with me and I was wearing stiletto heels. I staggered into the next table, spilling drinks all over the place.

"You bum!" a loud woman's voice shouted over the jazz band's rendition of Duke Ellington's "Do Nothing Till You Hear From Me." "You son of a bitch! What're you doin'

Check Up

with this tootsie?" The owner of the voice was a large, handsome woman. She gestured savagely toward me with her purse, the weapon that whacked the back of Dick's head. He was holding the back of his head as he glanced from me to her. Taking in the frightened rabbit look in his eyes, I felt sorry for him for a moment.

Then I got up and walked toward her. My intention was to take her gently by the elbow and ask her what she thought she was doing. After all, she had hired Chuck Eddy to get the goods on her husband. For that matter, where was Eddy? He should have seen her enter the bar. My mistake was thinking I could handle this situation discreetly. The moment I tried to take her elbow, she screeched, "Get your mitts offa me, you, you slut!"

"Sweetie pie," Dick said to her in a placating tone, "she doesn't mean a thing to me—"

This scene was, of course, the center of everyone's attention. I could see Joe getting up and coming toward me. Dick stood up and, avoiding my eyes, started toward his wife.

"Angie!" Joe said, concern in his eyes and a sheepish expression on his face. "What're you doing here?" He glanced at Dick's wife, who was still glaring at me, then to Dick, who was shrinking as fast as Alice after she polished off the DRINK ME bottle.

"Who the hell are *you*," Dick's wife aimed her rasping voice at Joe, "her pimp?"

I scowled at her. "For your information, lady," I said, "I am not a call girl." I resisted the urge to hit her. The lady had a mean right hook with her handbag.

"Angie? I thought your name was Sherri," Dick said to me before his wife thumped the back of his head again.

"Ow!" Dick cringed for a moment, then straightened up

and faced his wife. "You know, I'm getting really tired of that. Stop it."

She looked at him with no expression on her face, then whacked him upside the head again. "As soon as you stop hitting on anything that's wearing a tube dress," she said calmly, "I'll stop hitting you."

Joe's waif-like tootsie came up behind him to cling to his arm. "What's going on, Joe?" she asked in a velvet voice. She looked at me. "Who's this, your sister?"

Where the hell was Eddy? I wondered. This was fast becoming a disaster and I wanted out. I turned away for a moment to see if the recorder had done its stuff and found that it was, indeed, still working. I figured the rest of the evening was a loss. A large building was moving toward us. When it got close enough, I realized it was a bouncer.

"Is there a problem here, miss?" he asked, his eyes skimming me like I was a plate of prime rib.

"No," I replied, "nothing I can't handle. I'll call if I need you."

"I'll be right over there," he said, indicating a vague direction. I nodded and thanked him again.

When I finally had a chance to turn around, Dick and his wife were gone, but Joe was still there. I glowered at him and his coed.

"You okay, Angie?"

"What the hell do *you* care?" I snarled.

Joe suddenly realized that he had this unexplained appendage growing out of his arm. He had the decency to look embarrassed. "Oh, uh, Angela, this is, uh, Mariel." He avoided my eyes. A lot of men had been doing that to me lately.

"It must not have worked out with your wife," I said dryly, crossing my arms.

Check Up

Mariel looked up at him, her chin quivering. "Wife? You're married?"

"Uh, well, I'm, uh, separated right now," Joe replied. His eyes looked for an escape route.

"Gee, Joe, it only took you three days to decide that it wasn't working between you two?" I leaned toward Mariel in a confidential manner. "You see, less than a week ago, I was going out with him. Then, three days ago, he told me that he was going back to his wife."

Joe turned red. "Now, Angela, that's not exactly what happened—" Before we could hear his explanation, his sweet little waif grabbed Dick's watery whiskey, stood on tippy-toes, and dumped it all over Joe's head before marching out of the joint.

I smiled for the first time since Dick's wife spoiled the party. When I left the bar, Joe was still mopping the whiskey off his face and shirt.

I churned outside, ready to rip Eddy's lungs out for his sloppy surveillance. Eddy came out of the van before I got to it, a narrow look on his face.

"What the hell happened, Angie? You went in with the guy, I thought you had it all sewn up. Then I see him leaving with some other broad."

"What do you mean, some other broad?" I returned. "That was his *wife*, the woman who hired you."

Eddy pulled up short and blinked rapidly, then shook his head. "Naw, that wasn't his wife. His wife came into my office and—" He stopped and slapped the side of his head. I was witnessing an awful lot of slapstick violence this evening. "Geez, could that one tonight be a girlfriend?"

I shook my head slowly. "This is your mess to sort out, Chuck." I took the tape out of my evening bag and handed it to him. "I got what you want. I'm calling it a night. Drop my check in the mail." I stumbled to my car, my feet screaming with each step. Just as I unlocked the car, I turned to Eddy. "And Chuck?"

He looked up from examining the tape recorder. "Yeah, Angie?"

"Don't call me for another one of these gigs. I've just retired." I pulled the high heels off of my aching feet and tossed them in the back of my car, then got in and drove, barefoot, back to my place in East Boston.